10/22
$2—
D1501044
6/22

Ground Control

By KA Hough

There's no going back

Ground Control is a work of fiction.
Names, places, and incidents in this book are either the product of the author's imagination or are used fictitiously. Any resemblance to actual persons, living or dead, events or locales is entirely coincidental.

Copyright © 2021 K.A. Hough

All rights reserved.

No part of this book may be reproduced or used in any manner without written permission of the copyright owner except for the use of quotations in a book review.

First Print Edition 2021

Published in the United States by Lights Out Ink, LLC.

ISBN: 978-1-914152-09-2
eBook ISBN: 978-1-914152-10-8

Cover design by K.M. West

Lights Out Ink is an independent publisher of serialized, digital, and printed fiction. Visit www.lightsoutink.com to discover our full library of content and read extras online.

To Fis

I'd follow you anywhere

Chapter 1

"Why can't you understand that I need to do this? That I have to?"

Sarah took a deep breath to calm herself down, but when she finally responded, her voice was sharp and ragged. Ugly.

"For the same reason that you can't understand that I can't do this. You don't *need* to do this. You want to, and your wants have moved us around enough already. The kids need some kind of— of— stability, or something. We are not coming with you. Not this time."

Grant didn't respond. He just stared at her stonily, his blue eyes intent on hers. She crossed her arms.

"If you choose to go," she said flatly, "then you're giving me a divorce."

He looked surprised, then furious. "No."

"No?" she repeated. "You're choosing to leave us for God knows how long, maybe forever. Give us— give me the chance to live my life and take care of my family. A divorce, with full custody."

"We'll let them choose," he said, feverishly. "Maybe they'll want to come along, and—"

"NO!" Her head hurt. Her eyes burned and her throat was sore. "If you leave, you're leaving alone. I'm not going to live like that. My children are not going to live like that. They're children. Let them have their childhood, their friends, their playtime."

"The ship is set up for families," he pleaded. "There are teachers, other kids, lots of activities."

"No fresh air. No playing outside. It's not a place for kids."

"It is a place for kids! They have it fully set up to be sustainable and educational and interactive. It's an opportunity to be a part of something new, something incredible and historic."

"You're making it sound like a glorified Disney cruise," she snarled. "Not a stupid experiment. We're not going." When had she put her tea down? The smoky grey-blue pottery mug was cold to the touch.

He changed tack. "You're afraid that if I let them choose, Jack will want to come with me."

She looked at him, amazed. "Of course I am! And of course he will! But he's six! He's not old enough to make irreversible decisions about his future! They're children. Let them have their childhood... Besides, I'm already losing you-"

"You're not losing me," he interrupted softly.

She held up a hand, which he grabbed. "I'm already losing you," she repeated. "Don't take my kids away too."

She had tucked Maggie and Jack into their beds about forty minutes ago, bathed and sweet-smelling, and she wasn't sure that they were both asleep yet. Their tablets were both accounted for, charging on the bookshelf in the kitchen, but Maggie sometimes lay awake for an hour or so.

They were in the den. The den was a bonus room, added over the garage to the house about ten years after it was built. When they first moved in, they didn't know what to do with it. After London, it felt luxurious to have a bedroom for each kid as well as a guest room, let alone a finished basement and a family room, but the den was Grant's territory.

The walls were covered with his posters and certifications — "Finally, you're letting me decorate with my stuff" — at one end of the room, surrounding a large, ugly old Ikea desk and two decrepit filing cabinets, all piled high with papers. That was his zone, where even the kids — even the cat — feared to tread. This was where he went every night after dinner, while she helped the kids with homework or watched them play outside, or, more recently, as the evenings got colder, watched TV with them in the basement, the mindless, brainless pre-teen television that were as unfunny as the shows she had loved at that age.

Grant sat on the arm of the old couch, his posture erect and stiff, his dark hair tousled. Sarah stood tensely in front of him, and tucked her hair behind her ear again.

"How long have you known about this?" she demanded.

"It just became real today," he responded.

"But how long have you known it was 'probably' coming?" She put the air quotes in her voice.

He sighed. "A few months. Since Spring Break. That's why I had to go to D.C."

That break. The kids were off for two weeks. There was an early thaw, but the weather was still terrible: cold and damp, but the backyard wasn't snowy enough for fun. Patches of mud were starting to peek through the dirty piles of old snow, and there was slush everywhere. This kind of spring only meant dirty, wet snowpants and sopping wet mittens. On top of that, Sarah had a flu which nearly killed her, but she drove themto a cottage outside of Montreal for a little vacation, for time away surrounded by nature. Snowshoeing. Firepits. Drying the snowpants and mittens in front of someone else's grate. Grant had been planning to come with them, in his noncommittal way, but a week beforehand, announced that he had to fly to Washington for the week. This sort of thing wasn't unusual, and she and the kids were used to having their own adventures when 'Daddy's busy.' But that was...

"Three months?" she said slowly. "You've known for three months that you were 'probably' going to head off to outer space forever, and you thought you should wait until it was definitely a thing before telling me?"

He said nothing.

"When do you leave?" she asked, wearily.

Chapter 2

18 years ago
Kingston, Canada

"Systems!" Sarah yelled, hanging the office keys back up on their neatly labelled hook.

She took her coat from its hook (not labelled; she hadn't gone that far) and pulled her somewhat-unruly dark brown hair back into a loose bun. One piece escaped and fell across her forehead, as usual.

The student council office was still bustling behind her as she passed through the reception area, pausing for a moment to fill her travel mug with hot water from the dispenser. She picked a dead leaf off the plant on the reception desk and tossed it into the garbage can, then fished a tea bag out of her purse. On Fridays, she treated herself to a tea at the café across the quad, but today was Tuesday, so cheap tea would do. She clicked the cap on, pushed open the university centre door and stepped into the cool spring afternoon.

"See you tomorrow," she called over her shoulder. God knows what state they'd be in again by the morning.

The office was a good place to work: convenient, and she liked the energy and excitement of the place, the passion of the student council members, the ones who were going to make a difference on campus, then in the world. But boy, did they need help. She was quieter than anyone else there, but competent; she knew that she made it run more successfully, more orderly. She organized and sorted, did the budget, typed up correspondence, that sort of thing. She set up systems to keep everything running smoothly, which it did, when people followed them. Or hung the keys where they belong.

Because of her efforts behind the scenes, it all worked.

It was a good feeling.

She took her tea to the little square in front of the university centre that held a small patch of lawn and two teenage maple trees. Sarah leaned against the larger of the two, feeling the sunshine filtering warmly, greenly through its thin layer of new buds, dappling her face. One more year to go.

Her twenty-one years so far, and her pending undergraduate degree in Biology, certainly hadn't set her up to be an earthmover. She was a good student, no, an excellent student, when she applied herself. She had so much potential, her teachers had said since she was little. She grasped concepts easily and memorized facts without too much effort; she followed instructions and picked out patterns, and — was it only two-and-a-half years ago? — figured that she'd hold onto her entrance scholarship, thank-you-very-much, as long as she didn't get too lazy.

She almost held onto her scholarship, just .1 away, which was still far enough that her bank account and her ego took a bigger hit than she expected. So much for potential. She was an A student with a B+ average, and tuition, books and rent to pay; food was optional. Soup here, ramen there and a supply of teabags in her desk. She'd get by.

The dance studio, where she taught preschoolers on weekends, paid fairly generously for the six hours of classes she taught a week, but she had needed to supplement that with more. The student council office was right on campus — she could go straight from class or the lab — and flexible — she could work any time as long as deadlines were met and hours were put in — and she knew it would look great on a resume. Like she was a leader. Then, with her degree in Biology and her resume, her drive and ambition, she would go out there and be more. She would work and test and cure and invent, and on the side, she would dance and achieve and meet a handsome man and she would be more.

She reached out with one hand to place it on the slender trunk, the bark still light brown and smooth, cool under her palm. Inhaling deeply, she closed her eyes and lifted her chin, smiling up at the sun. A shadow fell across her face, and when she opened her eyes, Grant Harper was standing there, smiling too.

Overall, the students of different years didn't mingle much — each class was consumed with its own labs and dramas — but she knew who he was. Tall, slim to the point of being skinny, she assumed that he slept in his lab coat. His hair, so dark brown it was almost black, was always rumpled, too. She knew him as Grant, the genius. Grant, the intense. He was finishing up his Master's, known to be more brilliant than some of the professors, and acted as TA in one of her labs and one of her classes. He was quiet too, and serious. Now, though, she was hit by the force of his blue eyes and surprising dimples. You don't see dimples in people that never smile, she reminded herself. He knew her name, though.

"You're Sarah," he said. And that was that.

She went out for a sandwich with him — true, she was starving, as she was running low on soup — but it wasn't her hunger that made her accept his invitation. His whole long, lean body seemed to vibrate with... potential? She'd laugh at that later, but it felt true. He was passionate and bright; he had a plan for the rest of his life; he needed a sidekick.

That was something that she knew how to do.

*

She graduated with a solid B+ (she still cringed) with an honours degree in biology specializing in clinical research and took on a full-time project at the Dean of Admissions' office for the summer, something that she was flattered into accepting. She — and everyone there — knew she was more than competent. The office was a comfortable place to work, the money was good, and, well, she hadn't quite decided whether to pursue a Master's, let alone a PhD like Grant had. Grant had already begun his second year of his research and was in the lab day and night.

She contemplated whether her B+ would be enough to apply for the spring intake. She took on a few classes at the studio in the evenings and signed up for an adult ballet class at the university. When the end of August loomed, they offered her a full-time position in university administration, managing the Dean's office. She took it without hesitation.

Summer melted into late September. It was Friday night. She sat on her back porch with a glass of the cheap, bottle-your-own red wine that she and Nancy had made together in April, as a celebratory, we're-adults-now activity.

Nancy was sleeping at John's tonight. They were still best friends, of course. She had the same confident, adventurous spirit that had drawn Sarah to her — and to Ethan — in frosh week.

The night was warm, but she wrapped a light blanket over her knees and breathed in the sounds of the city as she watched the shadows lengthen on her small lawn. Her radio was on, playing softly through her open window.

The deadline for Master's applications was coming up in two weeks, but she still hadn't gotten past printing out the forms. Her thesis advisor, in April, had told her to be prepared to go all the way, that she'd only really be able to 'do something' once she had her PhD. Nancy had brushed off the professor's dire warning about the necessity of 'even further' education and had started her Master's in September.

For Sarah, though, it meant six more years before she could 'do something.' What Grant had accepted without hesitation made her rethink and second guess her skills and dreams. What did she, really, want to do?

She removed her dark-green-framed glasses for a moment to rub her eyes, the ones she'd chosen because they made her seem smart, serious-looking. She replaced them, tucking her flyaway hair behind her ears; it had escaped from her braid again.

She had been told over and over about her potential. God, she hated that word. *Potential.* Just another word for failure. As in, you have potential that you're failing to meet. That you're failing to try hard enough. You are not enough.

Grant poked his head over the fence, then unlatched the gate and crossed to the porch in a few long strides. He stooped to give her a peck on the cheek as he sat down beside her, but declined a glass of wine.

"McMaster wants me," he said, with no introduction, no hello. "They want me to finish up my studies there. It's a better facility, a Level 3 biocontainment lab, and they've already spoken to Dr. Menchel, in fact he was the one who contacted them, and..."

Sarah had stopped listening. She was no longer cuddled up on her porch with a blanket and a glass of wine and her boyfriend; her boyfriend of two years was just popping over to break up with her. Her hand felt like ice around the glass' stem, her eyes and throat felt dry. There was a sudden fluttering in her tightened chest. It was Friday night. She had to make it through the next two—

"Sarah? So, they'll transfer me over at the beginning of January, and I'll be all set. I can do my last two years from MAC, full credit, no problem. What do you think?" His face was too close, his eyes too eager, uncharacteristic for him.

She gulped and shivered. "That's— that's great, Grant." She managed a smile, without looking up at him. "I'm happy for you."

It was Friday night, and she was free. They'd been dating for two years with no real talk of the future, except of Grant's research, of his potential. He had his place, a ten-minute walk away, on the far side of campus, and she had hers. She was undemanding, helpful, *convenient*. Just what you wanted without really needing it. Or wanting it, apparently. Her jaw started to ache. She shook herself, and the blanket fell off her knee, making her feel even colder in the warm evening air. Sarah moved to stand up, to walk away with dignity and grace the way one does when one is an adult.

There was a ring in Grant's hand.

It wasn't a big ring, but it sparkled, brilliant in the dim light over her porch. She fumbled her glass, spilling half its contents onto her lap. Grant's gaze was more intense than she had ever seen it, and for a moment he seemed young, unsure, something he had never seemed from the first moment they met.

"You will— you will come with me?" he said. "I want you there, Sarah. I want you to marry me."

Of course she said yes — a flustered yes, dripping with wine. A shy smile, a kiss, and the ring, too big, slipped easily onto her finger. A new world opened up as a door closed softly in the background.

It was probably her upstairs neighbour going inside quietly, so as not to disturb a young couple so much in love.

The wedding was quick, quiet. A City Hall wedding, not fancy but just right. Their parents were in attendance, and Nancy and John stepped in as maid of honour and best man. Nancy and Sarah found the perfect dress, creamy white and belted, with little pockets and buttons. She felt sweet and pretty and quite bridelike, especially with the little clip-on veil. And with their little group, and the well-wishes of her coworkers at the university, she felt like she was leaving plain old Sarah Sheridan behind, embarking on a beautiful adventure with this strange, intense, brilliant man.

Chapter 3

"We're going to Mars."

Her throat caught, and she choked on the mouthful of water. She coughed and hacked, doubled over, her face bright red, tears streaming from her eyes.

Mars.

Sure, his projects for the past five years had been focused on the effects of microgravity on plants and animals. Sure, he was considered the top biologist in the country, if not the world, on this subject. And *sure*, space was the next logical step to go, *if one was in a science fiction movie.*

Every two to three years, Grant came home vibrating, and Sarah knew it would be just a matter of waiting till the kids were in bed for him to start talking about the new opportunity, wherever it was. About his work, he was intense, brooding. Everyone was an idiot. Scientists that the world considered brilliant were fools. The breakthroughs he could make with the right equipment, support, funding. The right team. So, when he banged in the door at the end of the day, she knew the same thing was happening again. A new job, probably in a new city, usually in a different part of the country. New schools, new house, new friends.

Same Sarah.

Her sidekick skills were well-developed. The kids were encouraged to celebrate the time they had with the friends they had made. The new city would be waiting for them, with friends yet to be made, activities already signed up for, and tested-and-true systems (Systems!) for the packing, move and unpacking. The cat (the damn cat) always sensed it coming, and made life harder than it really needed to be, but off they were going on a new adventure, and won't it be great. The places you'll go! The things you'll see! The world beyond the reach of most of your friends, that's where we're going.

So, when he whistled — actually whistled! — up the steps and into the kitchen this last time, Sarah squeezed her shoulders down and back, took a swallow of water, and turned to tell him he had six minutes till dinner, knowing that she'd hear all about this next big thing in a few hours. She could wait that long.

Mars. Grant had mentioned joining the Mars colony several times. It had sounded completely surreal the first time he mentioned it, and hadn't improved over time and retelling as the opportunities crystallized, when the first ship landed successfully, then the second. It wasn't just the possibilities that sounded bizarre and unreal, but the one-way journey; a ship made to take off from Earth and land on Mars wasn't made to take off from Mars and land on Earth. She had a ticket to Mars with no return. Ever.

Of course Sarah wasn't ready for this. Who could be? She had to choose between a one-way move or losing her husband. Both were forever.

Their year in New Zealand had been a big move. At the time, it had seemed so far away, literally the other end of the world. She went through the goodbyes, each a little death.

When they got there, she realized that life went on. She was fine. Another city, another house, another community ready to embrace Dr. Harper's wife. She spoke with Nancy and Anne about as often as she did now.

This, though, was obviously, necessarily different. Wellington had been only for a year, not forever.

Eyes streaming, nose streaming, she continued to sputter. Grant patted her on the back, bent over with her, trying to find her eyes with his. "It's happening, Sarah. I've got the funding. I'm on the next shuttle to Mars and—"

He stopped abruptly as her fingers shot out and fumbled to press against his lips, to stop his words.

"Later," she gasped. "Not till the kids are asleep." In her head was a silent scream. *No. I'm not going.*

Dinnertime was tense. Sarah put on a neutral, everything-is-totally-fine mask, one that didn't quite conceal the panic in her eyes. She put the plates at each setting, breathing deeply and slowly despite her tight chest.

"Jack! Maggie! Dinner! Go wash your hands!"

Jack banged in the back door and beetled through the kitchen on the way to the bathroom. A few moments later, he returned, giving her a small, close-lipped smile as he climbed into his chair. She reached over to remove his smudged glasses, then polished them and handed them back. "Where's your sister?" He shrugged, tilting his head on its side.

"Maggie!" Then, more sharply: "*Maggie!*"

Maggie came twirling in, her hands still wet. She flounced into her chair, then shot her arm across the table to grab the Lego figurine by Jack's plate.

"Give it back!" he shouted, knocking over his empty cup.

"No toys at the table," she taunted, holding it up.

Jack's hands balled into fists and he lowered his reddened face to look down at his plate. Sarah reached across the table to pluck the contentious figurine from Maggie's slender fingers, then righted Jack's glass. She rested her hand on his head for an instant, feeling the silk of his dark hair before letting it flop back over his forehead.

"That's enough of that. Maggie, no grabbing. Jack, you know the rules."

Fill the glasses with milk. Place the Lego on the counter. Sit down to dinner. Everything is normal. Everything is fine. She followed Grant with her eyes as he joined them.

Maggie had her elbow on the table, her glossy dark head propped up by one long, skinny forearm, her grey eyes flicking back and forth between Sarah and Grant. She swung her long legs under her chair, in protest against having to sit still.

"Elbow," Sarah poked her and watched her straighten up. *Act normal.* "How was ballet today?"

Maggie rolled her eyes with the eight-going-on-thirty superiority that she had developed since starting second grade. "Miss Patty says that my turnout is the best in the class, but Sophia sassed back and said that hers was the best." She prattled on. Maggie was going to be a dancer. She stretched every day with discipline that Sarah had never had. *How would that work, how would she still get to all of her classes?* Grant travelled a lot, but it would be harder to juggle everything if he was... well, gone.

She looked over at Jack, still slumped in his chair, sullen. His sturdy legs were wrapped around his chair, and he ate quietly, staring at his plate. He'd miss Grant the most. But he'd be ok with his books, his Lego and his cat. He always had been. *I hope.*

Grant's knee bounced under the table. His eyes gleamed, and he chewed quickly, washing down each bite with a sip of sparkling water.

"...but then Sophia missed her landing but mine was perfect, and—"

"Elbow, Maggie." Sarah looked up at Jack, surprised. He didn't usually fire the first shot. He had straightened up now, too, and looked steadily at his sister, his grey eyes challenging her behind his glasses. He was 22 months younger than Maggie, and quieter, less confident, but he was immovable when he wanted to be.

"Hey, buddy, it's ok. Not your job," Sarah said. He could obviously feel the tension in the air. *That something's up*. "But, yes, elbow, Maggie."

Keep talking. Anything to quiet the words whirling around her head. The kids would be ok. They were both resilient, not because of her, but because that's just how they were. They easily packed up for each move, their treasures carefully packed away in labelled boxes, systems (Systems!) that were followed just so.

The last move had been harder than usual, maybe because they were getting older; the friendships they made were closer, stronger. The promise of a new city, a new adventure awaiting, was still a pull, but she knew it would continue to get harder, the shorter or longer they stayed in each place.

Maggie, at least, was always on the lookout for the next adventure, which, in her experience, was probably only a year away at most, and definitely no more than two.

But what if her next adventure is losing her Daddy?

Dinner over, Sarah told them to play outside and cleared the table herself. Grant went into the den upstairs, which was his routine after dinner; he'd usually be reading scientific digests. Tonight, however, she could hear him pacing back and forth upstairs.

Don't engage. Not yet. She boiled the kettle for tea.

Through the open window over the sink, she could hear the children's voices murmur and rise over the buzzing sound of a neighbour's lawnmower. They reminded her of chipmunks fighting as they contradicted each other then started wrestling, anger turning into squeals and laughter. They were good friends when they weren't fighting, probably because they were so different. But that was probably why they fought, too. Her hands rested for a moment in the hot soapy water so she could hear them better.

They took turns now on the tire swing, Maggie pushing Jack till she was out of breath, then Jack pushing Maggie much higher, until she squealed, "Too high! Too high!"

These were her kids: Maggie was older, but Jack was stronger. Where he was too quiet to stand up for himself, she was fiery and more confident. Where she would jump in too quickly and say the wrong thing, he was level-headed and calm, up to a point. If he was pushed too far, she was the only one that could have a chance at calming him down. It comes, she supposed, of having each other — and only each other — every time we moved, until they managed to make new friends.

Sarah put the last dripping dish in the dishrack, draped the towel over her shoulder, and stepped out through the kitchen door. Rupert, the cat, sat in a pool of light on the back porch.

Grant had given him to her ten years ago, amidst still-unpacked boxes from their move to Wellington. It was her fourth home in five years — three months before their fifth anniversary — and she was officially the farthest away she could be from home and still be on the planet. And he was leaving for the airport already.

Sarah had watched Grant bustle about, going through his usual mental checklist, checking that his passport was in his breast pocket and that his boarding information was on his phone. He left the room briefly, then returned with a little mewling fluff of fur, which he placed in her lap, then turned away to zip up his suitcase, glancing over his shoulder once with a suppressed grin. At a honk outside, he bent over her.

"That's my taxi." He pressed his lips against hers and held her face between his palms for a moment, gazing down at her intently. "Maybe you won't feel so lonely now," he said. Then he was gone, and she was alone. She was on the other side of the world, still jet lagged, holding a kitten.

She had gotten used to following Grant around, move after move, packing and unpacking each time, falling back on her organizational skills for that and easy-to-get administrative work, but it was hard to make friends. Grant was always travelling, visiting other labs, lecturing at universities and conferences. Rupert was a confidante of a kind. A dog would have been a friend, but impractical for their nomadic lifestyle. Besides, he was sweet and cuddly, and hers.

In the calm of the evening, Rupert's tail twitched rhythmically, but otherwise he was still. *Such a beautiful backyard*, she realized anew. This last move had been a good one: more money, back in Canada, in Ottawa, a city with a far lower cost of living than in London. They could afford a house again, with space to spread out and a real backyard, instead of being squashed up together in a tiny flat.

"We'll live like kings!" Grant had declared.

We'll put down roots, thought Sarah. The house was on a quiet cul-de-sac in a walkable, child-friendly community. They did, indeed, have more than usual. Grant had left the world of academia after their year in Atlanta; he'd been headhunted by BioMars, and the larger salary that he had been paid to work and live in San Antonio, then London, went a whole lot farther here.

They had moved here only two years ago, and even though they were still a five-hour drive from her parents — Grant's were back East, a two-hour flight away — it had felt more like home than any place other than, well, university. And Ethan.

Ethan.

Where had that come from, she wondered. After fifteen years and countless moves, why would she suddenly think of Ethan in university?

She sat on the edge of the porch, holding her steaming mug of tea, her palms warmed by the cloud-coloured stoneware. The dewy grass was cold against her bare feet. Rupert stretched and lazily wandered over to her, like he didn't really care to, like he was doing so under duress. The night air hummed like his purring, and she absentmindedly stroked him while she watched the children play, their dark hair blowing up around their faces. They were so much happier outside, she thought.

She filled her lungs with deep breath after deep breath, smelling the freshness and coolness, a hint of charcoal — not charcoal anymore, she supposed — propane from a neighbour's barbecue, the greenness of the lawn and the trees. Everything was good here. Everything was right.

It was too soon to go.

Chapter 4

"Are we there yet?" Muffled giggles emanated from the back seat as the Prius turned onto the familiar driveway and slowed to a stop in front of her childhood home. Sarah turned around to look at Maggie and Jack, cuddled up in a pile of crumb-covered pillows and blankets.

"*Now* we are. You can stop asking."

Grant was away, as usual. Sarah had pulled the kids out of school after lunch on Friday to make the five-hour drive to her parents' house for the weekend.

Sarah hadn't mentioned anything to them yet about Grant's news, but they'd be expecting something. It was their normal pattern, moving every two years or so, so "We're moving" wouldn't be a surprise. But what would she say over the phone? The options were ludicrously bleak: "I'm leaving him?" No, "He's leaving me?" "We're getting on a spaceship and never coming back?" It had to be a face-to-face conversation.

It wasn't a bad drive. Once they got going, and their own little pillow forts were built, music was on, and snacks rationed out, it was no time at all till they passed the halfway mark, then stopped for a quick bite at the last big service station before they left the highway. Rupert was at home with two large bowls of water and an overflowing food dish, and the teenager next door would check on him on Saturday afternoon.

Dusk was falling as she pulled up to her old house. The streetlights flickered on as Maggie and Jack piled out of the car with their backpacks and ran towards the front porch, where her parents were waiting. They were squeezed first into big grandmotherly hugs, then a quicker one from granddad. Then, whooping, they dropped their bags in the entrance way and dashed through to the backyard, a cookie already tucked into their hands, and an extra for each in their pockets. Grandma was quick.

Sarah shook the blankets out one by one and wrinkled her nose as she surveyed the wreckage of crumbs and toys the kids had made of her nice, clean backseat. *Oh well.* She turned to grab her bags out of the open trunk.

"Jack can help me vacuum that out in the morning." Her dad reached past her and lifted her suitcase out before placing an arm around her shoulder. He kissed her temple. "Now, pass me those pillows." He had retired fifteen years ago, and though his dark hair was now grey, his teeth were white, his back was straight, and he played golf twice a week in the summer.

"Dad! I'll carry those!" she protested.

"Nope." Ron Sheridan took pride in his own garden and drive, repainted the trim on their house every few years, and still mowed their elderly neighbour's lawn, raked her leaves and shovelled her driveway and walk. He walked three miles every night after dinner, weather permitting.

She shrugged and closed the trunk behind him, then reached into the passenger seat for the cooler bag and her purse.

Her mom held the door open for him. It looked freshly painted in a soft blue. *Another change.* Jean was a few years younger than her husband and kept her hair a shiny dark brown with considerable help from a bottle. She had blossomed, Sarah thought, when Sarah had "given her" grandchildren, but since they always lived away from them, she had directed her energies into nurturing her neighbourhood, baking casseroles and cookies for neighbourhood kids and single moms and widowers. She gave her daughter a nice, comfortable hug and led the way into the kitchen, where a sink full of bubbles waited.

The screen door let in sounds of the kids playing in the backyard. There was a big tree back there that wasn't really a treehouse but was magical for having boards nailed into it like a ladder. The leaves, between June and mid-October, covered a wide saddle of branches easily big enough for the two of them to sit side by side. Sarah had sat in it for hours at a time as a child. *Her* friendly tree in a friendly yard, one that was richer now with children running about.

So many yards. This one was hers, would always contain her childhood memories. The one in Ottawa was perfect; they had made it home, too. And Colorado. And Georgia. Texas. For the most part, wherever they went, she had had a garden to tend. Their year in New Zealand was no different. They'd had a small patio, with just enough space to walk between the barbecue and compact two-seater bistro set. She could still picture little Rupert following her outside for the first time, his little grey striped tail standing straight up.

She had stepped onto the coarse grass of the tiny lawn. He trotted towards her, stopping just at the edge of the patio, uncertain, one paw lifted and quivering. “Come on, little one.” Sarah had scooped him up with one hand, and walked around the little yard, feeling the springiness of the grass under her feet as she counted five steps to the fence. Broad-leaved spiky grasses lined its perimeter, waist high and deep purple. She paused to let them prick her fingertips, then stood in front of an odd-looking tree clump of trees that stood in one corner. *Is everything here spiky?* she had wondered.

I will never explore another backyard. The realization hit her with a dull thud.

She put the leftover snacks in the cupboard as her mom plunged her hands back into the soapy water, chatting. Jean was keeping busy, as usual. She volunteered at the children’s library three mornings a week, golfed when other wives tagged along, and joined Ron on his walks as long as it wasn’t raining.

“Rain doesn’t count as weather,” he said, sitting down at the table with a newspaper. *Who still gets newspapers? Old people, that’s who.* Her parents, in their early 70s, had been in their mid-thirties when they had her, older than most of her friends' parents. Retired now for years, they were active, very young, still. *Still young*, Sarah thought wryly. The description fit her, as well, she supposed.

She grabbed a dish towel and wiped the dishes as her mom put them in the drying rack, the way she had done as a teenager. She still felt like a teenager, being in this kitchen with the wind blowing through the open windows, listening to her parents' affectionate bickering. *Home*. Each time her parents updated part of the house, removed wallpaper or replaced an old, worn-out piece of furniture, it felt like a mini betrayal to her, of her childhood. But it still felt like home.

The last dish away, sodden towel hung up to dry, she suddenly realized how late it had gotten. The screen door still creaked as she pushed it open. The kids were speaking in whispers, watching fireflies start to venture out in the twilight. From underneath the tree, all she could see of them was their feet, swinging slightly, just visible when she looked up at the branches.

"Time for bed," she called, and the feet stilled. "I see you," she said, and was rewarded with giggles. First Jack, then Maggie, climbed slowly down the makeshift ladder, and entered the warm kitchen, where Jean now busied herself with filling the kettle. Sarah's father had the newspaper spread out in front of him on the old, scarred kitchen table, and on each side of him sat a glass of milk.

Jack gulped his down, then wiped his arm across his mouth, as Granddad tousled his hair, while Maggie paused between sips. She smoothed her hair back from her forehead and fluttered her eyelashes at her grandfather over her glass. He waggled his thick eyebrows back at her and she giggled again.

"Your bags are up in your room, dears," said Sarah's mom. "And I've laid out some new jammies and toothbrushes for you. Granddad will be up in five minutes to read you a story, so get moving!" The kids raced off. Either Jack, Maggie and Sarah nearly always forgot to bring one or the other on their visits. It had become a running joke.

The kettle whistled, and Jean put peppermint tea bags into three waiting stoneware mugs. There had always been just the three of them, one for each, as long as Sarah could remember. Above them, they could hear the floor creaking as the children scampered and fooled around instead of getting into their new pjs and brushing their teeth. Sarah's dad heaved himself up out of his chair with a grunt and went up after them, calling out a warning on the way. There were squeals and Sarah smiled up at the ceiling, where their footsteps thundered overhead.

The room at the top of the stairs held twin beds, one with a blue bedspread, one with a pink, and Sarah knew that it would only be a few minutes till they were lying, all tucked up in them, listening raptly to whatever story her dad was telling them tonight.

Her own room they had transformed almost unrecognizably into an impersonal guest room. They had ripped out her faded pink carpet — "How could you!" she had exclaimed the first time she had seen it, when she had come for a visit from Hamilton, a new bride — hardwood flooring and an old-fashioned flowery rug put in, her twin bed replaced by a queen-sized bed, her walls painted a neutral cream. Not hers anymore, but pretty. Never mind that she was an adult, that she was married, that she hadn't lived with her parents for five years. It still hurt a little.

What will they do when I'm gone for good?

As the tea steeped, Sarah listened to Jean talk about the neighbourhood, about old Mrs. Hanson next door, about the new babies at storytime at the library. When her dad finally came back down the stairs and settled into his chair and his newspaper and tea, Jean took her mug and sat down too, gesturing that Sarah should join her.

"So," she said. "Where's he taking you this time?"

Sarah leaned against the counter. The mug felt uncomfortably hot as she fitted her hand around its familiar shape. Her mother had left her her favourite; they were almost identical, but if you looked closely, each had different patterns of tiny cracks in the glaze. She had already had this conversation with Sandra from spinning and with Linda at the lab, and with Nancy, who lived across the country now. With Nancy, it had been a talk-me-out-of-it kind of conversation, the but-of-course-I'm-not-going type. They didn't talk as frequently, with the kids and with the time zones, since Nancy lived 'three hours later,' but a bottle of wine and a phone charger had helped Sarah get through the discussion last Saturday night. They left it as a draw; Nancy demanded a visit to talk it through properly. Anne had pinged a quick response, *So excited for you!* — highly unsatisfactory — but she hadn't seen her in almost a decade anyway. It still stung.

Interstellar travel isn't like moving to another country, not even the furthest country away from where she lived. She wouldn't be just a 30-hour flight away in New Zealand for the rest of her life, extremely inconvenient for visitors, but possible. Most, if not all, of these goodbyes would probably be permanent. *No, not probably.*

There was always the chance, albeit one in a million (or more — she was sure Grant could tell her the odds, and if not, he'd ask one of his colleagues to figure it out for her), that she'd see them again. That the mission would work, and they'd join them one day; but that wouldn't be for years, ten or twenty at least. *'Still young' isn't young.*

She couldn't sit down; her tea was still too hot anyway. She knew her mom would ask; she had been rehearsing this response but choked. She poured out everything she knew, trying to remember how Grant had put it. There was the importance of the mission, the importance of his work, and how he would be a pioneer, the lucky one to take this voyage, to prepare everything for the next ship and the next after that.

She heard herself speaking too fast, giving too much information, saying how much she'd miss him and how selfish he was being, and why did he think he was so special and that it had to be him, that he had to do it. It was his choice, and—

"But you're going with him," Sarah's mother said.

"Till death do you part," Ron intoned, without looking up from his crossword.

"Mom, it means giving up, well, everything. My job, my friends, my home, my life. My *life*." She took a shaky breath and took her hand, her palm pink and swollen from the heat, off the mug. "You guys." She ran her hand through the back of her hair. "They have no idea if we'll ever be coming back, and even if we do, it won't be for years. You'll be—"

"We'll be gone," said her father firmly, putting down his pen. "But you'll go."

Chapter 5

Two years ago, she had unpacked into this home, the one that finally felt like a forever home.

The backyard was a dream when the mosquitos weren't bad. She had fallen in love with it at the viewing. It had a large tree that just begged for a tire swing to be hung from its big branch, a deck, a lawn, bushes to run around and hide behind; everything the kids needed to frolic and wrestle and run and spin. And more, for her: a place to sit with her tea on the weekends and a glass of wine in the evenings, breathing in the green smell of the cool damp air.

"You like it?" Grant had murmured quietly, so the agent wouldn't hear.

"I love it," she whispered back.

Within two weeks of moving in, she had bought giant planters to line the edges of the deck: two long troughs for her herbs, and a big round pot each for the kids. Too late in the season for planting from seed, she helped Maggie transplant colourful mums for the fall. Her long, slender fingers patted down the dirt gently. She buried her pointy little nose in the white, purple and yellow blooms, inhaling deeply before twirling away across the lawn. At the garden centre, Sarah had steered Jack towards chives and a few little pepper plants, hoping they would stand up to his somewhat overenthusiastic handling. He smooshed extra dirt around the roots, poured most of the contents of Sarah's watering can into his pot when her back was turned, then, covered head to toe with dirt, he ran to get a caravan of matchbox cars to drive through the clumps.

In September, for the first time in six years, Sarah could go back to full-time work without feeling like she shouldn't, like she should be spending every waking second with the children that she had wanted so very much.

Her first foray out into her new neighbourhood was, as always, to the closest gym that had spinning classes. Once that was sorted, and the house was in order (Systems!), the boxes and packing paper folded up and stored for their next move, she set out to look for a job.

A career would be almost impossible; they moved around far too often, and besides she had only finished her undergrad with that damn B+ average. She was hardly an attractive prospect at the campuses that welcomed Grant, and she would have been mortified to accept anything offered to her as a favour to him.

She often thought of furthering her education, and spent days, weeks, months considering what sort of project she could do for her Master's. But each time she got settled into a new home, she knew that it would only be a short time before Grant would be offered something new, something a little further up his ladder. Someplace else.

With the kids settled into school, she put her resume together again and reached out to her LinkedIn network for recommendations, then sent it out to a few local labs for positions well within her comfort zone and close to her neighbourhood. Within a week, she was invited to interview for office manager at LabX.

She wasn't nervous.

Why would she be?

She had gone through so many of these over the last thirteen years, and knew the drill: be polite, competent, professional. Wear a sensible blouse and blazer, and low heels. Keep the lipstick neutral. The admin's job isn't to lead, or to shine, but to quietly, and in the background, keep everything running smoothly.

She sometimes felt keenly the direct contrast to her and Grant, whose work, while it was extremely fascinating only to others in his field, was at least not just admin.

"Get over yourself." Nancy always told her. She was nothing if not blunt. Sarah's sidekick schtick, as Nancy called it, had gotten old even before she married Grant. "Your job is admin," she would say. "*You* are not just that."

You've got this, Sar, she told herself as a burgundy-haired receptionist led her into the lab director's office. She was surprised by how pretty it was: grey and teal, with light wood shelves and a functional desk, bare except for two frames, their backs to Sarah.

The director was probably in her late forties, she guessed, with short dark hair and caramel skin. Her glasses matched her charcoal-grey dress. She looked very efficient, very no-nonsense. Dr. Johnson leaned forward over her desk and read through Sarah's resume as she asked questions about her past jobs. She finally put it down, smoothed it out and gazed at Sarah. Behind her glasses, her brown eyes were sharp, almost shrewdly appraising.

"Why do you want this job?" she asked.

Sarah sat up taller. "I'm a natural organizer, I suppose. The kids are both finally in school all day, so I want my own... *thing* again. I know it's been a few years, but I've got a long background as an administrator and I'm familiar with lab work as well. I'm a quick learner, and I think I'd be a good fit."

The director blinked at her again, not looking away. "I don't," she said, finally.

Sarah's shoulders slumped a little. Her eyes flicked to a large abstract painting in soft blues and aquas over Dr. Johnson's shoulder — *how beautiful* — then back to hold her gaze steadily. "Well, thank you for your time, then," she said. She wasn't used to rejection, not for easy, completely-in-her-wheelhouse jobs. She ran her hands down her thighs and started to stand up.

"Michelle da Silva sent me your name before you applied. I've already spoken to two of the labs you've worked at, so I know you're capable of pretty much anything. You'd be a better fit as the lab manager," Dr. Johnson said. "Your resume is fine, your education is great, but I don't see you doing our filing, somehow." She smiled a little, her deep red lips widening. "We don't need a quiet mouse behind the scenes." Her nails, painted the same red as her lipstick, drummed on her desktop once. "We do good work here, but we need someone who can sort us into shape, train the staff on how to do their jobs better. More efficient. More effective." She drummed her nails again. "Etcetera."

Sarah had halted halfway out of her chair. "But Dr. John—"

"Call me Linda. Same hours, $25K more a year, your own office. You can develop 'systems' all you want and boss us all around. What do you think?"

Dazed, Sarah accepted. *What just happened?*

"Diane!" The receptionist popped her brightly dyed head into the office. "Show Ms. Harper her office, please, then get her started on the HR paperwork. She'll be starting—" she paused and whipped her eyes back to Sarah. "—When can you start?"

"Um... I guess Monday?" Sarah was reeling.

"Monday. Let me know what you think of the salary. I don't have much flexibility, though." Linda stood up and handed the resume to Diane. "Shred this, please." She extended her hand out to Sarah, now smiling warmly. "Welcome to LabX."

✷

In the two years since she was hired, Linda had been a cheerleader and a friend, a partner. She treated Sarah as a leader and an equal. Linda was right. The lab work was innovative, their equipment top-of-the-line, but their processes had been in need of updating, or of complete replacement. This was what Sarah was best at: following steps, working within systems, and seeing how systems revealed themselves in practice; anomalies and inefficiencies jumped out at her. Her role, it turned out, wasn't just to manage the lab and develop and test new systems — her favourite thing — but also to train the scientists and technicians on lab protocols. Her confidence grew as she realized that her staff followed her guidance without question, that they saw, as she was starting to, how good she was at her job; the work being done by her lab was starting to attract attention in academic circles. After thirteen years of following and settling, she was working in her field.

The children were older now, more self-reliant. Sarah was starting to think more about herself, her choices, her past and future. The potential that Linda had seen and believed in.

She had seen that potential re-emerge from under all those years as 'Grant's wife' and the kids' mom. So who would she be when she went with him to Mars, other than the mother of his children, the woman behind the great man, his sidekick? At work, she felt valued, intelligent, respected for what she said and did, what she thought.

And now she was going to have to give it up, again.

Chapter 6

Bedtime.

The routine was comforting in its sameness, wherever they were in the world. *Or off of it.* She cringed inwardly. Grant had left for San Antonio this morning, so she was flying solo with the kids for a few days. *As usual.*

Jack had bathed first, eager to test out a submarine he had built from Lego. Judging from the variety of noises emanating from the bathroom, it had depth-control issues and sonar capabilities.

Maggie sat in a wide straddle in the hallway, a book set out in front of her.

"Chest up," Sarah murmured as she passed by with Jack's robe. Maggie straightened her back and rested her elbows on the hall runner, her stomach almost touching as well. She re-pointed her toes and took an audible breath. "Don't push too hard, sweet girl; you'll hurt yourself."

She hung the robe on the back of the door, then knelt down on the mat to wash Jack's hair. He clung to his submarine, his strong little body floating while she rinsed the soap off. "Did you do a good scrub?"

"Mommy?" When he stared at her without his glasses, she felt like he could see through her, like those grey eyes could see the white subway tiles that lined the walls of the bathroom, or beyond, even through the row of ferns on the windowsill. It was unnerving.

"Jack, did you scrub yet?"

He blinked and focused his eyes. "Uhhh... no... Mommy?"

Sarah sighed and picked up his washcloth. She put a dollop of bodywash on it and lathered up his neck, giggling with him as she got to his armpits. "What's up, buddy?"

"What do you think it will be like... in space, I mean?" He was staring dreamily at the ceiling again already.

The kids had taken the news extraordinarily well last night. What kid wouldn't? Space was... well, *space*, and it was cool, the coolest thing in the... *I'm going to have to update all of my expressions.* They had bragged to their friends that morning at school and hadn't stopped strutting around the schoolyard since.

"I don't really know." This was truthful. She had been trying to imagine what their life would look like, for the nine months of space travel, for the rest of their lives on an alien planet, and each time, her brain just shut down. *Too big.* She could imagine packing up her office, packing up their house, starting the rounds of goodbyes... her eyes welled up with tears and she shook her head. "We'll learn more about our spaceship next week, but do you remember the video tours we watched about the last Mars ship?" They had devoured all the information they could find from the last two shuttles: images, videos, anything they could find.

The space shuttle looked... well, on the inside, it looked a lot like a cruise ship. "You'll have your room, and Lego, and school to go to, and friends to play with," she recited as she washed his shins, carefully dabbing at some new playground scrapes.

"And Rupert."

"And Rupert — that means you get to help with his litter box—"

"Yucky!" He scrunched up his nose, distracted for a moment. "And stars... what will the stars look like, up close?"

"Ok, all clean. Well, we're not going to be close to the stars. We'll just be more... *among* the stars. Up you get!" Sarah pulled him up to his feet and used her forearm to push a lock of hair away from her face. She sighed as she rubbed him down with a navy-blue towel. His hair stood straight up in spiky points. "I really don't know, buddy. It's going to be something we discover at the same time I think. Now, brush your teeth, please. Miss Maggie!" she called into the hallway. "You have five minutes till your turn!" Jack wriggled into his bathrobe, letting the damp towel pool around his feet. She scooped it up, then bent to pull the plug, and her hair fell into her face again.

*

11 years ago
Copenhagen, Denmark

Another beautiful day.

"Not a bad life, eh?" Sarah stretched out on the crisp white sheets, yawning, while Grant tied his tie. Behind him, she could just see the top of a building against a grey-blue sky. A tiny plane sketched its line across her view, the end trailing away into nothing. She smiled sleepily as he bustled around the hotel room.

They were on vacation — well, she was on vacation; Grant was presenting at a conference — in Copenhagen. He was travelling, as usual, and twice a year or so, she took a few days off work, or an extra-long weekend, to tag along with him. While he was in meetings and sessions, networking or whatever-it-was-he-did-at-these-things, she had the days free to explore the area. Beaches, museums, galleries, monuments... they went to places that she would have never chosen to go, but each time she was impressed by the newness and difference of the cultures.

And the sameness of the mothers.

Without exception, people outside of her hometown were louder, ruder, stood closer, made her feel like an outsider. But the mothers with babies: in strollers, in slings, strapped to their chests or backs... they were all the same, the way they held their little ones close and cooed and murmured to them, the way they stroked fuzzy little heads and proudly turned to show them off to this quiet stranger.

She hadn't been 'Sarah' for so long. She had been 'Grant's wife' or, more usually, 'Dr. Harper's wife' — not even 'Mrs. Harper!' — ever since they had moved away from her hometown. Why not be known as somebody's mother, then?

It would be slightly more of an identity, linked at least to something she herself had achieved.

Getting a dog or having a baby, she decided, was the way to go. Both are excellent ice breakers when you move to a new town. Both love you unconditionally and have a considerable amount of upkeep, slobber and poop. Both would be a challenge to train into respectable members of society.

Grant was allergic to dogs.

Decision made. But here she was, two years later, and no baby. Grant wasn't worried. "These things take time sometimes," he told her. They hadn't been trying, but they hadn't been *not* trying, either. All her very careful, meticulous contraception practices had slowly been abandoned, one by one, after their second anniversary. "Why not?" they had said. She was young, but why not? What else was she going to do?

She'd miss the travel. Tagging along after Dr. Harper had its perks, for sure. He presented at least six times a year, at conferences and schools in Europe, all over North America and was waiting for a formal invitation from New Zealand. She had been damp and cold in Scotland, just plain cold in Sweden, and completely impressed by Slovenia. She had wandered Disneyland all by herself for a day, which was lonely, but also advantageous for lineups; a single rider was a hot commodity. So many cities and countries, which hadn't been 'on her list' were suddenly part of her story.

Copenhagen was... *nice*, she mused, as she walked somewhat aimlessly down cobbled sidewalks. A clean city, if chilly, and felt constrained, reserved; a place where systems had their place. She liked that.

She paused in front of a window full of colourful pottery, then walked down the steps into the small shop, empty except for the woman behind the counter. She smiled tightly as Sarah browsed muted colours of stoneware in all shapes and sizes on the shelves.

A gurgling coo caught her ear and she turned, surprised. The woman pressed her lips together, then said something in Danish, indicating something tucked behind the desk. Sarah peeked over the counter. There, in a little playpen, was a plump baby — *What was he, six months old? Older?* — waving his fists and feet around and fussing. She smiled at the clerk and said, "He's beautiful." He *was*. His eyes shone as bright of a blue as Grant's, and he gave her a gummy smile.

The woman's face relaxed and she spoke quickly. "My babysitter couldn't come today," she said in good, but accented English. "He is usually no trouble." Sarah barely knew what she was doing as her hands reached toward the baby, glancing first at his mother for approval.

When was the last time she held a baby? She held him gingerly at first, then cuddled him closer and smelled his white-blond hair. *This is what I don't have.* She shifted him over to her left arm and walked through the shop slowly again, bouncing as she went, pointing at this and that item, repeating his sounds and squeals. It felt natural, right.

Sarah reluctantly returned him to his mother with a smile, then turned back to the shelves. She picked up a rustic hand-cast stoneware mug, the cool grey blue of the sky outside. It warmed in her hand, and she cupped her other hand around it, imagining holding a hot cup of tea. She picked up a second of the same and brought them to the counter to buy.

The shopkeeper wrapped them gently in paper while Sarah made faces at the baby, who was tucked back up in his playpen.

She placed the parcel gently into her backpack, then waved goodbye to the little boy. The woman held out her receipt, and as their fingers touched, Sarah felt that this stranger could see through her. She took a deep breath, smiled at her, and left the store quickly.

Three moves in four years, she brooded as she walked down more cobbled sidewalks. She wasn't lonely, exactly — there were always people to meet — other faculty members' wives, coworkers, friendly faces at the gym — but lately, she thought that she wanted something more.

She found herself doodling at meetings. Her sketches were of hands, and then of little hands holding bigger hands, then just of little hands.

She wanted a baby.

*

"Good night, Jackattack." He was snuggled under cool, light-blue sheets, his hair still tousled and damp on his pillow. Rupert sat at the foot of his bed, licking his back leg and studiously ignoring them both.

She bent to hug her little boy and was rewarded with his standard almost-too-tight hug. "Grrr," he growled softly.

"Oof," she said, returning his smile. She reached for his nightstand and turned his glasses over so that they weren't resting lens-side down, then neatened a small stack of books that threatened to tip over.

Jack's personality was showing in his room more each year. It housed a growing collection of books; he was a surprisingly avid reader, though he had just started getting into chapter books. She loved to watch him without him noticing, as his pale grey eyes scanned a page then fixed dreamily on the wall. Sarah had put up shelves and cubbies for his Lego, too; he was an Advanced Lego Builder, he said, and constantly rotated a display of his creations. His two good friends at school were like him in personality, if not in form. Tucker and Jackson were scrawnier, more nerdy in appearance, but Jack could nerd with the best of them. *He's young. He'll make new friends. But it won't be the same,* another voice argued back.

"See you in the morning, buddy. I love you." She paused at his doorway for a moment, her finger on the lightswitch. Rupert looked up and leaped down from the bed to follow her out.

“Aw...” Jack’s eyes were already closing. “Mmmm... I love you too.” She closed the door softly and crossed the hall. The bathroom light was still on, and Maggie’s book still lay where she had been stretching. She flipped the switch and picked up the book.

“Systems,” she muttered under her breath.

Maggie had her PJs on, a long nightshirt of lilac Tshirt material. She lay on top of her pink duvet, knees bent, feet in the air, her hair twisted up into a towel turban. Her head was bent over a pink clipboard in front of her, and she held a pompom-topped pencil in her hand.

Maggie’s room was artistic, pretty, just so... so *Maggie*. Sarah had first helped her pin up her own drawings on her side of the tiny room she shared with Jack in London, when she was four, as a way to make it feel like her own space. At first, there were just a few childish drawings of ballerinas with big heads and stick arms and legs, big pink triangle tutus. Over the next four years, the drawings added to the collection got better and better, more lifelike, more in scale. They now covered the entire bottom half of her bedroom, some with ribbons dangling from them. When the window was open like tonight, or the door was pushed open, the ribbons fluttered delicately. They swayed as Sarah reached down to pick up Maggie’s damp bathrobe off the floor and returned it to its hook. She put the book back on the bookshelf.

“What are you drawing now, Miss Maggie?” She peered over her shoulder. Maggie tilted her head to the side to allow a clear view of a full-skirted ballerina — *of course* —

reaching her arms up in a field of stars. She grinned. "That looks about right."

Maggie smiled back at her, then drew a circle around her dancer's head. "That's her helmet." Her toes, always pointed, drew little circles in the air as well. Sarah lowered herself down to lie on the bed, shoulder to shoulder with her daughter. She waited. Maggie added a few more stars.

"I'll colour it in the morning," she said, and wrapped ribbons up the dancer's long, slim legs. "I'm going to bring all of my drawings with me, and my ballet shoes and all of my leotards and barbies." She paused. "Sophia said that when I leave, she'll be the best dancer in class, and I said that ha-ha, then that means that *I'm* the best dancer now." She looked squarely at Sarah now, as if daring her to disagree. "Because I am."

Sarah rolled her eyes. "I know, Mags. But you know that it's because you work so hard at it and try so hard and love it.

"So hey... you've had a full day to think about the move, so what do you think?"

Maggie shrugged, and her eyes dropped. Then she grinned. "I'm going to dance in the stars."

Sarah's eyes misted up again as she hugged the skinny little body close and kissed her cool cheek. "That you are, Miss Maggie."

She took the clipboard and pencil from her and put it on the bookshelf, then helped her unwrap her hair. It fell to just below her shoulders. "Do you want it dried tonight?"

"No thanks, Mom. Just bed." She crawled under the covers and fanned her hair around her on her pillow. It would be dry, shiny and smooth when she woke up. *It's not fair*. Sarah gave her a kiss on the forehead.

"Sweet dreams, sweet girl."

She went to the door and flicked out the light. Slowly, on the ceiling, stick-on constellations began to emerge from the darkness. In the lamplight from Maggie's open window, she could see her daughter's eyes gleaming in the dark.

Chapter 7

The preparation for space travel was worse than she'd expected. Test after test at the doctor's office, scans, sample after sample of blood, of urine. Linda had been understanding about taking time away from her job. No, not her job, she reminded herself again. Her *career*.

Sarah sat in the near-empty waiting room, flipping through her notes, mentally rehearsing her points and statistics. A woman across from her leafed through one of the lab's dated magazines, sighing deeply every minute or so. *Don't engage, Sar. Focus and review.*

Linda was as excited about this presentation as she was.

"This is ridiculous," she grumbled again as she walked back into her office, hanging her coat up on her hook and picking up her lab coat. "I'm spending all of my time at a different lab, when I could be doing these tests myself. Or LabX could be getting the money for it." The philodendron on her bookcase looked limp. *Water*. She made a mental note.

Linda had followed her in. She grinned. "It's fine. It's exciting, and we can manage without you for an hour or two."

Sarah groaned. "I just feel like it's an hour or two every day! When are you going to fire me?"

"I don't need to," said Linda. "We'll be rid of you soon enough." She put her hand on Sarah's arm for a moment, then winked. "Now, look sharp. The new partner's coming at eleven to see our successful operation, and I need you in fighting form. Are you sure you're ok?"

"Yeah," said Sarah. "They didn't take much this time."

The inside of her elbow was sore, but she could deal with it. The kids weren't coping as well. Despite their initial bravery and the still-real excitement of boarding a space shuttle, the repeated prodding and poking was wearing them out, and they looked more tired and twitchier every time she picked them up from school for another round of tests. Jack had sniffed out a few uncharacteristic tears during this latest blood sample. *Quiet, strong Jack.* Maggie had sobbed, of course. Sarah gritted her teeth and choked back the words she wanted to say to Grant, who seemed to be feeling fitter and healthier each day.

All four of them had to be in perfect health; BioMars could still pull them off the trip. Part of Sarah — a big part, if she was being honest — was hoping for a nice, little, easy-to-cure tumour somewhere, or a recurring UTI, something that was a nuisance, but not terminal. Just enough to keep them here on Earth. Their dental health was minutely examined, their eyes, their ears, their lungs... they were onto the phlebotomy portion of the testing, and then just had the gastrointestinal bit left.

Save the best for last, she joked.

It wasn't funny at all.

She peeled the tape off her arm and tossed the soiled cotton ball into the biohazard container, then shrugged into her lab coat. She leaned over her desk and woke up her computer, dropping her head down to stretch out her neck. A stray lock of hair had slipped out of its clip, and she nibbled at it absentmindedly as she raised her eyes back to her screen.

"Sarah?"

She jerked upright, startled by the familiar voice. A tall man stood in the doorway to her office, his blue dress shirt and grey pants well-fitting but slightly creased. His eyes, still the same grey as her own, twinkled as they looked her up and down.

He looked older — *did she look that old, too?* — and broader across the shoulders, more of a man than the boy she had loved in university. There were little lines around his eyes when he smiled and his hair, cut short, was a little duller than it had been.

She hadn't seen Ethan, *officially,* since graduation. He had given her a friendly handshake and a shy kiss on the cheek, despite — or maybe because of — Grant's sombre presence beside her. "Good luck, Sar," he had whispered in her ear.

"Ethan!" She came out from behind her desk and embraced him too formally, the way that diplomat's wives do. It embarrassed them both, and they were both a little pink-cheeked as she drew away. She laughed nervously. "What are you doing here?"

Last she had heard, he had finished his Master's and was working as managing director of a medical lab out west. She chose not to follow him on social media. She hadn't heard from him in six years, had figured he had stayed out there, met someone and settled down. But here he was, in her office. Flustered, she tucked her hair behind her ear again.

"Ethan! You made it! Sarah, this is Ethan Michaels. He's the new directing partner at LabX." Linda's crisp voice came from the doorway. She was holding her laptop and looking back and forth between the two of them, clearly aware of something going on. "But I see you know each other already. Shall we?"

Sarah gathered up her notes and laptop and followed Linda to the conference room, sensing Ethan's eyes on her back.

She had been thinking about him more and more frequently lately, ever since Grant had announced their next move. She knew that it had never been an either/or situation, that had she not gone off with Grant so completely, it in no way guaranteed that she would be with Ethan today. It had been... *oh my God...* eighteen years since they had dated? People change in much less time than that. They grow and argue, and the easiness and support of their relationship would have probably — *definitely*, she told herself — felt the strain of growing up.

She had forgotten again how tall he was — only an inch shorter than Grant, with long arms and legs too. Where Ethan was relaxed, casual, warm, where his long arms were made for hugging and holding and punching you in the shoulder with a joke, Grant's height was reinforced by his strict upright posture. She was 5'3" — just out of the petites section, and her spinning, weight sessions at the gym and a very careful diet kept her from being stocky like her dad, like Jack. Maggie had been lucky to avoid her genes. Grant was over six feet, and still rangy, just by luck, not with exercise, and it seemed like Ethan was still lean, too.

"Are you still running?" she asked him as she organized herself and threw her presentation up onto the screen, avoiding his eyes. *Stop blushing.*

It was the only thing she could think to ask him.

This would be harder than she expected.

She had written the presentation over two days — deadlines make the world go round — and she knew her subject cold: the statistics, the protocols, the cost savings and staff efficiencies — these were all protocols that she had developed, after all. But to have to give this, frankly, *boring* presentation, to be serious and professional in front of Linda, when all she wanted to do was apologize, then laugh and reconnect; this was going to be a stiff and dry meeting.

She kept catching a glimpse of Ethan's lip twitching and his eyes sparkling as she worked her way awkwardly through the presentation. She knew her stuff, but it just wasn't coming out right. The damn man knew she was uncomfortable and wanted her to sweat. *Fine.* Linda's forehead stayed creased, but she filled in numbers and added extra information when Sarah left it out, and eventually, she was done.

"Any questions?" She still hadn't clipped that piece of hair back, and now it hung over her forehead. She brushed it back impatiently and met his gaze.

"It's a lot to consider," he responded. "Your protocols seem sound, and if your statistics are right—"

"They are," said both Linda and Sarah at the same time.

He smiled. "Let me take tonight to look at it more closely. I promise I'll have questions in the morning, but for now... it's a lot to take in all at once. May I have a copy of your presentation and your stats?"

Linda smiled and stood up. "I'll get Diane to email it to you now. She'll schedule you in tomorrow as well. In the meantime, I've got a new distributor to meet." She shook Ethan's hand, then rushed out of the room, shooting a pointed glance just once at Sarah, who kept a straight face.

As soon as her boss had left, Sarah put her head down on the desk. "That was awful. I'm so sorry." Ethan started laughing and she joined in. "It's good to see you."

"It *was*. And it's good to see you too." He watched her disconnect her laptop, grinning. "You and your systems. I should have known Sarah Sheridan was the genius behind all this. Listen, I have an extremely boring document to review this afternoon, but maybe we could grab dinner? Catch up, for old times' sake?"

Sarah busied herself with her notebook. "It's Sarah *Harper*, and I can't, I'm afraid. The kids, you know."

Ethan wrinkled his nose. "Ugh, kids. Can't you tie them to something and leave out a bowl of cat food?"

She grinned. "You know I can't, but maybe I can rustle up a babysitter. Let me give you a call later?"

"You bet." He reached out to take her hand again. "I hope I'll see you." He swivelled his head towards the door. "Who am I supposed to see? Dina?"

"Diane," she responded. "She's the receptionist with the nametag that says 'Diane.'"

*

Back at her desk, she pulled out her clip and shook out her hair before pulling it back somewhat neatly again. She rolled her shoulders back and waggled her head side to side, releasing the tension that had built up.

She sat lost in thought for a moment. *So many memories.* She'd be saying goodbye to him all over again, this time forever. Permanent, for once and for all. There would be no pressure to say anything, to come clean, to do the right thing.

For whom, though?

Tea. She needed a hot cup of tea.

But first, she picked up her phone and started scrolling through her list of babysitters.

Chapter 8

Where is the support? Sarah fumed, her legs pumping.

Her parents had accepted that she'd be leaving forever in a few months, too easily. Her friends pushed her to 'keep the family together,' all except Anne, whose "So excited for you!" text she left unanswered. *What the hell kind of response is* that *to "I'm leaving forever?"* She pumped her legs even harder.

It felt good to transfer her anger into exercise, to let it out. At home, she was snappy with the kids, frustrated to be doing something mundane like folding laundry or making the beds, instead of what she wanted to do. She wanted to ... she didn't know exactly, but if her 'time on Earth' was limited – *no wonder it's a euphemism for dying* – she wanted to make the most of every second. Another lunch eaten outside, on the lawn at the park. Another evening spent watching the kids play in the backyard, or a Sunday afternoon leaning against the trunk of the big tree with a book.

Another spin class.

She turned the dial up further than the instructor told her to. Her heart pounded and she gasped, sweat running down her wrists and calves.

"That's how you know you're working!" the instructor shouted at her over the music. "If your wrists are sweating, right?" Sarah gave a half-smile and kept pushing. There had to be another way, another option, other than just going along with Grant on this crazy trip, giving up her world.

Who was she, really? She felt like she had only started to find out when Linda had offered her the job managing the lab. After years of sidekicking, of following, she was asked for her opinion. People now listened to her in meetings, took what she recommended seriously. She was using her brain and remembering that yes, she was intelligent, not just as a spouse and a mother, but as a person. She'd be giving that up.

Interval over. She sat back and slowed her legs, letting them spin with very little resistance. Feeling her heart rate start to slow, her breathing ease. What would she even feel like, in space?

"Time!"

She turned the dial and started climbing that hill again.

✷

It's a good thing she was working so hard at the gym, she mused as she stepped out of the shower, her face still red. Last night, they had gone to KFC. She had taken the kids to McDonald's on Saturday. Those weren't her favourite places to go, but they had asked, and she had started making a list of 'lasts.' Last meal at McDonald's. Last playdate at the trampoline park. Last trip to Grandma's. She pushed this last out of her mind; it hurt too much.

Her shower had been lukewarm, but restorative. She was still vibrating, tingling, as she dried off with her gym towel. She had burned a lot of the day's stress away on that spinning bike, put more effort than usual into her class.

She slipped into clean under-things, then put her work clothes back on; they would have to do. Her cheeks were still flushed from her workout, and she quickly drew an approximation of an evening eye with eyeliner and two coats of mascara. Sarah combed some anti-frizz serum through her damp hair and scrunched it up to bring out its waves. A shine of lipgloss, and she was ready.

She rolled her damp clothes up into her gym bag, and zipped her spinning shoes into their little pocket, then cursed as her tights caught on the edge of the locker. A run quickly laddered its way up her calf. *Dammit dammit.*

"*Dammit!*" she said out loud. Two older women looked over at her, then away.

What, were they going to have an infinite supply of pantyhose on the ship? Would they be able to order them, to arrive by shuttle in only one short year? Would they synthesize nylon in the lab and weave them themselves? Was she really mourning the possibility of a life without pantyhose? What was she getting herself into?

She glanced at her watch.

Dammit again. What was she even doing?

She was going to leave the Earth behind and see what else was out there waiting for her.

And before she finished her time on Earth, there was so much to do, to touch, to see. *To eat.*

And hence the spinning classes and the extra turns of the dial.

*

Grant would be at his lab till ten at least, frequently even later. Since he had accepted the offer from BioMars, she saw him even less than usual. He came in after the kids went to bed, sitting up in the den most nights till after she'd retired for the night. Sometimes she saw him very briefly in the morning before he dashed out the door. He had more travel now: a speaking tour of the universities, networking with industry reps whose companies supported the mission. Sarah often felt like a single mom.

Janelle from next door had been happy to pick up the kids from aftercare, to take them back to her place until her teenager came home from school, so that was taken care of. Sarah was rarely ever able to both work out and shower before leaving downtown, so she took advantage of the time she had. She still had almost 45 minutes before she was supposed to meet Ethan, and she stepped into the nail salon in the lobby, just on a whim.

Thirty-five minutes later, she sat in the bar in the hotel lobby, admiring her short, pearly-pink manicure and sipping a glass of red wine. She had put her phone on silent and checked it quickly — no messages from the babysitter — then dropped it into her purse and took part in a bit of people-watching.

A slim 60-something man, quite dapper in a checked sport coat and close-fitting pants, joined a silver-blonde woman with bright red lipstick in a booth by the window. He kissed her on the cheek dramatically once, twice, three times, then put his arm around her shoulders, the two of them grinning like they owned the world.

Longtime lovers? An affair?

Sarah blushed. *That's not what this is*, she told herself. Further down the bar, a group of businessmen leaned against the bar-top, obviously into their third or fourth beers, their discussion of something financial, something about markets and this or that trade getting louder and more raucous. Money had been made today, that much was clear. *And what was* that *woman's story*? A lone woman at the bar, her eyes darkly rimmed, sitting alone… *oh.* That mysterious woman was her.

What *was* her story?

"Always punctual, Miss Sheridan!" There were hands on her waist and a kiss brushed on her cheek. Sarah's eyes flicked up and her mouth broke into a grin almost as big as the couple's in the booth. It felt good to see Ethan. It always was. He was kind and supportive and warm, three words that had never seemed to fit Grant. Grant was a good provider. He was ambitious. He was intense, blazing with a white heat. But he wasn't Ethan.

It was odd. When she had met Grant, she had left Ethan behind, immediately grown out of him. Had he mesmerized her with those blue eyes, convinced her without having to convince her that she only needed, only wanted him? For the last two years of undergrad, she had barely noticed Ethan, who was still in her classes and labs, but not her partner anymore. He had quietly switched with Nancy, and that was fine. She hadn't minded. After graduation, too, he just felt like another one of her classmates, an acquaintance that she had shared an experience with — *four years!* — but hadn't left a hole in her life.

Seeing him again now, though, brought memories rushing back of the fun they had had as students, as partners. The ease with which they had fit into each other's lives — Sarah felt as though she always had to fit into Grant's life. *God, we were so young.*

She hadn't thought of Ethan at all for years after university. The wedding, all the moves, all the excitement of Grant's breakthroughs, the loneliness when he travelled, that damn cat. The challenges and pain of trying to start a family.

And that was when she ran into him. Nine years ago. Grant's career had taken them to Boulder, and he was a rising star at University of Colorado's biology department. She was 29 then, and the fittest she had ever been. She had a lot of time on her hands: her not-challenging job meant that she could funnel any extra energy she had into exercise and nutrition, and her focus had been on being as healthy as possible. Maybe that would help her get pregnant.

She had been wandering rather aimlessly up and down the aisles of the supermarket on a Thursday night, looking for something that would taste good enough to cheer her up without having too much fat or sugar in it. Grant had been invited to speak at the University of Nebraska's biology department dinner, then act as guest lecturer the next day, so wouldn't be home till Saturday morning at the earliest.

Her cart was half-empty (*that's how I know I'm a pessimist*, she told herself wryly), piled with oranges, kale, dried beans and vegetable broth. She was pointing her cart towards the chicken breasts when a voice behind her made her whirl around on the spot.

"Dear Lord, if that isn't the most depressing grocery cart I've ever seen!"

"Ethan!" The flood of memories, the internal fight of the last few years to be something other than somebody's assistant and sidekick, threw her into his arms. Her head hit him squarely in the middle of the chest, her arms wrapped tightly around his waist.

"Oof! Hey, it's good to see you, too! What the hell are you doing in... uh... Boulder?"

She didn't let go, just kept squeezing, now digging her chin into his sternum as she looked up at him with wet eyes. He looked older, stronger and wore glasses now. But it felt like coming home.

"What are *you* doing in 'uh... Boulder?' I live here!"

Ethan smiled down at her. His eyes were still as familiar as her own. "Sorry, Sar. I've been travelling for a while. It's hard to remember what city I'm in sometimes."

He had been on an eight-city tour of tradeshows for Quest Diagnostics — "A booth babe," he joked — and had two more to go after Boulder. He looked tired, but the same. She hadn't seen him in seven years, but somehow it was still easy to talk to him, easy for him to fill her cart with 'good food': some chocolate, chips and salsa, fresh sausages, crackers and cheese. A bottle of red wine. "Come on, Sar. I can't let you go home with just kale."

His basket had chips, oatmeal and orange juice in it. "And beer," he said, grabbing a six-pack from the shelf. "The minibar is highway robbery."

They walked out to her car together and he watched her load her few bags into her trunk. He pointed at his rental. "That's me." He paused, then, his hands in his pockets, suddenly looking again like he had when she had swiftly, suddenly, chosen Grant.

"Do... would you like to grab a bite to eat? With me?"

She watched his headlights in her rear-view mirror and saw his glasses flash in the streetlights as he followed her to a Thai restaurant nearby. They walked in together and looked at the menu while they waited to be seated. Sarah realized how hungry she was. *Starving.*

"Everything. I want one of everything on the menu."

"What about spring rolls?"

"Three of those."

It was so easy. To agree on what dishes to share, to talk about old times. Careful not to mention Grant more than once or twice, Sarah told herself that she was happy, as convincingly as she told Ethan. Her job was boring, she admitted, but she was able to focus on other things, on hobbies and herself instead of just a microscope. It was so easy to laugh and laugh.

And easy to follow his rental car to his hotel.

The next morning, she called in sick to work; they wouldn't miss her. The ten o'clock sun was warm on her hair when she left the hotel, when she crossed the parking lot to her car and opened the trunk. She took the chicken and sausages out of the grocery bag and dropped them in the garbage can by the sidewalk before getting in her car and driving home.

✷

How strange, even amazing, that she rarely thought about it afterwards, like she had erased that night from her mind as easily as she had left him the first time.

Almost two years later, she ran into him again, this time back in her hometown. Her parents had taken little Maggie, just 13 months old, for the weekend, so that she and Grant could go to a bed and breakfast for the night — ostensibly to reconnect and have a romantic getaway, but really, Sarah plotted, for the first good night's sleep she'd have had in a year.

Two days before their reservation, Grant called her at home in the middle of the day, something he never did. *Dammit,* thought Sarah. Her instinct was correct; he was being called in to consult on a project. "But this weekend?" her voice was quavering and babyish. Maggie fussed and threw her giraffe.

"I'm sorry, Sarah. Duty calls. We'll do it some other time."

She was tired — *God, she was tired.* And she was too embarrassed to tell her mother that Grant had bailed on their romantic night. She kept quiet, packed her overnight bag, and dropped Maggie off to her mom as planned. She'd take advantage of the in-suite hot tub herself, then, and that California king bed was calling to her.

She stopped to fill up her car — no longer pristine, cheerios all over the back seat — and recognized Ethan's tall frame at the pump across from her. His cheeks went pink, and he hastily replaced the nozzle. He crossed to her in a few long steps and touched her arm.

"I— I tried to get in touch. I couldn't track down your phone number. You're not on Facebook, but I sent a few messages to your old email address."

She had seen the messages in her inbox, deleted them without reading them. It had been a mistake, and there was no point revisiting it. It was better that way.

"I haven't used that email in years!" she said brightly, carelessly. "And don't worry about me. How are you?"

They had coffee together, tea for her — he remembered — and a slice of pie. She waved away his concerns, his unasked question, and subtracted three months from Maggie's age. Being a mom was lovely. She's beautiful. My eyes, Grant's hair. So rewarding.

When they ended up back at his hotel room this time, she wasn't even surprised.

Chapter 9

Sarah turned the key quietly in the lock and eased the door open. It was 11:30, later than she had planned on staying out, and when she texted the sitter an hour ago with an apology, she was dismayed to read her response: Grant had just gotten home, no problem at all.

Ah.

She had been counting on him being out. *Oh well.*

His car was in the driveway. She had pulled in behind him; she'd have to move it in the morning, earlier than she'd like to be up, but it would be easier than facing him tonight. She straightened up, walked in her own front door the way she imagined she would have had she not just spent the last two hours wrapped around another man. She dropped her gym bag and purse on the mat, then hung her coat on the empty hook. Sliding off her shoes, she said out loud, "Well, that feels good," hoping that Grant would hear.

The main floor was mostly dark; the over-the-stove light was left on in the kitchen, which probably meant... yes, that the dinner dishes were waiting for her. *Deep breath.* She emptied her sweaty gym clothes into the basket in the laundry room behind the kitchen. Above her, she heard Grant cough, and she tensed. *Am I hoping more that he won't come down or that he's developing a harmless-yet-career-limiting lung disease?* She wasn't sure which, but after a few seconds she relaxed her shoulders.

She pushed up her sleeves, poured a glass of water, and turned on the hot water to fill the sink. While the bubbles were growing, she wiped down the stove — tomato soup — and the table — *so, so many crumbs* — and gathered the dishes into a stack on the counter.

The warm water felt good on her hands and wrists. She felt light, clean. The bowls and plates, glasses, pots and utensils all came clean easily, too. Once they were rinsed and stacked in the dishrack to air dry, she pulled the plug, sighed and dropped her head down, stretching out the back of her neck again. She'd have to make an appointment with her chiropractor.

Hands on her waist, a kiss on her cheek. She forced herself to stay still. The sounds of the water slurping down the drain must have muffled his footsteps behind her.

"Hello," he said.

She could smell alcohol on his breath. *Scotch? Bourbon*? She couldn't tell them apart. Grant never drank *too* much, but on quiet nights he would have a small glass of something civilized. Grownup. As always.

She pulled her shoulders back, pasted a suitably tired smile on her face and turned around. She blew that lock of hair out of her eyes and leaned against him. "Hi," she said in a small voice.

"I didn't know you were going out tonight."

It wasn't a question. That was the thing about Grant. He could make statements that anyone else would want explained, and he sincerely wouldn't care. He just meant that he hadn't known.

Her head was turned to one side against his chest, her still-damp hands on the counter behind her. "It was a last-minute thing," she mumbled, surprised at how sleepy she suddenly, actually, felt. "Big presentation to Corporate today. I was terrible, but Linda and I celebrated anyway. I thought I'd beat you home."

His finger went under her chin, lifted it so that she was looking up at those blue eyes, the angle of her neck uncomfortable with the height difference. "Drinks?"

"One before, one with dinner," she recited. "Then I switched to water, Dr. Breathalyzer." The strict control that he kept over himself meant that he was the designated driver almost all of the time. She knew how he felt about her drinking anything and getting behind the wheel, even four hours later. "I'm ok," she murmured. "I promise. I'm just ti-i-i-red—" she stifled a yawn. "We sat there and talked for longer than I intended. I'm sorry. I'll move my car in the morning."

She put her hands against his stomach, and he backed away from her touch.

"Wet hands," he grinned.

She smiled back and turned away, waggling her neck, then slowly climbed the stairs to their bedroom. *God, she was tired.* It was all she could do to get into her pyjamas and brush her teeth — she decided that her face had gotten clean enough after her second shower. She peeked her head into Maggie's room, ribbons fluttering as the opened door stirred up the air inside, then into Jack's, whose floor was booby-trapped with a swath of razor-sharp Lego. His glasses were sitting, lenses down, on his bedside table. She sighed as she turned them over. She'd clean it up with him tomorrow. He was a good little guy. Those two… they made everything worthwhile.

Grant was in their bathroom when she climbed into bed. He had already turned his bedside lamp on, so she pulled the covers up under her chin, tucked herself into a ball facing away from the light and closed her eyes. She meant to fall asleep right away, to fall back into her real life the way she had done each other time, forgiving herself, erasing what she had done. She waited for Grant's power, his sense of order and right, his confidence in his own abilities and in her, to draw her back to him like magic.

The bathroom light went out and she felt Grant climb onto his side of the bed. He smelled of toothpaste and some drugstore-brand men's face wash. She heard him rustle to get comfortable and heard the click of the lamp as he turned it off. He rolled over and gently put a hand on her shoulder.

She waited in the dark. *Was he hesitating?*

"I love you, Sarah."

"Mmm," she responded, but her eyes were suddenly open in the blackness, not yet accustomed to the dim. He had the same routine every night, him coming to bed after her, his light left on while she slept. She did love him. He was her rock, her star. She had hitched her wagon to him and had seen so much of this beautiful world with this incredible, brilliant man. And their kids — they were magical. All their travels, and the sacrifices they had both — no, all made, all culminating in this impossibly incredible next step.

After tomorrow, she would never — literally never — see Ethan again.

Her wide-open eyes filled with tears.

Chapter 10

Sarah yawned again, her knee jiggling under her desk. Her neck was aching again, and she had reheated the same cup of tea three times already. She had gotten up with Grant, to move her car out onto the street so he could reverse out of their driveway and drive down their cul-de-sac towards his lab. He didn't look back in the rear-view mirror, didn't see her waving, her pyjamas covered by her robe.

She had stumbled back into the house and squinted at the clock on the stove. 6:30. *Ugh.* She debated between falling back into bed for twenty minutes or using the time constructively.

"Man up, Sar," she said aloud. "Be a grownup." By the time the kids got up at 6:50, she had straightened her hair and applied a little bit more makeup than usual.

"You look pretty, Mommy," said Jack, between bites of granola. He had a milk moustache, and his dark hair stuck up like hers had, twenty minutes before. Maggie had already brushed hers smoothly back in a ponytail. She liked to get dressed and ready before breakfast, so that she could organize her school supplies and make sure she was neat and presentable, and more importantly, ready before her little brother.

How is she mine?

Sarah asked herself for the millionth time.

She wasn't sure how long she had slept last night, if at all. She got up for a glass of water once, then once to pee, without turning the bathroom light on. Her eyes had been open for hours in the dark; she could see just as well as Rupert by then. She had decided that her best move would be to take so much extra care in her appearance this morning that neither Linda nor Ethan could tell there was anything wrong. A simple wrap dress, low heels. Tasteful, appropriate, extra blush to bring a pretence of life into her pale face, a swipe of concealer to hide the purple circles under her eyes.

Once the kids were on the school bus, she put her travel mug of green tea in her car's cup holder, and off she went.

Her lab was a 23-minute drive away. She used to feel guilty for driving instead of finding her way by public transit, but it took an hour and five minutes by bus if she made all of her connections. Add that to the infrequent but always urgent-when-they-came calls from the school to pick up a vomiting child, and it just wasn't worth it. She felt the need to justify it, still: she drove an eco-friendly, second-hand Prius. So there. It was hers, and barring road trips with the kids, kept it free of garbage — no gum wrappers or used tissues — and loved the solitude of driving alone. Life was funny; after years of missing Grant so much when he was away and pining for children that just weren't coming for so long, she had discovered the perfect happiness of driving herself in her own car with her own music, twice a day. *Bliss.*

Today, she listened to newsradio, letting bad news after shooting after bombing wash over her for a few minutes after she parked. Her eyes burned. She sipped her tea; too hot, it scalded her tongue.

With her shoulders pulled back and down, Sarah settled an alert face onto her tired features and walked briskly into the office. Diane wasn't on the phones yet, though the lights were all flashing. She had a strict policy against answering the phones a second before 8:30. She was intent on her computer — *probably Facebook*, Sarah thought — but chirped, "Good morning," without even looking up, her burgundy hair pulled back into two braids over her shoulders.

Linda was already in, suited up again, and looked up when Sarah paused by her door. She had hoped to drop a quick greeting before slinking off to her own desk, to drop her professional, awake act for a few minutes, but she called, "Come in, lovely! Do you have time to prep before Mr. Corporate's return?"

Ethan was due to meet with them at ten. *The lucky bastard was probably still in bed*, thought Sarah.

"I do," she said, trying to look lively and perky. "Let me just drop my coat and refresh my tea."

At 9:45, Linda popped her head into Sarah's office. "Hey... conference room?"

Oh crap. Sarah massaged her cheeks, finished the rest of her cold tea — *does jittery count as alert,* she wondered — and brought her laptop and notebook into the large room. Linda was already there, insulated coffee cup steaming away.

“I’m so sorry,” Sarah babbled. “I was reviewing the stats again to make sure I’ve got the answers this time, and-”

“Forget it,” Linda said warmly. “You’ve got this. *We’ve* got this. I want to know what’s going on with you and Ethan.”

Sarah opened and shut her mouth a few times.

“We dated in university,” she managed, blushing. “For years. And it— I was shocked to see him again like that. I— I haven’t told him... that I’m leaving, and I don’t know how. It just made everything a little more overwhelming.” She averted her eyes as she poured herself a glass of ice water from the jug that Diane had put on the conference table. “Where was this yesterday?” she joked. “Maybe it would have helped.” She took a long drink and swallowed. “I really want to ask you about the wording on this part, though.” She clicked to a graph.

Linda was still staring at her appraisingly, but with softer eyes. “Oh, this isn’t over, my dear.” She focused on the screen. “Now, what am I looking at?”

*

When Ethan arrived, shortly after ten, Sarah turned pink again. She shook his hand, which was warm in her cold grasp, and smiled nervously. She needn’t have worried, though. He was Ethan, calm and friendly, and even though she wasn’t at all at ease, she answered his questions thoroughly, referring to her notes only to put the stats up on the screen.

Finally, he seemed satisfied. "I can take this back to Corporate. I wish I could bring you with me; you're incredible." Sarah flushed again; *why did she blush so easily?*

Linda leaned back in her chair. "This is why you're irreplaceable, my dear. We're going to miss you."

Ethan's eyes flicked to hers. "Moving again, Sar?"

Sarah gathered up her book and stood up. "It's a long story." She turned to Linda. "Would you like to join us for lunch?" *Please say yes*, she pleaded with her eyes.

Was that a subtle wink?

Linda sighed. "I'm afraid I can't today. Duty calls! Actually, a pedicure calls, but it's close enough." She smiled broadly and shook Ethan's hand again. "I'm looking forward to hearing the way forward on this soon. When can I expect an answer?"

The new systems could give LabX a very real edge over the competition, and Linda's leadership over the project would be a feather in her cap. She'd be due a bonus, if not a raise. Sarah would be identified as a leading contributor, and possibly rewarded as well, but...she was leaving.

It would be her legacy on earth, she thought.

How... sad, but how nice, too.

I finally did something worthwhile.

*

She had chosen a restaurant within walking distance from the lab. She hopped into Ethan's car, but planned to walk back to her office afterwards, to use the exercise and fresh air to clear her head.

She had picked a nice place, one of those white-linen-tablecloth, three-fork kind of places. The kind of restaurant where a waiter filled your water glass after every second sip. Polite, dignified and a terrible place to make a scene. *Perfect.* It was also too expensive, which was what lunch with corporate types was for, wasn't it?

She followed him to a table, noticing again that he looked taller, more confident than she remembered. A quick, bird-like movement of his head reminded her of Maggie. His eyes, studying her intently behind his glasses called to mind Jack mulling over a problem.

He waited till they had ordered their lunch, making small talk about her work and her presentation over drinks, light comments about Linda and the expected next steps with her research. When the server turned and walked away with their menus, he folded his hands in front of him and looked directly at her.

"You're amazing, Sar. You're the smartest person I've ever met. You should be running that place — no, you should be running this *company*, instead of following that—" he stopped himself, and shook his head. "There's potential for a new position at Corporate, Director of new innovation—"

"Potential. I hate that—" Sarah lifted her hand, and he grabbed it.

"—and you've got the brain, the ideas, the skills to back it up. You're good. You can't just move away, stand by your man and take a job doing someone else's filing again. Promise me?"

Sarah bit her lip and looked down. "I'm— I mean we... Grant is leading the biological research team on the next shuttle." He looked at her blankly. "To Mars. We're all going."

"You're... going... to Mars," he repeated. "I... I mean I heard rumours, but that's— would you be mad if I said that's insane?"

Her lip twitched, and suddenly they were both laughing. She covered her mouth with her other hand and Ethan slapped the table. "Where's Sarah?" he asked. "Oh, she went to Mars. She's in space. *Filing.*"

She couldn't stop laughing, so hard that tears were in her eyes. He was right. All of this, her life, her potential. She was giving up everything and moving to *Mar*s, for God's sake. It was absurd and ridiculous. It was pathetic. Ethan was still holding her hand. They were still wiping their eyes and snickering when their soup arrived.

"Woo," he said softly, still grinning. "So, you're going into space. How does that work? Tell me all."

"Well, there's enough room on the ship for 2000 people, about 400 kids. There's school and sports for the kids, activities... I'll be helping to teach art and maybe some dance classes, and probably helping out with other things with the kids as well. Each cabin is responsible for a garden plot, exercise programs to follow. It's sort of like a commune but with an Important Mission" — she pronounced the capitals — "for the Fate of Humanity. And Grant's leading the bio research. His... his whole life has been working towards this."

"Good for Grant. But what does it mean for you? You're just going to follow him, do part-time volunteer jobs and that's it?"

"His research is important. It's everything to him, and he's my husband— he's everything to me."

There. She had said it. She wasn't sure that she was telling the truth — in fact, she knew that she wasn't, but that's what she did. She followed.

They had never done this, never discussed that she was married. Everything was changing.

"Are the kids excited? They're what, seven and five?"

"No, eight and six."

She had spoken without thinking. She ducked her head and didn't see him furrow his brow as he did the math in his head. Nothing was said for a few minutes.

Ethan seemed to be having a hard time swallowing his spoonful of soup. His face was bright red, and he didn't meet her eyes.

"How long will you be gone? Years, I guess? How long *is* a return trip to Mars?"

She shook her head. "The shuttle's not built to come back, or to even take off again. It means... it means not coming back. It means forever."

He crumbled his bread into smaller and smaller pieces, practically crumbs, his head still down. "What about the kids?"

Last night, staring blankly into the dark, she had imagined this. This would be the right time, maybe the only time, to say something. To tell him about Maggie's quick brain and easy confidence, Jack's perseverance and strength. The way they were kind and cared about other people. The best parts of them, they got from their father. He didn't know — he couldn't possibly know. But she should tell him, shouldn't she? He didn't have a family, maybe he didn't have a girlfriend — he'd never mentioned one, but then again, she never mentioned Grant, and they'd been married fifteen years.

Her brain was whirling, as it had been since getting into bed last night. Would it be better to fly away and for him to never know? Or better to tell him now and fly away with him knowing, never able to see them. Either way was wrong, impossible.

She was a terrible person.

"They're coming — they're excited. Spaceships and stars, what kid wouldn't want that? They're pioneers and colonists — I mean, they'll be making history — they *are* real, live history. It's going to be great."

The waiter came back to clear away their soup. Out of the corner of her eye, she saw a second waiter approaching with their mains. She asked for a second glass of wine.

*

He had driven her back to her office after all. He placed his hand over hers, and held her eyes with his, so she saw again the shining grey of his eyes, almost the same grey she saw when she looked in the mirror, when she looked at—

"Goodbye, Ethan," she'd said quickly. Her eyes were filled with tears too, and she got out of the car quickly.

"Sar!" he'd called after her, but she was gone.

Chapter 11

Nancy lived a four-day drive away. They hadn't lived in the same city at the same time since graduation. They hadn't seen each other in person for over two years, in fact, but managed to keep their best friend status intact with monthly calls when schedules allowed. Sarah drove to her parents' house, dropped Maggie and Jack off for the weekend, and flew to Calgary.

After Sarah and Grant's wedding, Nancy and John waited a full two years before following suit. Nancy finished her Master's and was hired as a pharmaceutical sales rep. John had passed his bar, and the two of them started their life together with long hours of work and great income.

Sarah took a cab from the airport to the restaurant Nancy had suggested. She'd be there as soon as she could, she had said. Despite their enviable rapport, world travel and wealth, and sparkling chemistry, Nancy and John lasted four years before separating, just after the surprise that was their daughter. Nine years later, they were still separated, still co-parenting a funny and creative nine-year-old, and seemed, well, the same. Sarah was surprised to see them both at the restaurant when she arrived.

"Who's watching Lily?" she asked, grinning. The two of them looked healthy, fresh, even sparkling. The natural rewards of wealth and loving what you do, she supposed.

"Nanny," responded John, giving her a big, squeezy hug. He still looked like the big teddy bear she knew in university, albeit now one in an expensive suit. Nancy's hug was longer. She looked slim and pretty in a bright orange wrap dress, her hair looked great, and she had a large diamond ring on her left ring finger. Sarah didn't know whether to keep her mouth shut out of respect for what was technically still her friend's husband or grab her hand and demand the whole story. She didn't get a chance.

"Ta-daaaah!" Nancy waggled her hand inches from her nose. "Guess what?"

Sarah looked between Nancy's big smile and John's beaming grin.

"Ummm... I have no idea," she said weakly. "You're back together?" She took a drink from her water glass.

"Oh, God, no!" laughed John. "Fool me twice, shame on me!" Nancy punched him in the arm.

"Shut up. No, come on. Guess!"

"Honestly, it's weird that you're still even friends. Actually, it's weird that you're still married, too, so I'm not even going to guess."

Nancy and John kept laughing, while Sarah sat with her arms crossed, pretending to not care. "Ok, what? *What?*" she demanded.

John sighed, still smiling. "I'm in love. And it's not with her. Sar, I'm getting married! Unfortunately, she said that she'd only marry me if I divorced my wife. Some ultimatum, eh? So, I thought I should do the honourable thing and buy the mother of my child one last sparkler for the road. She's worth it." He grinned at Nancy, then glanced at his watch. "Speaking of my love, I've got to run. I'm picking up the bride-to-be at her office in ten minutes." He got up, still chuckling at the look on Sarah's face, and bent down to kiss her cheek, placing a large hand on her shoulder. "I just wanted to say goodbye in person." His smile faded. "You're ok, though? You're sure that this is what you want? The final frontier, and all that?"

Sarah smiled, and placed her hand on his, her eyes watering the tiniest bit, her voice catching in her throat. "I am. And you, too, the best of luck. She's a lucky lady, whoever she is."

"Oh, I know she is." He squeezed her shoulder and raised a hand to Nancy, who was watching Sarah. "I'll see you Sunday night to drop off Lily. Bye, Sar. You take care." He dropped a kiss on Nancy's cheek and walked away.

Sarah didn't even watch him go. She immediately swivelled in her chair to look accusingly at Nancy. "When was this? You didn't tell me! Are you ok? First, let me see this ring."

"First, a drink."

✷

The last of the second bottle of wine had been poured into their glasses, the bottle removed. There was still a half inch at the bottom of Nancy's glass, but Sarah's was empty.

"You're really going." Nancy played with the stem of her wine glass, eyeing her pensively.

"I am. It's what he's worked for, always."

"But it's forever. Like, *forever*. You're giving up everything again for him, but this time, it's literally *everything*."

"Nancy, don't." A pause. A deep breath. "I know all that, I've struggled with it, but I'm going. Hey," she smiled crookedly. "This feels just like the night before my wedding again."

That night. Their kitchen floor had been piled with Sarah's moving boxes, taped shut and labelled, ready to be shipped to Grant's apartment in Hamilton.

"The night is young. What say we get some fresh air? Let's not let these bad boys go to waste," Nancy grinned as she indicated two open wine bottles. "I know, it's late, but it's ok, they're half empty."

"Pessimist." The women had bundled up in their winter coats and mittens, snickering. Nancy grabbed the wine while Sarah picked up the old, crocheted throw from their couch. She draped it across their laps as they sat on the back steps, huddling together for warmth in the frosty December air. They each held a bottle between their bemittened hands.

Sarah leaned her head against the post, and Nancy rested hers on Sarah's shoulder as the crisp air pinkened their noses and cheeks. The grass was already covered with a good coat of snow, but little blades, black in the darkness, still stuck through here and there.

"I'm going to miss this, you know," Nancy said, raising her bottle to her lips. "I'm going to miss you. Running away to get married, following your man... humph."

Sarah grinned. "I'm going to miss you too. But you'll have John, and a guest room! Did you ever think you'd have a guest room? That'll count for something, won't it?"

"I'd rather have my friend," Nancy said sullenly. She sat up straight. "To friendship!" she announced. They clinked their bottles together and each took a swig. "And one day, I will only drink good wine. To good wine!" They drank again, and settled back, gazing out and up.

They sat in silence for a few minutes, Sarah looking up at the few stars she could see in the clear patches across the night sky. She took a drink as well. *Was that one a star, that extra twinkly one*? She watched it travel across the clearing between the clouds. *No, either an airplane or a satellite. Those ones, then... ah.* A constellation she recognized was slowly revealed as clouds drifted across the sky. Sarah tried to pick out the stars in Orion's belt.

"Sar...?" Nancy's voice was quiet again, uncertain. Uncharacteristically so.

"Mmm?" There they were, twinkling in their little row.

"You're not really just going with him?"

"It's sort of too late for that," Sarah replied, smiling quizzically into the darkness. "The wedding's in... um..." she checked her watch. "Thirteen hours. Besides, I'm jobless as of today, and homeless, too. Where am I going to live, your new guest room?" She kept her tone light. "Besides, what else am I doing? I can coast for a few years, choose a subject for my Master's—"

"You're already coasting," Nancy interrupted. "I love you, Sar, but you're just following a man."

Sarah felt her shoulders tightening up towards her ears. "Stop saying that. He's not just 'a man,' he's Grant. And yes, I've been coasting, so what difference does it make if I do it here or somewhere else? I'll figure out what I want, and why not tag along with Grant while I think about it? It's about time you and John officially moved in together— about time he started paying rent." She shot a pointed look over at her friend.

Nancy had spent less and less time at John's place ever since Sarah announced her engagement. John was in his second year of law school and claimed to be reading all the time, but he'd been coming over after dinner most nights lately. Sarah didn't mind; he was good company, and he'd be living here soon enough. They had big plans: wealth, travel, adventure...

"Why Grant?" Nancy blurted out suddenly.

The question took Sarah by surprise. She stared at her friend; eyes wide.

"Because! He's... Grant. He's a grown up! He's smart and mature and ambitious... he's everything I'm not, and— "

"Bullshit," Nancy said. "You are the smartest person I know, Sar. You're my best friend. I don't know why you're not already doing your Master's, or working your way up in a lab, or at least looking for a job that fits your skills and education! You know you're good, you know you can do it, but instead, you're coasting. You're hitching your wagon to someone else's star, and you could be your own star, so easily!" She waved her hands agitatedly, wine sloshing around in her bottle.

She had sat up now and was facing Sarah, talking quickly but quietly, angrily. "I understand leaving Ethan for Grant — I don't but I do — but don't sell yourself short just because Grant doesn't believe in you."

Sarah stood up quickly, the afghan falling to her feet. The cold air swirled around her legs, matching the chill she felt in her chest. "I am getting married *tomorrow*," she said, just as quietly, through gritted teeth. "This is not the time to bring this up. Do you know when would have been a good time? Anytime at all in the last two years would have been a good time." She put the bottle down on the step beside Nancy. "I'm going inside."

"Don't!" Nancy grabbed at her leg and held tight. "Don't. I'm sorry, Sar. I shouldn't have— I've had too much wine and I'm going to miss you, that's all. Don't listen to me. He's a good man, and I'm happy for you. I want you to be happy, that's all. I'm sorry." She didn't let go, looking up at Sarah with wild eyes. "Stay. Sit with me. It's our last night."

Sarah had looked away, across the little yard, up over the trees and into the night sky. She was so cold she was shaking. The sky had cleared, and a dome of glittering lights stretched before her. The air felt cleansing, fresh, and smelled of woodsmoke.

Her head drooped and she felt her shoulders slump. She sat back down and let Nancy spread the blanket over her knees, accepted the proffered bottle and raised it up.

"To friendship," she said.

They drank.

Just like tonight.

Nancy looked at her now, across the table, her fingers still. "What about Ethan?"

The only recrimination Nancy had ever had was that she hadn't told her right away, not till months after Jack was born.

"You can date Ethan! You're single now." It came out more bitterly than she expected.

Nancy looked at her, her eyes suddenly full of tears. "I want *John*. I never wanted to break up. I wanted to be cool. I thought he'd come back."

Sarah looked at her friend, her mouth open. "Oh Nance, I'm sorry. I was trying to make a joke. But— but *nine years*. You're so successful at coparenting and such a good team, and—"

"I know, I know. He thought he was being so funny, going down on one knee with that diamond," she said, bitterly twisting it around on her finger. "I thought he was coming back to me, Sar. And I've lost him." She sniffed suddenly, wiped the back of her hand across her eyes, her mascara smearing a bit towards her temple. "But we're not talking about me. I'm going to be fine. He's still here, I still have Lily, my job..." she grinned. "... Fresh air, trees."

Sarah raised her hand to the server. "Could we get the check, please?" They were in for a long night.

*

Waking up all alone in Nancy's beautifully decorated guest room, Sarah stretched in what would have been a luxurious way, had she not had a pounding headache. She had woken up a few times in the night, knowing that she should get up and drink a glass or two of water each time, but enjoying the soft sheets, the heaviness of being drunk, the sweet taste of wine still in her mouth. *You'll regret this*, her inner voice said. *Go 'way, m'so comfy*, another voice whispered back.

There, on her bedside table, was a full glass of water — *I'm an idiot* — a little packet of Emergen-C, and a pair of old-lady wraparound shades, probably leftover from Nancy's laser eye surgery twelve years ago. *This* was a friend.

She put on the glasses, staggered to the upstairs bathroom and proceeded to mix the powder into the water. She downed it as quickly as she could, then turned on the shower. *You always feel better after a shower*, she told herself, wincing as the water hit her.

Fifteen minutes later, she stepped into the kitchen, still in the sunglasses, but now clean, damp and dressed in sweatpants and a light sweater. She had packed for a visit with an old friend. Nancy was at the stove, frying up potatoes and bacon.

"How do you like your eggs?" she asked, waving a spatula.

"Shhhh." Sarah pointed to her head. "Just... shhhh. You know how I like my eggs, but I'm not sure I can this morning." She filled the kettle and put it back on its base, then searched the cupboard for a mug. She hoped there was tea somewhere; Nancy ran on coffee.

"Above the kettle," Nancy indicated a cupboard with her spatula. There was an unopened box of cranberry green tea beside the coffee grinder. "Don't say I've never done anything for you." Sarah grabbed her friend and hugged her, her breath catching. "Get off me, or I'll throw up on you," Nancy laughed, looking away quickly. "Now, open up the champers. We're having mimosas."

The fried breakfast was just what she needed; Sarah realized. After the agonizingly loud juicer had produced fresh orange juice, she popped the cork softly and topped up each glass with... yes, it really was champagne. No 'sparkling wine' for Nancy. Looking around her spacious, modern kitchen with top-of-the-line appliances, skylit dining room, and professionally-tended garden, she wondered how she would have adapted to such wealth — would it make her a nicer person? Kinder? More relaxed? *Too late now*, she realized, *unless...*

"I've changed my mind," Nancy declared, her mouth still full, waving her mimosa around. The giant diamond sparkled in the late morning light. "You should tell Grant. Then he'll leave, and you'll stay, and you can move in with me and we can live together, and the kids can be siblings — Lily would love to have Maggie as a sister, and she's always wanted a little brother... ok, no she hasn't, but she loves Jack — and we'll grow old together. You and me."

Sarah smiled. It sounded wonderful, but — "No, I can't. I— should tell Ethan, though." The champagne definitely helped round out the edges. She felt less defeated, more confident. "Maybe I'll stay. The kids and I can live a normal life and—"

"Don't be an idiot, Sarah."

Sarah blinked. "But you just... It works for you!"

Nancy put her glass down. The smile left her face. "Joking aside, Sar, we've been through this. What for? You're going to tell him that he has two children — that you've never let him meet — and that you're taking them away from him forever? Literally forever. It wouldn't be fair."

"But if I leave, if I just go, and I haven't told him, then what am I?"

Nancy shook her head gently. "You're a mother. You're a sweet memory for him that he'll always have, that he'll think about and strut a little still. To tell him, though, that would be cruel. It would destroy him, Sar. I mean, poor Ethan!"

"You don't think he's still in love with me, do you?"

"In love? Oh, probably. You're gorgeous." Sarah rolled her eyes. "He's sweet. He's never found someone to replace you."

"He's dated lots of girls," Sarah protested.

Nancy's tone sharpened. "Yes, but *dated.* He wasn't broken when you chose Grant, but geez, Sar. This would *break* him. You used him to get what you wanted—"

"I didn't plan to—"

"Withdrawn." Lawyer-speak learned from John, no doubt. She picked up her glass and took a large sip, then turned to face her squarely. "But you used him. And you got what you wanted. Let him have his sweet memories, Sar. You'd destroy him, knowing that his kids were lost to him forever. There is no happy ending here. There's no possible universe where this would turn out ok. Do you think that you'd tell him, he'd propose, and Grant would blast off, leaving you and the kids with New Daddy? What would that do to them? God, I wish I still smoked."

She picked up her champagne flute and threw back the rest of it. "I love you, Sarah, and it's killing me — *killing* me — that you're leaving. That I'll never see you again. You're my best friend. But you can't scorch the earth behind you. It's not fair. The rest of us will still be here, still have to go on with our lives." She picked up the bottle of champagne and filled her glass again, leaving no room for orange juice. Sarah toyed with her stem, looking down at her plate. Tears were streaming out of her eyes.

Like death. That's what this all felt like. Like she was dying — or like everyone she knew and loved, aside from Grant, Maggie and Jack, were dying. She knew it was coming, and she knew that it would be goodbye, actual goodbye, instead of 'see you later.' And, for all anyone knew, it meant actual death, too. What if the ship's systems failed? What if the supply shuttles couldn't make it? What if the new colony had been swept away by the time they arrived? What the hell was she doing to her family?

What was the point of all of these goodbyes, other than to drag out the pain?

Chapter 12

She hadn't even wanted a cat. Or rather, like the children, maybe she had liked the *idea* of a cat, not realizing how much work he would be, and how much of that work would fall to her to do. Rupert, whom she had christened Rupert Catburden the Third (though there hadn't been a first or second), or just Catburden when she was feeling particularly put upon, was a sleek tabby with a cat's lofty airs and general disdain for all humans.

Grant had never revealed where he had come from, meeting every question only with a quirk of an eyebrow and a flash of a dimple. "I'll never tell."

"I feed you. I let you in and out. I clean your litter box. I protect you from being dressed in doll clothes. Usually." She bustled around the house, grumbling, trying to grab any older item, no longer worn, used or played with, that would be donated or sold, or left out on the curb. She had signed Maggie and Jack up for an extended-day camp and extra playdates in the evenings, both to keep them out from underfoot for most of the packing — she preferred her Systems the way she wanted them — and also to give them as much outside playtime with their friends as possible before they left: more the former, if she was being completely honest. In the two hours she had between work and the kids arriving home, she sorted through their clothes mercilessly, packaged up their dishes and old toys, working methodically from room to room. She had thought about putting a few large, sentimental items into storage: the piano, perhaps, and the dining room table that had been her grandmother's. But no, there wouldn't be a storage locker to come back to. They were never coming back.

For a moment, she felt dizzy again as the enormity of that washed over her. There were less than six weeks till moving day, till they flew to Florida for a two week-quarantine before boarding a... well, a spaceship. She hadn't been able to fully absorb the reality. It was still too much to wrap her mind around.

A sudden jingling made her jump.

Rupert lay on his favourite chair, a sunbeam striping his already-stripy fur. He blinked at her insolently before stretching his long body even longer and looking away. One of his stupid jingly-ball toys lay on the floor beside his chair. *Jerk.*

But she admitted now, he was the only constant in her life for the last ten years. The string of jobs, of moves. The kids were born and were always growing, changing. But not Rupert. He was sort of good company, she supposed, and a good listener. Not that she thought he was listening, but he never interrupted with a complaint or a demand. He would never wait for her to pause, then jump in with a long story involving abrupt tangents and science and, well, expecting her to listen back. *Like Grant.*

Rupert's carrier was set out in the hallway, with food, water and a blanket inside. As always, the idea was to get him used to it ahead of time, maybe enough to even wander into it on his own. As always, he refused to go near it, to the point of avoiding the entire hallway. He entered and exited by the back door only, and the way he levelled his gaze at her seemed to say, “and it’s all your fault.”

Having a cat on your lap had always been a rare and precious thing in the Harper household. Rupert was not by nature affectionate and was less of a pet than a presence. *Or a nuisance*, thought Sarah. On ‘special days,’ as she called them, only once in a while and only when Grant wasn’t home, Rupert would leap up onto the couch and climb onto her lap. It happened so rarely that she would then sit still, even if she had to pee or was thirsty, even if her phone was ringing on the other side of the room.

Some nights, when Grant was away, she’d wake up to silence that gradually developed into the bass of his purrs and his warm weight behind her knees. Rupert wasn’t allowed on the bed when Grant was home — or indeed at all — but for the last four years or so Sarah had been looking the other way, enjoying a bit of companionship, escaping the loneliness of her big bed. She kept a lint brush in her closet and made sure to remove any evidence in the morning. Sneaky. She lay there, trying not to move, willing the cat to stay even when she shifted position. It sometimes worked.

So, there he was: her companion, who tolerated her presence, who demanded her attention, who dirtied his litter box when it was raining or snowing or windy. And who left a much larger hole in her life than she expected when he was hit by that car. A distraught woman rang their doorbell at 10:47 at night, two days before he was to enter his own four-week quarantine.

Grant held her as she cried... kind of, awkwardly patting her on the back.

"But you didn't even like Rupert," he said. "It's one less thing for you to worry about before we leave. He would have hated the ship, anyway."

This was all true. Rupert had enjoyed being outside, loved to come and go as he pleased. The checks and preparations for him had seemed even more stringent than for the children and the shuttle staff made it clear that their pet was considered a frivolous luxury, a concession they made only because of the brilliance of her husband. He had not been a great pet, not even for a pet cat (for which the standards as an animal companion were low to begin with), but he had been there.

She thought back again to that night in Wellington, when Grant had given him to her as he packed his suitcase, as she unpacked moving boxes. "Maybe you won't feel so lonely now," he had said. He left the rest unspoken.

To make her feel less lonely. To make her not want a child so badly. To have something to hold, to care for, to love, besides him. He was heading to... everywhere else, and despite the cat's demands and messes and indifference, at least he was there. And now he was gone.

The kids were heartbroken.

"He's family," sobbed Maggie after breakfast the next morning, holding Jack tightly. Sarah was heartened and heartsick to see them cling to each other like this, as if they only had each other to cling to — *which would be the case soon enough, wouldn't it*?

Rupert had been a key piece in convincing the kids to buy into this 'big adventure.' They were going as a family, Rupert too of course, and Mommy would be there after school, and Daddy wouldn't have to work as much — well, there was no commute anyway, if no less work. Rupert had been part of the package.

Grant, ever the biologist, had no trouble retrieving the body. He wrapped him up in one of Maggie's old sweatshirts, leaving just one unscathed paw out for the kids to hold and say goodbye to. They all huddled together and watched as he placed Rupert into a boot box and dug a hole under the tree, the side away from the swing. Sarah had called the kids' summer camp and said she was keeping them home. Linda had taken her absence well, too; she still had a lot of vacation time to take, anyway.

Only later that night, as she washed his dishes and got ready to dump out his litterbox for the last time, she felt suddenly free. She had been about to scrub it out, but then realized that she could just throw the whole thing in the trash, litter and all. They were leaving Rupert behind, under his favourite tree, and they weren't coming back, not ever. She placed the litterbox, litter and all, into a garbage bag, and put it outside the back door, in sight of the large stone, painted with 'Rupert' in blue paint, that marked where the earth had been filled back in. She packed the food dishes into his crate and set it into the garage sale pile, humming.

Maybe it was for the best.

Chapter 13

"We're still on for tonight?" Linda popped her head into Sarah's office, her glasses pushed up on her head. Her suit was immaculate, as usual.

Sarah looked around at the boxes and stacks of paper and grimaced. "This is a disaster zone. I can't believe I left it so long. But yes!" She ran her fingers through her hair. "Um... sitter's lined up — there's no way Grant will be home before ten — and I. Will. Have. This. Office. Clean."

Linda shook her head and smoothed down her navy blazer. "Don't be hard on yourself. We've got all your work saved and shared already; your systems have backed up all the important stuff. All this stuff can just be..." She trailed off.

"Recycled. I know," Sarah finished ruefully. "My life's work, gone!" She tried to sound dramatic instead of depressed. *Don't think about it. That way lies madness.* She was getting better at ignoring the sudden rising sense of panic. She was pretty sure that nobody could see these brief episodes, the ones where she suddenly remembered, where she felt her world was dropping out from under her.

"I won't bother you again till five." Linda's head disappeared from the doorframe.

Sarah was dressed down today. Jeans and a flannel shirt, appropriate for emptying filing cabinets and moving boxes. *Not so much for a wine bar*, but it couldn't be helped. She found the work soothing: sifting through two years' worth of notes and files, sorting them into piles. She turned off her mind, let the mundane task quell the little flashes of hysteria that kept flaring up.

By four forty-five, she had restored order to a solid standard of good enough. There was a lot of dust, and the carpet needed a thorough vacuuming, but she had distinct piles for garbage, recycling and shredding. Her desk was empty except for a few of the kids' drawings, a small mauve sculpture of a melting popsicle and the framed photo that sat beside her monitor.

Definitely not a professional shot, it was colourful and lively. In it, all four of them were on a park bench on a calm, sunny autumn afternoon two years ago.

Grant was staring directly into the camera, his hands on his knees. His blue eyes seemed to glow, and there was a half-smile on his face, not quite enough to see his dimples. Maggie was draped over him from behind, her skinny arms wrapped around his neck, sticking her tongue out at Jack. Little Jack stood on the bench between Sarah and Grant, his eyes sliding sideways towards his sister, giggling. Sarah was half-turned, gazing at them, a smile on her face.

She picked up the frame now, remembering that day. Maggie and Jack had been wearing their new fall jackets, still bright and clean. They had been taking a long walk along the river, the path lined with trees brightly dressed in their autumn finery. They had stopped by a wooden bench to let the kids rest their legs for a moment. An older couple had walked up and offered to take a photo of the whole family. They had taken three shots, she remembered; of these, one had them all looking at the camera, smiling but stiff. Another had blurry shapes where Jack and Maggie were muppeting around, and there was this one, imperfectly perfect, their personalities shining through the image.

She put the frame in her purse, then added the children's drawings to her recycling pile with a sigh.

A few minutes in the bathroom, a quick wipedown with paper towels, a comb through her hair and a swipe of lipstick, and the Sarah looking back at her was moderately presentable. *As good as it's likely going to get today,* she told her reflection.

At five, she knocked on Linda's open door, her purse over her shoulder, a folder and the popsicle sculpture in her hand. Linda was typing something, but waved her in. She placed both of these on her boss — her *friend's* — desk.

"Ok, done." Linda closed her laptop and smiled wistfully up at Sarah. "Your popsicle? I couldn't—"

"Keep it. I can't bring it with me." She gestured towards the folder. "Here's my handover for the new guy. It's all on the drive, but I wanted to make sure... He's inheriting my plant, too. Tell him to keep it alive for me."

Linda stood up and came around the desk. She had changed into jeans, a plaid shirt and sneakers. She followed Sarah's eyes and laughed. "Solidarity." She put her hand gently on Sarah's shoulder. "You're a treasure, Sar. We owe you so much." Her eyes were shining, and to her horror, Sarah felt hers well up in response. This office was where she had been *seen* for the first time in years. It hadn't changed, except for a large cactus that she had given her boss for her birthday last year.

"Prickly, like me?" Linda had grinned.

"Strong and tough. Nourishing," Sarah had corrected her.

The two framed photos still sat on the desk, their backs to her, but she knew that one was a portrait studio picture of Linda and her son when he was a fuzzy-headed two-year-old, and the other was his most recent school photo. Alex was a nice boy, a good boy. Linda believed in him as much as she believed in Sarah. *It makes a difference.*

She sniffed and shook her head. "No crying! Are you ready to go?"

"You bet. Let's go class up that wine bar."

✷

The bar was louder than she had expected. *Do people always go out on Thursday nights?* All around her, people in business wear gathered in twos, threes and fours, toasting and laughing in the dimly lit restaurant.

She and Linda had wound their way through to an empty table on the vine-lined patio. Brighter outside, if not quieter, a soft breeze ruffled through their hair. Much better, they agreed.

Fairy lights sparked into life around them as it grew darker. The server opened a new bottle of wine and topped up their glasses, then placed it on the table between them, clearing away the one they had already emptied. A plank of wood contained the remnants of cheese and charcuterie.

"We're still nibbling," Linda said to him, then turned back to Sarah as he walked away. She lifted her glass to Sarah's in another cheers. "And *I* am taking a cab home. And you are too." She leaned back into her chair for a minute, then sat up straight. "So hey, Ethan. What's the story there?"

Sarah stared into her wineglass and swirled the deep red liquid around and around. She lifted it to her nose, still swirling, her lips parting as she inhaled. She could feel Linda's eyes still on her, and she drew out the ritual. She returned her glass to the table, then lifted her eyes to Linda's. She would never have to face her again. She made up her mind. *Well, why not?*

"It's complicated," she began. "I— I need to ask you about— I need to talk to you about something. I need to tell you something."

✷

"And Grant doesn't know? And Ethan doesn't know? And you're sure?"

"I know. It's awful. I'm a terrible person."

Linda hesitated before answering slowly, not meeting her eyes. "You wanted a family," she said. "And so did Grant. You did the right thing for you. Your kids are gorgeous, no-one will ever know, and, well, that's it. What's done is done." She smirked. "Twice."

"But shouldn't I tell him?"

"Grant?" Linda snorted. "No. What's the point? Why bother? You'd just ruin the rest of everyone's lives. And why *now*? You'd be giving him what, a *week* to decide if he wants to be trapped on that damned spaceship with someone that betrayed him. He might not be able to forgive you, and then it'd be too late. *Or* he'd get mad enough to leave you behind, then regret it forever. And you'd be a single mom. You don't want that."

Don't I? "But what if I tell..."

Linda looked at her, her eyes soft. "Ethan? Oh, Sar. I think that ship sailed a long time ago. I don't know him as well as... as well as I thought I knew you," — *Ouch* — "but God, that would be a blow to anyone. And how would you even tell him? 'I'm leaving my husband, and these are actually your children. No pressure.' And the kids!" She rubbed her hand across her eyes. "'Old Daddy's gone to Mars. Kids, meet New Daddy.'"

That's what Nancy said.

"Linda! It wouldn't be like that. But... doesn't he deserve to know?"

"Again, why bother? I'm your friend, Sar. But this is a take-it-to-your-grave sort of secret, especially now. If you tell him and stay, there's pressure, expectations. If you tell him and leave, then you've stolen his family. There's no good choice here. You're going to have to let him go."

She reached her hand across the table to hold Sarah's.

"I know I asked, but I really wish you hadn't told me this."

Sarah pulled her hand away and nodded miserably. Telling her had been a mistake. She'd lost Linda's respect and it was too late. That awful, shaky feeling inside threatened to spill out again.

Linda was right. Nancy was right. This was too big of a deal, and too late to turn back now. She knew that. She knew — of course she knew — that everything wouldn't work out, that Ethan—

"What's done is done. Keeping your secret isn't hurting anyone. And you'll do what you're going to do, but be careful, ok?" Linda reached for the bottle and topped up their glasses. "To the best damn employee I've ever had, to adventure, and to...uh...interplanetary friendships!" She winked. "I want to hear that you're taking over that spaceship."

Chapter 14

"Can we go outside?" Sarah asked the night before they entered the quarantine bay. They had checked into the BioMars isolation facility in Cape Canaveral a week ago, with a few changes of clothes and pretty much nothing else. "Before we take off. We're still here for two weeks before we actually launch, so can we still go outside? Stock up on, you know, nature and fresh air?" She paced back and forth between suitcases, ferrying clean laundry, folding and refolding sweaters and pants.

Grant looked up from his laptop without expression. "Sarah, you know we can't. I'm sure I told you. It was definitely in the briefing documents that you signed. The crew routines, the system checks, the disinfectants... we can't have airlocks being opened and a bunch of new pathogens introduced every day. Once we're in, that's it."

The kids were finally asleep in the twin beds in the other room. They were hopped up and excited about the next day, even though she and Grant had tried to calm them down by reminding them that it was really just another moving day. They were simply checking into another 'hotel' the next morning, but the loading shuttles weren't leaving — blasting off — for two weeks yet.

Sarah's parents had driven up to Ottawa to help with the kids as they finished packing up the house. Sarah leaned against the tree while Maggie and Jack rolled around on the front lawn of what used to be their home, and they all watched the cleaners drive up. They had decided, after all the sorting and organization, to turn what was supposed to be their moving day and garage sale into a street party, a going away extravaganza. Over the long weekend, various trucks and vans had pulled up and loaded up the furniture, toys and clothes that were being given to charities and shelters. Their piano was going to the community centre. Friends, families, colleagues, neighbours... all came out to wish them well and to walk away with a plant or a bottle of something from their cabinet. Sarah's cheeks were sore from smiling — *Can't anyone see I'm screaming?* — as she accepted hugs and well-wishes with a lump in her throat.

At the end of it, they were left with an empty, if dusty, house. Maggie and Jack's friends were back at school, and all that was left to do was to supervise the cleaning; their lawyer would hand the keys over to the new owners.

They had sold the house for a song. The nicest house they had ever had: four bedrooms, the den, the large eat-in kitchen, the finished basement that had acted as the kids' playroom, Jack's fort and Maggie's dance studio, *gone*. It had been bright and big, and *home*. The big, green yard had been beautifully landscaped with just enough wildness mixed in. The new family had wanted to keep the tire swing. *Well, we can't use it*, Sarah thought wistfully. They had listed it at market value, and when the first offer came in too low, Grant looked at her and shrugged.

"We can't take it with us."

They couldn't. They wouldn't need to. The ship and the colony were set up as communes, with all supplies, all equipment either being grown, produced, or manufactured onsite or delivered in few-and-far-between unmanned shuttles. There would be no economy, no pay. With the sale of the house, they could pay off the rest of their mortgage, cancel all of their insurance policies, and divide up the rest between their families.

Sarah sold her Prius to Linda for a dollar. "Alex will want a car next year," she said. She had set up a small-ish college fund in his name as well, just enough to help out a single mom. She had left the certificate in the glove compartment; she'd known Linda would put up too much of a fight if she told her in person.

Her parents had been scandalized when she tried to give them some, too. "We've saved for this," her dad had said gruffly, insulted. "We're not taking a cent."

Her mom was no easier; Sarah had been counting on Jean being willing to accept the gift. "Give your money to someone who needs it. We'll be fine." There was a steely edge to her mom's voice. She knew she wouldn't win this one, and, unlike Linda, would only be insulting them further if she left an envelope hidden somewhere in their house.

At least it's a nice day. Maggie and Jack had retreated to the backyard for — *Oh God, don't think about it* — one last afternoon on their tree swing, and Jean had gone out to pick up takeout coffee, tea and donuts. They sat on the back deck, quietly sipping, and enjoying the early-September sunshine.

The kids, who had initially been ecstatic to hear that they didn't have to start school, instead getting an extra day of being underfoot and running wild out back, seemed to feel the weight of the day, too. Jack squinted up at the clouds from where he lay on the lawn, his mouth powdered in sugar, and Maggie dangled languidly from the tire swing. A few feet away, on the other side of the tree, the paint on Rupert's stone was already starting to fade.

Sarah's dad dragged one last bag of trash to the curb, then returned, dusting his hands off.

"I don't know about the rest of you lazy bones, but I've worked up an appetite. Who's ready for an early dinner?"

She looked around as hard as she could, willing her eyes to take in every tiny detail, to commit it all to memory: the deck, the tree, the lawn, the swing. Rupert. *Keep it together, Sar. Deep breaths.* Grant stood in front of Sarah, holding out his hand. She turned to hide her tears against his old sweatshirt as he pulled her into a tight hug.

"Thank you," he whispered into the top of her head. "Ok, kids!" he called. "Say goodbye to the house!"

"Bye, house!" they chorused cheerfully. Maggie did a lopsided cartwheel towards them on the lawn, and Jack gave the tire swing one last spin.

The chain Italian restaurant that Ron had chosen was, as always, far too expensive for such bland food. The service was slow, and they brought Sarah the wrong meal. She waved the server away.

"This looks good, too," she said. Maggie and Jack busied themselves with colouring their placemats and the adults shared a bottle of overpriced wine.

The mood was surprisingly fine and upbeat; her parents were very matter-of-fact about the whole thing. *Are they acting? The way that I've been acting?* Sarah wondered.

"It'll be like that year you spent in New Zealand," her father said. He put his hand over hers, maybe to stop her from screaming, *It's not the same thing!*, from upsetting the children and making a scene in front of all the other diners. "We'll miss you, of course, but we'll have the webchats. It'll be just like being there." Sarah's cheeks were sore from trying to smile, and her eyes were stinging. "And we'll send you care packages!"

There would be no visits, no return trips, but there was an unmanned shuttle that could reach them on the voyage and at the colony. Care packages *were* something to look forward to, she supposed.

The goodbyes were short: a squishy hug from Grandma, a gruff squeeze from Grandpa, and Sarah was the only one who cried. "I love you," she whispered, so soft that they couldn't hear. "I love you."

They took a taxi to the airport and boarded the plane to Orlando. They'd spend the night in a hotel, then move into the isolation facility, away from the other families, for a week before entering full quarantine. They'd sit in there for another two weeks before blastoff. They had three weeks left on Earth.

Grant had said goodbye to his dad over the phone, calling the kids over for an awkward few minutes each with his parents. Sarah hurt for her in-laws as she heard the kids respond, robotic, monosyllabic. "Yes." "No." "I guess." Grant seemed fine throughout the conversation: not unemotional, but oddly indifferent for someone who would never see their parents again except on a screen.

But that was beside the point. He *hadn't* told her that this was her last night of feeling like she was still on Earth, or if he had, in all the excitement and confusion, she didn't remember. She had read and signed so many forms. She was so wiped out, so tired.

And this was her last night, her last chance, to... to go outside. Ever. There was no "outside" on Mars. How could something that sounded so small be so big? She could still call her friends and family, could connect in every other way, but she would never — *never* — again feel the wind in her hair, shiver with a mist of real, honest-to-goodness rain on her face, or breathe in the damp, cool air that creeps into your skin as you pass a meadow at night.

She grabbed his hand. "Let's take a walk," she said.

He looked over at the door to the kids' room. "We can't leave the children alone," he said. She looked over, too, then back at him, her eyes wide and pleading. He squeezed her fingers gently. "Go ahead," he said softly. "I'll hold down the fort here."

The night — their *last* night — was cool, with a light breeze. She pulled her fleece a little more tightly around her neck, and crossed the parking lot to a little field, fenced in but still undeveloped, behind the building. The air was chilly for a September evening in Florida, but it felt fresh. Crisp. She closed her eyes and breathed deeply, smelling the pine trees that dotted the lawn, a little bit of exhaust from the nearby highway. The sound of traffic, of crickets. She opened her eyes now and looked around. Nobody was there. She sat down on the curb and slipped off her shoes and socks. Leaving them there, she stepped back onto the grass.

It felt cool, wet with dew, alive under her feet. She wiggled her toes, letting the blades of grass tickle her soles and between her toes, dropping her head back and taking another deep breath. Then another. It caught in her throat and her breathing grew ragged and shaky.

She felt the tears running down her face before she knew they were there, trickling towards her ears. She sniffed and tilted her head forward so that they ran down her cheeks to the corners of her mouth where she could taste the salt. Hinging forward from the hips now, her hair covered her face as her tears dripped from the tip of her nose.

This was it. Her last night here. This was her home. Every move, every time they picked up and left, there was always the knowledge that they *could* come back, that their friends, their acquaintances, their lives were still within reach. All the excitement and adventure of being a pioneer, of forging a new way ahead for the rest of humankind could just...

She fumbled in her pocket, reaching for her phone. She had to re-enter her PIN three times with shaking fingers before it would accept it. She scrolled through her emails to find the one she had sent herself from work, a forwarded meeting acceptance from Ethan. Nowhere else had she written down his number, and she wasn't about to put his name in her search field. His email signature at the bottom of the page had his mobile number on it.

She dialed. She clenched the phone to her ear with cold hands, now shivering, bare feet freezing in the grass, the hem of her jeans wicking up the dew.

"Hello?" He was someplace noisy – a restaurant, or maybe a bar.

"Ethan, I—"

"Karine? Where are you, babe?" His voice was warm. "I've already eaten the appetizer. Hurry up, or I'll eat another one."

Oh.

She pressed 'end.' She put the phone back in her pocket and stood, shaking, looking up at the night sky. The stars were almost invisible in the glow of the lights around her: floodlights that illuminated the building, a brightly lit sign for the gas station across the highway, lights dotting the fence.

Later, she tiptoed back into their suite. Grant had left the light on in the bathroom, but the room was otherwise dark. How long had she been out there, looking up? She had tried to see *something* up there in that haze of black, something that her mom and dad and everyone she had ever known would maybe be able to see as well and remember that she was here.

She felt like a fool. Of course she wouldn't have professed her love to Ethan, then heard him tell her not to go. Of course she wouldn't have told him about the children. Of course she wasn't hoping that he'd beg her to stay. And of course, at any point in time, including tonight, she could have changed her mind, told Grant that she wasn't coming with him, that she and the children were going to stay here. That they weren't his anyway. That she was going to be the main character in her own story for a change, from now on, not just a sidekick. She was a fool, too, for telling Linda. For losing her respect.

She blew her nose, washed her face with cool water and brushed her teeth, then, leaving her damp jeans on the bathroom floor, slipped into the bedroom. In the sliver of light coming from the curtains, she could see that Grant had laid out her pyjamas on her side of the bed. She put them on quietly, crawled into bed behind him and cuddled up to his heat.

Chapter 15

The onramp wasn't scary, not really.

From the end of the corridor, it felt just like boarding a plane, but bigger, wider, shinier. Fancier.

Sarah pulled a small wheelie bag and carried her purse, which still contained — and here she would have laughed, if she could have — her passport and her phone. The kids each wore a backpack that contained their blankets and stuffies and a book or two. Everything else would have been loaded up already, sent ahead on another transfer shuttle, and, once they docked with the main ship, she had a few days of unpacking and organizing ahead. That was good. It gave her a focus, a feeling of familiarity and competence. This was what she did.

She held her hand out to Maggie, but watched her lithe form run ahead with Jack, both in jumpsuits, pushing past Grant so they could be the first to step on to the ship.

The docking gate that they were on was still, lifeless, covered in worn blue industrial carpeting, with scrapes and rubs on the walls that indicated that big things had been dragged and shoved and loaded this way.

A crew member greeted them. "Good morning, Dr. Harper, Mrs. Harper." She grinned down at the kids, who were hopping from side to side, perceptibly vibrating with excitement. "You must be Maggie and Jack. Come with me and I'll get you all strapped in." She flicked a glance up to

Grant. "All protocols have been followed, sir?" At his nod, she extended her smartbook his way. "Just sign here, and we're off."

The jumpsuits, the diapers, the enemas. *The glamour.* The night before had been stressful, the kids too excited to sleep, then being extremely-and-understandably resistant to being 'cleaned out' this morning in preparation for the six-hour transfer. Between trying to keep the children calm and pretending that she was fine with it too, Sarah felt like she had been through several wars already today.

The cabin already held four adults, two on each side of the aisle. They each nodded warmly to Grant as he passed. The crew member helped Sarah and Jack strap in tightly, then moved back a row to secure Grant and Maggie.

"I'm not going to use this diaper," Jack whispered for what must have been the twentieth time. His eyes looked unfocused without his glasses. They had been packed in his backpack for safekeeping, just in case.

"Just in case what?" Sarah had asked Grant. He hadn't responded.

"Your water tube is here, buddy," she responded. "Drink if you need to. And here's the controls for your headphones—" *Right.* He was already plugged in and scrolling through music. She fiddled with hers for a moment or two, then decided to leave them off. More passengers filed past, three more adults and a family with a toddler, who looked sleepy. *Fingers crossed he stays that way.* She could see past Jack to the window. Outside, the sky was grey. Technicians milled about, each doing something, she realized, that could mean the difference between her living or dying.

She closed her eyes and tried to control her breathing. *In-two-three-four, out-two-three-four.* One more hour on Earth, ever. The last two weeks didn't really count, but this was *really* it. What the hell was she doing? It wasn't too late. She could turn around, tell Grant that she had changed her mind, that she didn't want to go. That their kids were really just *her* kids. She could watch his face fall, see his eyes grow cold. She could be stuck on the ship, on a new planet, having made him hate her.

She felt a hand touch her hip. *Still an hour to go.* She could hear Maggie chattering away behind her. She reached her own hand back to hold onto Grant's knee. She breathed.

At the briefing, blast-off had been likened to a plane taking off. *This is much worse than a plane taking off.* The shuttle was shuddering and shaking, the engines screaming, even before they started to move. Sarah wanted to feel angry about being deceived, but was pressed back too hard into her seat, squeezing Jack's sturdy little hand too tightly, and yelling over the din that it was going to be fine. Her chest was tight, her eyes wide, though she couldn't turn her head enough to see out the window again. She was too scared to feel angry. She was too excited. She was actually going to space.

In less than fifteen minutes, everything suddenly went quiet. Jack's water tube floated away from its clip, and his face split into the biggest grin she had ever seen. Outside the window was black, dotted with infinite pinpricks of light. It would still take another three hours or so to dock with the large shuttle, and another one before the hatches opened and they could step foot on their new home. The Earth was right there, huge and shining, but separate. Apart.

"So, what do you think?" Behind her, she could hear Grant's smile in his voice.

"Cooooooool," breathed Maggie.

"So cool!" Jack said. She wasn't sure what, if anything, he could see without his glasses.

Sarah couldn't stop from smiling, even as tears gathered in the corners of her eyes. "Yeah," she agreed. "Pretty cool."

✷

When her heels touched the deck of the ship, they clicked on the newness of the... *well, it wouldn't be linoleum, really, could it?* It wasn't quite a pristine surface, but close. She could feel warmth, and an almost-imperceptible hum rising up from the soles of her feet — not unpleasant, but there, just the same. Like the ship was alive. It would take some getting used to.

Grant had been so eager — of course he was — to step onto the ship. He was just ahead, and he turned back to smile at her, blue eyes shining, a dazzling, boyish grin that she hadn't seen in years. *Those eyes, those dimples.* Fifteen years of marriage and he was still intense and handsome. He had been on a model of the ship on Earth and was familiar with the layout of his lab. He had supervised the stocking of supplies, and now he was excited to see her reaction to this place, the culmination of all his hard work.

He waited till she caught up to him, then rested his hand on her neck and kissed her temple. "Tell my wife I love her very much," he murmured.

"She knows," Sarah responded, a wry smile on her lips. She took a deep breath. The kids were already out of sight down the corridor, squealing and giggling. "Which way?"

The colony on Mars was small but surviving. The first Martians had set up basic facilities: shelters and air exchange and existed on what rations they had left while waiting for the next ship, only twelve months behind them, long enough to be sure that the settlement was viable. The next group had been bigger; a crew of doctors, engineers, technicians, the kind of people that you want to problem solve and sort things out. Food systems, water recovery, waste management, crops.

This mission was even larger, with a wider cross-section of livestock, plants, families. If there was a theme, *and there was totally a theme*, it had to be biodiversity. Sarah wasn't foolish enough to think that everyone on board was a brilliant addition to a new colony.

She had been given a map of the ship, floor plans and layouts of each deck, descriptions of the facilities, all in the briefing they had attended three weeks ago. "Just like a freaking Disney cruise," she had murmured again to Grant.

There were a lot of similarities. The ship had everything. Though not luxurious, with no servers or Disney characters hovering around, there were plenty of spaces to gather, to dance, to play, to grow, to create, to be alone. Each cabin had its own fully equipped kitchen and dining area, but there was a buffet-style cafeteria, two coffee shops and two restaurants. There were two gymnasiums, an ice-like surface that could be installed and skated on, an auditorium-slash-movie theatre, a cluster of dance and fitness studios, a weight room. The assigned garden plots were set in the bowels of the ship, three stories in a row, and Grant's lab was in the very aft, "a ten-minute commute, unless there's traffic," he had joked. The school rooms were divided up over two decks, each for a grouping of grades and ages, and had a comprehensive curriculum comprising standard academics, arts and trades as well as practical, survival-type lessons.

"Home sweet home. Welcome to Harper Quarters." Grant opened the door to their quarters. Maggie wriggled past Jack, and the two scrambled into the apartment, running and pointing and shouting. Grant held back, beaming at Sarah. "After you."

Their cabin was surprisingly homey, Sarah admitted, putting her purse on the kitchen table. The living area felt like a modern — but not *too* modern — condo, with large windows that showed the views outside. *This can't be real.* There were three bedrooms — no need for a guest room here — and two bathrooms. The kids had chosen their own paint colours already, and each room held the approved-weight, UV-sanitized boxes of clothes, bed coverings, toys and decorations, ready to make these walls, ballet-pink and dark purple respectively, their own. The twin beds already had standard white sheets and pillows on them, but one of the first icebreaker sessions would be to decorate their own sheets with special fabric paints. The beds were currently down, but they folded up into a wall cabinet when not in use, giving each family a bit more space to spread out, to play, to be, with a sun lamp emitting varying levels of UV from 7am till 7pm on each windowsill. The windows currently looked out into blackness, but she was looking forward to seeing the fifteen sunrises and sunsets a day while they stayed in orbit.

Will it get tiresome? she wondered.

The master bedroom and ensuite were almost as big as the one they had left behind. Grant followed her as she went from room to room, his eyes watching her carefully controlled face. He had let her choose the wall colour, had left all the decorating decisions to her, really. It was the least he could do, he said, and she agreed.

Literally, the least he could do.

Already their rooms showed their personalities. Maggie had brought along a heavily edited collection of her drawings; the rest, Sarah had captured as photos and sniffled loudly as she rendered all but a few early pictures to the recycle bin.

They had been allowed to bring 20kg of personal effects along each. It didn't sound like a lot, but the ship — and then the colony, when they'd make the transfer — was so climate-controlled that they wouldn't need boots or jackets. The kids had chosen five stuffies each, and five favourite books, knowing that they'd be able to access millions of titles through the ship's computer on their smartbooks. Jack had struggled with paring down his Lego, but Sarah had worked with him over an entire afternoon, armed with a few big ziploc bags, a scale, and too many deep breaths and hugs to count, to come up with a manageable selection of blocks and specialty pieces.

Grant hadn't used his full 20kg.

"Really? You're not bringing anything sentimental?" she had asked him, exasperated, as she struggled to close another box.

He had grinned down at her and placed an old label maker into its own box. "This is sentimental," he said. He lifted her chin. "Besides, everything else I care for will be on that ship."

Maggie had insisted on ballet shoes, and on Sarah purchasing her two more pairs in larger sizes — if that's what it would take, then fine — after all, money was really no object.

For her part, she 'invested' in high-end skincare products, things that would last maybe six months, maybe a year, then would regret ever buying them when she had to start to do without or have to have them sent by unmanned shuttle. She cringed in advance about requesting them. She'd have to beg Grant to make her something in the lab, she told herself. She was going to look old, *no, worse*: middle-aged. No more highlights, no fancy conditioner, no manicures, and the lighting wouldn't be flattering either, she bet, but who was she trying to impress? The other husbands?

Ethan would have found that funny, but... well, she would never be able to tell him that, would she?

Chapter 16

Whatever technology they had used to get such a huge piece of machinery from the ground, to orbit, to Mars, Sarah was pretty sure that Grant only pretended to understand, too. Unless it had something to do with varying patterns of cell division in microgravity, which was the last thing he had worked on that made *any* sense to her, she was sure that he was as awed as she was at the magic that science had wrought. *Behold! A great big cruise ship to Mars!*

They had warned her in the orientations that they would all feel some queasiness for the first week or so, but she was unprepared for the force of the nausea. Both kids threw up in a suspiciously regularly alternating schedule for four days straight, then lay around the cabin moaning and being mean to each other for the next two. Sarah didn't throw up. It felt just like the morning sickness she had had during both pregnancies, though; lots of nausea, feeling like death warmed over, but no vomit. As she had then, she thought that if she could just throw up, she'd feel better. She was up and about, back to herself on day five, refereeing the weak squabbling and comforting the miserable sobbing. And Grant? *He was fine, damn him.*

On the seventh day, they were up and bright-eyed, chomping at the bit to go run around and look out from every window.

The view was stunning. A far cry from the starless sky of her last night outside, here there was no light pollution to outshine the glory of the universe. From this new perspective, her constellations were gone, but little pinpricks of light were everywhere, in the full spectrum of colours, from reds to blues. The moon was much less impressive than she had expected. Sure, it looked bigger than it did from her old backyard, but not much.

But the Earth, the Earth was staggering in its size, its beauty, its colour. In its holding everybody anybody ever knew. She found herself as excited as the children, as excited as Grant, following its progress around the ship, watching sunrise after sunset, trying to recognize which country, which city they were passing over.

Can anyone see us? she wondered.

If I screamed loud enough, would someone hear me?

They'd be leaving this orbit tomorrow, leaving this last link to home far behind, heading out towards one of those pinpricks. In this shuttle, it would take nine months and four days, if all went well. Nine months to get to Mars, to start a new life, a new home.

She wondered if they had planned it that way on purpose.

That first week flew by in a haze. Despite their nausea, the kids were more eager about the adventure than she had ever seen them, because of course they were. A routine quickly formed: up early with Grant, then another orientation meeting planned around the ship, a safety drill, then they had the rest of the day mostly free to explore and figure out the layout of the ship. The kids had already made friends, in fact, several new potential best friends for each of them. They seemed happy.

In the late afternoons, there were safety briefings and facilities and activities seminars, to make sure that everyone knew what was available on the ship. Tonight's was in the auditorium, a huge room with a wide stretch of windows; this one was about the school and extracurricular activities available. Tomorrow was their turn to plant their gardens.

The unpacking was quick. She had gotten that down to about a science after so many moves. Setting up house was the same routine anywhere, but she kept feeling a hum of anticipation, of adventure, which she hadn't expected. Their quarters were more than adequate for the size of their family, the layout was smart and efficient, and the kids loved having space to play in their rooms when their beds were hidden in the wall. Or, more likely, she mused, they loved being able to hide their beds without making them first.

Pick your battles, Sar.

Jack had built seven different Lego spaceships so far, each of them displayed on his shelves, beside his small stash of books and stuffies. That first day on board, Maggie had put up her very best drawings on the hidden magnetic strips in the walls. She was currently at their dining table with glue, ribbons and magnets, so that when she danced into her room, or turned the fan up high, the ribbons fluttered like they had at home. Jack sat at the table, too, his short legs wrapped around the legs of his chair as he painstakingly drew the plans for the next spaceship with a ruler and a pencil while Maggie glued and tied.

Sarah supervised their work with her hands wrapped around her mug of tea, lost in thought. Most of the supplied dishes were a lightweight melamine-type material, but she had used up 850 precious grams of her weight allotment by bringing the two mugs that she had bought in Copenhagen.

She considered a list of requests, things they still needed or wanted to make the trip and their new life more manageable. Packing stuff in a box and weighing it was one thing, but now that they were unpacked, the boxes removed and recycled, they had a chance to review their choices and request substitutions or more items.

What if she traded one of her mugs for another framed photo of her parents? Grant rarely used his, preferring his stainless-steel travel mug. She wanted more craft supplies for the kids, she had noted on inspecting the studio space she'd be sharing with the school and other artists on board. What if she found two other families willing to share a casserole pot? Would it really be too much of a hassle?

In the lab, Grant was in his element; he had spent the weeks leading up to boarding ensuring the conditions, filters, air exchange and safety measures were in place, that the freezers and biocontainment units were functioning and manuals, protocol sheets and replacement parts easily available. He was now setting things up the way he wanted: his office just so, his filing cabinets labeled and computers organized, his files backed up and shared with his staff. He had started briefing his team this morning.

He had even joined them for lunch. Sarah was stirring together a quick soup when he walked into their cabin with a bright smile on his face. The kids both jumped up and squealed, "Daddy's home!"

Sarah grinned at them. He rarely came home during the day. *More like never.*

"This is different," she teased.

"This is what this can mean for us," he said, giving her a kiss on the cheek. "And Sarah, I have a surprise for you after lunch."

She ladled the soup into the brightly coloured melamine bowls. She had let the kids choose the dish pattern, and they were certainly colourful; bright blue, orange, green and yellow rings alternated around the rims and down into the bowl. The plates were white with the same colours around the rims, and the eight glasses ('plastics,' Sarah called them) were solid colours, two of each.

Jack had set the table with spoons and glasses and a bright blue salt mill and an orange pepper grinder. Maggie had gotten the milk out of the fridge. The sun rose again.

Just a regular lunch.

When they had all been served, she sat down and picked up her spoon. "So," she said, "What's the surprise?" *Don't let it be a cat.*

Grant smiled his thin-lipped smile.

Oh, those dimples.

"You'll see soon enough."

"I'm curious. Can't wait." She watched him as he spooned the soup into his mouth. He was happy, she realized. They were living on what amounted to a cruise ship, and he seemed actually happy, for the first time ever. Gone was his feverish excitement, his standard twitchy start at a new lab, a new position. He was calm, content.

She could get used to this.

After lunch, Grant had cleared the dishes off the table and wiped it while Sarah quickly washed the pot and utensils. The kids started their crafts again while she refilled her mug with boiled water from the dispenser.

"I'll send the surprise down in a bit," Grant said, kissing her temple. "I can meet you at the theatre at four."

Her tea was still warm when there was a knock at the door. Maggie looked up, but Jack stayed focused on his spaceship. He had made a little snowdrift of eraser crumbs.

Sarah got up to answer the door, and there, one arm propped against the doorframe in an exaggeratedly casual pose, was Anne.

"Oh hello there," she drawled. "Isn't this a coincidence?"

Chapter 17

Sarah had gotten used to being alone. She rarely thought about being lonely; she liked her routine, her freedom. Each job she took was taken with the knowledge that it wasn't going to be for very long, and the work was often so mindless — not because of its complexity, but because she was naturally efficient at organizing and sorting. She didn't have to feel challenged at work or learn new systems; after all, she'd be moving with Grant in a year, no more than two.

Grant was brilliant, well-respected, and climbing fast. He had very interesting ideas about cell biology. Groundbreaking. Important. Or so Sarah had been told at all those gatherings full of older scientists. When she was with him at one of these events, her bachelor's degree had given her enough of a background to understand the basics of what Grant's colleagues discussed, and his dinnertime conversation supplied her with more, but she kept that hidden; she always felt too young, too carefully, casually, or stylishly dressed among so much tweed.

At cocktail parties and faculty events, or those long, boring, oddly uncomfortable networking conference dinners, she would feel like she had an interesting story. The places she had travelled, far beyond where she had ever expected to go. The sights and monuments she had seen in person, that most people had only ever seen in movies or travel shows — these all were fascinating ways to join conversations. Until she explained that she had gone because her husband had a meeting there. Until the other people in the cluster realized that she was just a sidekick.

Grant was gorgeous. When he mingled at these events, sipping soda water with a wedge of lime, his intensity seemed to shine from his whole body. The group around him were always listening intently; the men were impressed by his research, the women, even as tweedy as they tended to be, by his tall build and those blue, blue eyes.

Those nights, Sarah would accept a glass of wine when they arrived, "but just a small one," then another and another as the night went on, as she was pushed to the outside of the groups.

One night in December, she had sat alone on a window seat, breathing crisp Cambridge air through a slightly cracked window. MIT's Head of Biology had invited the faculty and their wives to his stuffy home. She was looking at his collection of microscopes on a nearby bookshelf when another body plopped down beside her with a sigh.

"It's a lot, isn't it?" A stunning brunette in a red sweater dress swung a curtain of shiny hair over her shoulder and smirked. "These things always kill me." She gestured a red-sleeved arm at the display on the bookshelf. "Half of them are museum reproductions. How original for a biologist to collect microscopes, right? The least they could do is not insult our intelligence with obvious fakes." She turned to look at Sarah, who smiled back. "I'm Anne. I work with the esteemed Dr. Grant as often as I can. He's the only man here who isn't stuck in the past." She jabbed her hand out for Sarah to shake, then took a big sip from her wine glass.

She grimaced. "Well, that's a lot of port."

Sarah burst out laughing, loud enough for Grant to hear. He glanced over at the two of them sharing the window seat and shaking with laughter — *snorting* with laughter, Anne corrected her later — and pressed his lips together before looking back at the tweed he was speaking to.

"Oh, I'm in trouble now," Anne murmured, and Sarah covered her mouth with her hand.

"I was going to say that *I* was in trouble," she said, and they collapsed again.

At the end of the night, Grant, sober as always, had driven Anne home too. She entertained Sarah with amusing stories of the lab — "I didn't know *interesting* things happened at the lab," quipped Sarah — from the back seat. As Anne got out of the car, she leaned forward and put her hand, then her head on Sarah's shoulder.

"I'm glad to have met you," she said, a little too loudly. "Grant needs someone like you." With that, she swung her legs out into the snow, swore, and stumbled up her front steps. Sarah watched her go, a big grin on her face.

"I like her," she said. "Please, can we be friends?" Grant's lips had disappeared again, which Sarah found hilarious. "It is possible that I may have had too much wine," she declared. "Take me home, sir!"

Grant had taken a position in New Zealand two months after that party, just in time for the first semester. It had been wonderful, though, to have found someone to connect with for a change, to laugh with over a bottle of wine. Anne had worked just as hard as Grant but unplugged from the lab as soon as she left it at night. "A girl's gotta live," she said. "I'm too cute to be locked up with these nerds all the time."

And now, here she was on the shuttle, leaning against their front door.

Sarah shrieked and threw her arms around her, squeezing her friend tight. "Oh my God oh my God oh my God," she chanted. "What are you doing here? Are you really here? I mean, *here* here?"

Anne laughed and hugged her back. "I am, m'dear! When I got the call, I wasn't going to turn this down! Are you kidding? 'Excitement, adventure, really wild things?' I eat that stuff for breakfast!"

Maggie and Jack were looking at them curiously. Mom didn't usually squeal like a teenager, but here she was, wrapped around this pretty lady in a lab coat.

"Maggie and Jack, I want you to meet Ms.—"

"Anne," said Anne firmly, walking up to the table and sticking out her hand, her short nails painted perfectly as always. "I'm Anne. Your mom and I are old friends, from back before there *was* a Maggie and Jack. Now," she paused, looking back and forth between them, keeping a straight face, "which one's which?"

Sarah made a cup of coffee for Anne in the other stoneware mug, milk, no sugar.

"'*So excited for you!*'" she mocked. "That was cruel!"

"I thought you'd like the surprise!" Anne exclaimed, laughing. They took their drinks and sat on the sofa while the children worked on their projects. "Are they always like this?" she asked out of the corner of her mouth.

"Like what?"

"Quiet, diligent, Grant-y?"

Sarah laughed. "Not always, but they can be. And hey! I can be quiet and diligent, too."

"You could, but luckily you've got Grant to be that instead. What do you think about your new abode? Mine is a quarter of this size, of course, but then again, I'm a quarter of the people, so." It wasn't a complaint, just a statement.

"How long has it been?"

"Since I had a boyfriend? Let's see..." Anne pretended to count on her fingers.

"No, since we've seen each other."

Anne took a tentative sip of her coffee. "Hot! Damn, too soon. Well, definitely not since you had these little people. So, what's that? How old are they? Four and five?"

"I'm eight, and he's six!" Maggie's clear voice rang out behind them, indignant. "And I'm finished my magnets for now. Can we go call on Dana and Evan?"

Jack whipped his head around at the mention of Evan's name. "I'm done too." He dropped his pencil and stood up, wiping his hands on his pants. His glasses had slid down his nose a bit and he pushed them back up.

"Ok, go, but stay together. And you have to come home by 3:30, and I'm saving your mess for you to clean up when-"

They were already gone.

Anne watched them go, then turned back to Sarah.

"Cute kids. Your eyes. The last time I saw you was... huh... it must have been New Zealand. Ten years ago?"

Ten years. How did she go so long without reaching out to her friend? She had been busy, of course. Having the kids had meant that she didn't tag along on Grant's conferences anymore, and their babyhood was a blur, overwhelming, and moving, always moving, then finally landing in Ottawa two years ago, when both kids were in school, starting her job at LabX and working hard... but still.

She didn't have time for friends, which is why she didn't have any. No, that wasn't true. She had Linda. And Nancy, of course. She and Nancy could live at opposite ends of the earth and not talk for twenty years and still be best friends. Coworkers and neighbours were pleasant enough, if replaceable and interchangeable. Spinning instructors and gym friends? They come and go. But Anne was the first real friend she had made since school, and she hadn't seen her in a decade.

She was still gorgeous. When they'd grab a coffee or lunch, men's heads would turn, they'd look at Anne's long legs or the curves of her hips. Sarah didn't mind — really — she had never turned heads herself, and *of course* Anne was attractive; Sarah had been drawn to her *because* she was beautiful, confident. Her hair was shorter now, just to her shoulders, but still dark and shiny — she possibly had a bit of help to keep it that way — and she had a few extra little lines around her expertly made-up eyes and around her mouth. But overall, she looked great, as beautiful as ever. Under her lab coat, you could see about an inch of her dress, something dark grey and silky.

As she listened to Anne explain her career trajectory, how the call for biologists in her field went out, how she had seen Grant's name as the lead and reached out, how she, too, had sold everything she owned, but apparently with a lot less regret, Sarah was suddenly aware of her comfortable clothes: jeans and an old sweater on her slim frame, her hair pulled back in a ponytail, a bit of eyeliner and mascara her attempt at vanity this morning. Aside from that last meeting with Ethan, she'd have been hard-pressed to think of a day that she had made that much effort — or looked that seemingly effortlessly good — for work.

Anne drained her mug — Sarah's was still in her hand, almost cold now — and put it on the table.

"Are you going to the orientation at four?" asked Sarah.

"Nope: no kids, no need. I'll read the Coles notes later," she said. "Can we meet for a drink tomorrow night? Eleventh floor lounge at eight?"

They hugged again and Anne walked away, headed back to the lab. *I have a friend onboard.* Sarah closed the door behind her and smelled Anne's perfume in the air; it was a little spicy, a little musky. Sexy. She looked down at her unpolished hands again, frowning slightly.

Chapter 18

Can't make it tonight.

Boss is a monster.

Raincheck? x Anne

Sarah sighed. Well, the ship was small, and they had nine months to have drinks together.

And the rest of our lives.

She had the kids put on old jeans and dark shirts and followed them down to their garden plot right after breakfast. Months ago, she had sat down with lists of plants and graph paper, put her orders in, and was excited to bring it to life. The three almost-mature apple trees had already been transplanted in raised beds to allow their roots room to spread. The horticulture techs had provided lightweight gardening tools, and their chosen seeds and seedlings had been delivered right into their unit.

The garden plots were, she had thought at first, a sort of apologetic attempt, an atonement for their exile from the outside world, the natural. But when she stepped over the threshold, from the smooth corridor to the spongy earth, she stopped, her eyes widening and nostrils flaring. She felt at home for the first time, immersed in this comparative wilderness, green and fresh. She filled her lungs with a huge breath of moist air and slowly exhaled, her shoulders moving away from her ears for the first time in weeks.

Their plot was one of about a dozen in this unit, set up like a line of so many yards. Theirs was going to be laid out in rows of herbs and vegetables and surrounded by the little trees. They weren't yet big enough to bear real fruit, but their trunks were just about spannable by Jack's meaty hands.

In the plot beside them, already dirty up to their elbows, a couple waved and smiled. Their thickly planted border indicated that they'd been there for a while already. A technician was patiently explaining that the seedlings needed to be planted further apart.

"First things first." Sarah took an elastic from her wrist and grabbed Maggie's hair. "Tie it back, miss!"

"Mom!" Maggie twisted out of her grasp. "I can do it!" She twirled away, then stopped suddenly. "Daddy!"

Sarah whirled around to see Grant at the entrance, wearing old clothes and holding out a bunch of latex gloves like a bouquet. He smiled as Maggie threw herself at him, then bopped Jack on the head with his fist.

"Need a hand?" He helped the kids put the gloves on, the fingers drooping comically from their small hands, then cleared his throat dramatically. "How Things Grow 101."

He took Jack and Maggie over to one of the trees and explained basic principles of plants and how they grew, in simple and clear language. Sarah's eyes shone as she watched him point out the components of the garden: the soil, the roots, the bark, the leaves. He was a natural teacher. *I never knew that.*

He busied the kids with planting the herbs in pots. To the sound of Grant explaining how the light was programmed to cycle for a realistic Earth day and growing season — *You're losing them now* — Sarah raked, turned over and dredged five rows in the centre mound of soil, spaced about two feet apart. It smelled divine.

"Ok, I need helpers for these seeds!" She shared a grin with Grant as Maggie and Jack, their faces already smudged with dirt, scampered over. "I've got carrots here! Who wants to plant carrots?" She handed the seeds to Jack, who, under Grant's strict guidance, poked the holes and pushed in the seeds.

"What do you think, Miss Maggie? Beets or beans?"

Maggie pulled a face. "Not beets."

"Beans it is, then!"

Grant's schedule, for that first week in orbit, was a new experience for everyone. He joined them for breakfast, then was in the lab by eight, home by five, plus or minus his six-minute 'commute.' He came home for lunch every day, dinner every night. He smiled and joked with the kids at the table. Sarah found herself forgetting to lift her fork to her mouth, sitting back and watching him, dazed. Who was this handsome man, lit from within? Was he really Grant? Was he really *hers*?

He sat and reviewed supply lists and equipment specs as she cleaned up the kitchen, as she tucked the kids into bed. But after that, he talked to her — *at* her — about his experiments, the plans and what he expected. His team on

Earth had been confident in their research, that their hypotheses were correct. They felt Grant's job was just to verify this, reproduce the expected outcomes. This bored him already — where was the fun in that? He chattered brightly about surprising outputs and variations that they had to quantify, like the faster growth cycles they'd already been observing, even in that first week. He smirked. The seeds they planted today should germinate quickly, sprout, and grow even faster the farther they got from Earth. He complained about the Earth technicians, the red tape and how long it was going to take to receive unforeseen components via the unmanned shuttle, if it even arrived on schedule, and wondered out loud whether they would have enough time to send required parts ahead to the colony.

For the first time in years, he was talking to her and involving her in his world. He needed to tell her everything, all at once, about who he was and what he did.

She hadn't met this Grant before, He was exhausting.

This is our life, I guess, she thought.

In a month, she had left everything behind. In just a week, they had acclimatized to this orbit, settled in, gotten used to wandering through the hallways and greeting faceless neighbours, all of the orientation sessions complete. Sarah watched as many of the sixteen sunrises and sunsets as she could, taking long last looks at the planet below. *Home* thought Sarah continuously. A mantra.

Then, it was gone. Well, not gone, exactly, but after the week of orbit, after getting used to seeing it out the windows all day and night, she watched the Earth slowly slip away behind them. The change ravaged her equilibrium again, so for a few days, at least, she was too sick to care. For that, she felt lucky.

Chapter 19

Sarah didn't know how anything could feel like home ever again, not this shuttle, and especially not some faraway, alien planet. She supposed, however, that after nine months on this cruise ship, she'd be happy to stand on the ground again, whatever ground that was. If all went well, they would never see Earth again, except as a large blue ball, still visible but diminishing from the aft windows; well, they wouldn't if all didn't go well, either.

Everyone recovered faster this time. On the third day after breaking orbit, with the Earth still large in the stern windows, their equilibrium was restored. The kids started school.

Maggie's Grade Three class met on Level 3. Seventeen other children arrived in various states of neatness and disarray, but all loudly, and the chaotic drop-off had the reassuring feel of any other first day of school.

"Have a good day, sweetie. I'll meet you here at lunchtime, ok?" Her lips barely brushed Maggie's cheek with a kiss before she broke away.

"Ok, bye Mom!"

The teacher smiled warmly at Sarah over Maggie's head, and then they were off to Level 2 to bring Jack to his classroom.

This classroom was even louder; fourteen Grade One kids ran in circles around the room, some over desks, some hiding underneath, and at least one in three in tears. Jack, shy but stoic, pushed his glasses back up the bridge of his nose and gave her a little close-lipped smile in response to her kiss, to her "Love you, buddy." He squeezed her hand a little tighter, then slipped into the classroom, where she recognized two of the boys he had played with during their week on the ground. He was resilient, that kid. She shared grins with some of the other moms as she watched the teacher and teaching assistant trying to wrangle the various personalities into some semblance of a storytime carpet. It really was so ridiculously, amazingly normal.

Well. That was done.

She walked away down the corridor feeling light and free. The sounds of all the youngest kids still rang out: the nursery, the day care, kindergarten and Grade One were all here, as were the art studios, where she had volunteered to help out. *There but for the grace of God go I*, she thought to herself wryly. *Until they want me to help.*

She paused for a moment at the entrance of the stairwell. *Do I have time?* She could go sit in the garden plot for a while, see if anything new had pushed through since yesterday. She was curious about the faster growth but didn't know how soon to expect it. Grant hadn't gone into detail, for a change. She glanced at her watch and sighed.

Not this morning, I guess.

She took the steps back up the six flights to their quarters and opened the door. The place — no, *our place* — was quiet and empty. The breakfast dishes were piled in the sink, the table covered with crumbs. In their rooms, the kids' rooms were, well, disasters. Jack hadn't done anything with his bed, and clothes and toys were strewn around from the morning's panic. Maggie's, though: every item of clothing she owned must have been thrown onto her unmade bed — *Good Lord, and she's only eight* — because the compartment that housed the bed during the day was propped open from the height of the pile.

Sarah sighed. She had only one hour to herself, but at least she was finally alone. These last weeks of having the kids around all the time had really worn on her. She loved them, of course, but returning to the role of housekeeper, babysitter, clown, cook, chauffeur... she was out of practice, that's all. These last two years as a respected grownup among other grownups had ruined her for this reality, she supposed. This was her role now.

She set to picking up, sorting, folding. The beds hid themselves away nicely, and all was well in the bedrooms. The kitchen, too, was quick, but when she finally sat down at the table with a hot cup of tea, she was dismayed to see that she only had fifteen minutes left. She brought her tea into the bathroom, hopped into a short shower — she had washed her hair last night anyway — and quickly applied a little amount of makeup.

She still wasn't sure how to go about the makeup thing on board. Makeup was a vanity and a foolish luxury, she knew, worth rationing, but she was still in the First Impression portion of her new life. She had done this before.

Might as well make the effort.

She dabbed on a little blush as well, and an extra coat of mascara. Her hair was back in a clip, of course. A simple, lightweight longsleeve in cornflower blue, and black tights, and she was ready to go. She picked up her bag and water bottle.

The studio was quiet when she arrived. She backed out to make sure she was in the right place — yes, Studio 2 — then stepped back in and left her bag and shoes by the door. She had entered a big room, painted a soft cream, the floors a light maple that matched the barres covering three walls. Interior rooms like this didn't have windows to the stars, but the lighting was nice, and the mirrors made it just what it should be: a dance studio. The kind of place that she had spent hour upon hour dreaming and stretching and twirling and jumping, that Maggie now lived for, and that she'd be spending most of her free time in, if Sarah knew her daughter.

She turned slowly, frowning at her reflection from every wall. Would Maggie's motivation be the same, now that the stage wasn't really an option as a goal. *Wasn't an option at all,* she corrected herself. No matter what instruction she had, no matter the hours of dedication and practice, would she still want to dance if there was no chance of becoming a prima ballerina? Prima in the first National Ballet of Mars? That was ludicrous.

Unconsciously, her arms had moved to first position, and her bare feet had too. She tried a little plie, then a larger one, her knees complaining a little. It had been too long. She stepped briskly over to the barre, placed her hand gently on it, and began. She drew herself up, shoulders back, chin level, shoulders down. She pulled her belly in firmly, tucked her tailbone under and turned out from her hips. She started by breathing. Just breathing. Realigning her posture with each breath, finding and rediscovering her body as it had been.

"I'm terribly sorry!"

A voice blurted out, and Sarah's eyes flew open. She didn't even notice when they had closed. Framed dramatically in the doorway of the studio was a tiny person, with a tight bun of white-blonde hair and fierce black brows. "I absolutely *detest* being late."

She strode — yes, *strode* — into the studio with so much presence that Sarah found herself intimidated. This bird-like personnage must be Katriahna — "*Ms.* Katriahna" — the woman who would be managing the dance programmes on board. Sarah had put in her name to teach ballet to the younger children a few days a week. As a volunteer, as indeed every position on the ship that wasn't essential to its trajectory or research was, she expected to be accepted on the spot, to be assigned a class, and to pick up where she had left off before she had married Grant.

But here she was, at an actual, honest-to-God audition. To teach three-year-olds how to plié on a spaceship. She could have said no, but... well, what else was she going to do?

Katriahna was teeny. She gave the impression of looming over Sarah, while being less than five feet tall. She was imposing.

"You were a dancer, yes?"

"I-I... I *tried.* I mean, I was more of a teacher than a dancer, and—"

"You will dance."

Katriahna turned away to touch a panel on the wall, and Sarah furtively wiped her hands on her pants.

Oh right. Mirrors everywhere.

Why was she so nervous? A piano piece began quietly.

Back at the barre, she went through a general warm up, as dictated tersely by Katriahna. Breathing in, out. Plié down, up. Tendu. Relevé. First, second, fourth, fifth. It came back so easily. She was a dancer again, light and graceful, not the sad woman with the middle-aged mother-of-two body that had walked in here this morning. The years fell away, and she was—

"Not wonderful." Katriahna's little hawk eyes looked her up and down again and again. Up close, she looked to be at least seventy. "You need to tighten up. To be less—" she plied, puffed her cheeks out and stuck out her stomach, creating a sway-backed caricature of a ballerina — "and more—" she straightened her posture and immediately looked regal and poised, forever a prima ballerina. "But you will do."

Back in her cabin, Sarah collapsed onto the couch, face down. She didn't know whether to laugh or cry. She felt shaky, like she'd attempted three spinning classes in a row, and fragile. She didn't feel like she'd been successful, that she had won her position to work for that awful little woman. For a moment, she had felt like the future was hers again, that she was a dancer, young and full of hope, but... the pose Katriahna had taken to show her how she looked. Could she really have been so ridiculous?

Her tea, grown cold as usual, was still on the counter. She added more hot water to it, then tapped out a quick message to Anne: *Worst. Interview. But I got the job!*

A message flashed up almost instantly.

Course you did. Drinks on Friday at 8? Grant'll babysit.

Sarah snorted, and replied with a thumbs up, then leaned against the counter. She looked around at her nice, neat apartment, empty of children and life, then turned away from her steaming mug. She quickly changed into her cycling gear. She could fit in forty-five minutes of exercise before the kids came home for lunch.

Might as well.

Chapter 20

It had been... different being with Grant, having him home with them. *Different good?* Sarah often wondered over that last month in isolation. She wasn't used to him, really. For so many years, he had been around on the periphery, the pins holding down her corners. She had never really known him on a day-in, day-out routine of breakfast, lunch and dinner. Even when he was in the same city, he was never home for more than one meal a day with the kids. With her. And now, there he was, and after dinner too.

The shared lunchtime, at least, had stopped abruptly when the children started school. He had rushed in on their first day, but with the kids underfoot, clamouring for food, demanding snacks to bring back for the afternoon break, Sarah's focus had been on them. She had barely returned from dropping them off again at school when he pinged down a message. *I'm thinking of taking my lunch in the cafeteria tomorrow*. Fine by her.

Tuesday morning, she taught her first class. Katriahna had given Sarah two classes on the schedule: preschoolers on Tuesday morning and kindergarteners after school on Thursday afternoons, while Maggie was in Studio 1 doing *proper* ballet and Jack played soccer on the turf fields. She delighted in her first class. The little ones, boys and girls alike, were good kids, even the troublemakers. Some were too young or too unfocused, or just uninterested in learning the magic of dance... they were all sweet, and some had real potential. She cringed at that word, but no, they did. She knew that Katriahna recognized it too, in the way she'd shoot a swift glance at a natural turnout or her brows would raise with a four-year-old's well-executed relevé.

Sarah hoped that her own technique would improve with practice. She demonstrated the warmups with the children, and stretched with them as well, only sometimes getting up to manually correct them. Even in her first class, she felt longer, stronger, more graceful, well, until she caught a glimpse of Katriahna's purse-lipped look, but overall, she felt wonderful, glowing, for that hour, anyway. She had forgotten how much she enjoyed teaching little ones. She hadn't been a teacher since she graduated from university, but it was just like she remembered.

Loud and messy and a lot like herding sheep, but fun.

She collapsed onto her couch afterwards, with an hour until she picked up the kids for lunch.

They had all fallen back into routines as normal as those they'd had on Earth. Kids at school each day, home for lunch. Maggie had her ballet on Tuesdays and Thursdays, and Jack, begrudgingly, had his soccer. They had time, finally, to have relaxed playdates, to run wild at the playground or on the turf fields. Last night after school, she'd brought them down to the garden plot to explore, to observe the little shoots already, miraculously, poking through the soil. The kids were different in there, she felt quieter, calmer. They brought books with them, and read them silently, sitting on the raised beams that surrounded the little trees, reaching out now and then to touch the smooth, cool trunks.

Everything was right there, a ten-minute walk away at most, and they could easily stop to play with other children before or afterwards. The community really was a true community, where maybe she'd make friends, trade babysitting as easily as a recipe exchange.

Maggie and Jack had already made friends. Young as they were, they could wander the ship freely, call on their friends, far more safely than they could have in their old neighbourhood. Aside from having to set aside time to see nature, Sarah thought, she'd almost agree that it was better. Maybe, soon, she could put herself out there and become part of it too. *But not yet*. Some of the other moms seemed nice, and she knew she should make the effort to get to know them, but that effort just seemed like a bit too much. She felt like a brat. The kids' routine was the most important, Grant's the strictest. And hers... well, here she was again. Really, though, what was she going to do with her time? Anne was in the lab all day, and she didn't know anyone else.

With the school runs and teaching, it only left her with... thirty-two hours a week with nothing to do.

*

"I'll start the dishes," said Grant. Thursday evening, Jack had disappeared into his room and his Lego after dinner, and Maggie was in the shower. Grant cleared the table as Sarah finished her glass of water. She considered helping but changed her mind; she had picked the kids up after school and brought them to ballet and soccer. She had taught the kindergarten class after school. She had made dinner. She moved to the sofa and picked up her smartbook, tucked her feet under her. She felt Grant's eyes on her. He was still by the sink but had only washed two plates.

"What is it?"

"I... I have a project to check up on at the lab," he said, tentatively. "I could go now, or I'll have to go back there after the kids are in bed. What... what would you prefer?"

Sarah hadn't ever seen him this hesitant. He didn't usually ask her permission, not about his schedule, at least.

It's not that *bad*, she scolded herself. And it really hadn't been. There was a very pleasant side effect to just turning off one's brain and following along, being told what was happening and how it would happen. But it felt very odd to be asked what she thought over something so small. Odd, but touching.

She went over to him and gave him a quick kiss. "Why don't you go ahead now? The kids are occupied, and I can finish cleaning up. You won't relax while you're thinking about work" — this was true — "so go get it out of your system. I'll see you later."

His face melted into an expression of relief. He held her for a second, then pulled away to look in her eyes.

So blue.

"You're doing ok? So far? This is... ok?" His glance seemed to encompass the cabin, the ship, the vast reaches of space between her and her home.

This was a big ask, but he was asking. This was his dream, and she had agreed to it, in the end. She smiled, not really having to try too hard.

"I'm ok," she said. "This is ok. The people are nice, the garden is lovely, and the dancing..." She drew her brows down and pretended to be Katriahna. "... It will get better because it is bad." Grant didn't know who Katriahna was, how she talked or moved, but he laughed anyway.

"Great. Thanks, Sarah." He kissed her quickly on the forehead, placed the damp cloth into her hand and was gone.

Sarah turned to the sink. She had overestimated his progress. One dripping plate sat in the drying rack.

*

The kids were in bed. When she got out of the shower, Grant still wasn't home. She towel-dried her hair, slipped into her pyjamas and poured a glass of wine, then sat down at the console in the kitchen. She took a deep breath and touched the screen.

A few moments later, Linda's image appeared in front of her, her mouth in a wide smile.

"Sarah!" she exclaimed. "It's too good to be true... is it really you? Tell me everything. Wait." She held up a finger and disappeared from the screen. Sarah could see the dimness of Linda's living room, neat as always. A muted beam of light flashed, then went out. In a minute, Linda was back, holding a glass of white wine. "Cheers, my friend. To long-distance friendships."

It had been, what, five weeks since they had had that awkward goodbye, since Sarah had told her what she shouldn't have told anyone else.

"It's honestly not exciting," Sarah protested. "Grant works like always, the kids have settled in, and it's like living in a small town." Linda peppered her with questions, some about the people, but mostly about the systems on board, how the lab runs, the routines, their systems of safety and disposal. These were all things that Sarah had regulated for LabX, and she realized how much she didn't know about what was going on in the ship's lab.

"You should get involved, Sar," Linda suggested, draining her glass. She moved out of sight again, and the light from her fridge glowed again briefly. She returned to the frame with a full glass and lifted it in another toast. "You're brilliant at this. We miss you so much around here. I mean, we're busy, and you've been replaced by a younger, better-looking model, but you're missed." She winked. "I don't want to hurt your feelings, but the new guy is more my type."

Head Office had approved Sarah's protocols and was starting to apply them across their network. "Everything is running well here without you, but it's all because of you." She took another sip. "I get to see Ethan fairly often."

Sarah kept her face neutral. "Oh? How is he? Is he as good to work with as I remember?"

Linda put her glass down. "I think — I don't know, but maybe you should talk to him, Sar. I've been thinking, and it's none of my business, but he's said some things, and maybe he... maybe he knows about the kids."

Sarah felt the blood drain from her face. Behind her, she heard the door to their quarters open. Grant walked in and stopped. She couldn't tell from his face whether he had heard, or whether he was just surprised to find her on the console.

"Come say hi to Linda, Grant," she said in a strangled voice. He crossed the room and stooped down to give a little wave to the screen.

"Hi Linda. How are things?" His voice seemed strained, but then, he had never warmed up to her.

"Hi Grant! Working hard as ever, I hear. I was just telling Sarah that she should get involved with the lab operations. She really saved us here." Linda's voice was bright. Too quick.

He glanced over at Sarah, then back to Linda. "Oh, I think she's probably enjoying taking a break," he said. "I'll let you two talk; I need a cup of tea and a shower." He waggled his fingers awkwardly, then moved offscreen, over to the cupboard, out of which he withdrew one of the blue mugs. He popped in a tea bag and filled it with boiling water.

Sarah used her eyebrows and darted her eyes to the side to indicate to Linda that he was still in the room. "Could you make me one too, please? Chamomile?"

Linda grinned. "I'd like one too, please!" Grant reached behind the melamine cups to get the other pottery mug from the back of the cabinet. He filled it from the dispenser as well, but as he brought it down to the counter, his elbow hit the first one, which Sarah watched fall towards the tile floor as if in slow motion. She made a convulsive movement with her arm, though she knew she couldn't reach it in time, knocking her wine glass over as well. The two vessels smashed almost in unison; the sturdy pottery fell apart in chunks, and the thin, slim-stemmed wine glass broke into shards.

Grant had jumped back reflexively, and boiling water from the mug he was still holding sloshed over his hand. He swore in pain, and Sarah watched in horror as her second prized mug cracked into pieces. A watery mess of tea and wine had splashed up the cupboard and spread all over the kitchen floor. "I have to go!" she blurted out and cut the link to Linda. The screen went black.

She moved as quickly as she could, gingerly trying to avoid the splinters of glass and pottery on the way to the sink. Grant was holding his hand to his stomach, his teeth clenched in pain.

"Here," she said, turning the faucet on. She gently took his hand and put it under the cold flow. "This will help."

He was scalded, there was no doubt about that. She kept his hand under the cold water for five full minutes, then softly patted it dry and bound it loosely in a clean cotton dish towel. He headed for the shower. How he was going to manage washing without getting the hot water onto it, she didn't know.

She quickly pulled up first aid procedures for a scald. Yes... yes... yes, she had done everything right. She knew she had, but... well, she didn't fully trust her instincts. Linda would be horrified by that.

She used another dish towel to mop up the wine and water, then swept the pieces up. She separated the glass from the pottery, then threw the thin pieces of glass into the recycling container. The stoneware, she laid aside. She didn't know why, but she wanted to keep them.

My favourite mugs. Then, *Eight hundred fifty grams. Wasted.*

She swept the floor again, making sure she got every little particle, then poured more boiling water into a melamine cup. Grant had understandably not wanted hot tea after this, so she brought her mug to the sofa and sat down, cupping it in her hands.

It warmed her palms, but felt plasticky, unnatural, not like her stoneware mug. Not the same, at all.

She picked up her smartbook and sent a quick ping to Linda. *All ok. Sorry. Let's do this again. xx S.*

She lifted the teabag out of her cup and set it aside. *Hmmm.* Maybe Linda was right.

She searched up the ship's documents. Yes, there was the research section, broken down across the disciplines. She found the protocols for the bio lab and scrolled through, skimming. They weren't considered secure. Too boring for most, she knew, and nothing that would cause problems if anyone read them.

She heard the bathroom door open and wondered how Grant's shower had got on. She considered checking on him but knew that he'd be cranky by now. He hated being injured, sick. If he needed her, he'd ask.

Grant had approved these protocols himself. Sarah wasn't sure if Anne had helped, or any of the other scientists that worked under him, but knew that they had been approved, reviewed with a fine-toothed comb, by both the FDA and SLPSRA, NASA's Space Life and Physical Sciences Research and Applications. But, as Linda had reminded her, this was her specialty, what she was good at — no, what she was *great* at. Even if she wasn't going to be working in her field onboard, there was no reason why she shouldn't take a look and get herself up to speed. Who knows, maybe Grant would hire her.

Two hours later, she tiptoed into the bedroom. Her melamine cup was washed and back in the cupboard, her smartbook charging on its pad. She had gotten through about a quarter of the documents — not exactly absorbing reading — and had highlighted and jotted notes as she went through.

The experiments were unfamiliar to her. She had to admit that she was way out of her depth when it came to the effects of space and space travel on living things, but the laboratory principles were the same as on Earth.

Grant was already in bed, had been there, she assumed, since after his shower; he hadn't reappeared. He had left his bedside light on. His injured hand, now bandaged, was on top of the covers, and he had propped himself up with an extra pillow to stop himself from rolling over, or snoring, she supposed, or — more likely, she realized as she saw his smartbook beside him — just fallen asleep reading.

Her face softened as she looked at him. The poor man was exhausted. He'd had a long day in the lab — *so much for a different lifestyle* — and he would be furious with himself for taking one of his hands out of commission. It would slow him down, make him depend on others.

He was a good man. He worked so hard and was good at what he did. That's why they were here.

He looked so much younger when he was asleep. His eyes were softly closed, and the bedcovers hid his length. Without the piercing blue of his eyes and his stature, he looked ordinary, plain. Not the kind of man that inspires and creates.

She bent down to gently kiss his forehead. She'd check his hand in the morning, if he'd let her. She padded off to brush her teeth.

Chapter 21

Grant was up and out early on Friday morning, his hand brightly bandaged. *How's your hand?* she sent after school drop-off. No response, nothing from him until right before dinner. Her smartbook pinged.

Stuck here. Am sending Mike's wife to babysit.

What? she responded. *Who?*

No answer.

There was a knock on their door at 7:45.

"You must be... Mike's wife?" Sarah was glad she was already dressed up. She had brought so few dresses — *why would she?* — but wore a simple black sheath and small heels. She expected Anne would look as gorgeous as ever, but this woman looked effortlessly beautiful, too.

"I'm Erin," the woman smiled. "You must be Grant's wife." Her eyes twinkled. On closer inspection, Erin's curly blonde hair was carefully styled, her soft blue eyes lightly made up. *We're all making first impressions*, Sarah realized. "And this is Bridget." Beside her, a miniature version looked around their quarters with wide eyes.

"Bridget!" shrieked Maggie. Over the high-pitched squeals, the women's eyes met again.

"I guess they know each other already. I'm Sarah. Thank you for doing this! I owe you one."

"No worries. It takes a village, right?"

The children were playing cards with Erin when Sarah kissed them goodbye, wearing another coat of mascara and a little bit of silver-plum eyeshadow.

Like everything else on the ship, the lounge was a short walk away. She passed by two elevator bays on the way, choosing instead to take the stairs, to continue to explore her new world on foot. Already she noticed differences in hallways, recognized doors along the way. Resist it as she may, this was her neighbourhood; this ship was becoming home.

The cocktail lounge was up on the eleventh deck, at the very front of the ship. Giant windows curved around one entire booth-lined wall, and skylights striped the ceiling. After the sudden, sustained swirl of dizziness earlier this week, the view seemed static; their movement through space was almost imperceptible most times, excepting the aft view of Earth still slowly shrinking behind them.

Anne was there already, waving her over to join her at the bar. She had freshened up too; her hair was shiny and smooth, her lipstick bright red, and she wore a slim black skirt and a deep, midnight-blue blouse, very chic and well fitting. The bartender looked dazzled as Sarah leaned in to embrace her friend. Same perfume. She looked tired, tonight. And wary.

She had ordered them each a martini — "Just the one," Anne had insisted. "It's another early start tomorrow" — and led them to a tall booth against the window. Stars twinkled all around them, from the wrap-around windows to the skylight — *Is it still called a skylight?* — above.

"I will never get tired of this view," said Anne in a hushed voice.

"It's pretty spectacular," agreed Sarah. "So."

"So," said Anne. She looked into her glass. The single olive rested on the bottom, as the angled sides fogged with condensation.

"It's been a while." *Where do we even start? My kids? Her career? Our oh-god-what-have-we-done?*

"To old friends." They clinked glasses gently, but not quite gently enough; a drop sloshed over the side of Sarah's. She took a sip through tight lips and almost managed to suppress a shudder at the sharp, cold liquid. Anne burst out laughing and took a sip from her own. "Still a lightweight! God, it's good to see your face, Sar."

Sarah set her glass down, grinning, and shook her head. "Yours too. Next time, I'm ordering, and it'll be wine."

"This is more festive." Anne took another sip.

"What are we celebrating? Leaving everything behind?"

Anne's gaze didn't waver, but her shoulders slumped a little. She responded brightly. "You've just got to change how you say it: 'Leaving everything behind!'"

"I left my jazz hands on Earth," Sarah began.

There was a discreet cough at Anne's elbow. They turned to see a uniformed officer standing by their table, the captain's executive assistant. He looked uncomfortable, and very young.

"Good evening, Mrs. Harper. Can you come with me, please? There's been an accident, and—"

"The children?" Sarah was already standing up, her drink untouched except for that one sip, that one spilled drop. Anne reached out and held her hand.

The young man dropped his eyes. "No, ma'am, not the children. If you could just come with me."

"Grant?" Anne's hand tightened on hers.

He looked over at Anne. "I'm sorry, Dr. Coyne, but—"

"It's ok. She can come with me." Sarah watched from outside herself as he walked ahead. They followed him quietly, still hand-in-hand, like little girls following a teacher to detention, to the entrance of the lounge, through the corridors, not stopping until they reached the closed door of the Captain's quarters.

A month before boarding

She was going to be late picking up the kids from camp. Again.

Get your act in gear, Sar.

She thought she remembered being organized and efficient, she and her systems, until lately. Until this job, she admitted to herself.

When they moved to the neighbourhood, she had been one of those moms that dressed their kids appropriately and took them to interesting places, talked to them instead of being on her phone. She had dropped the kids, the magical little beings that she had so desperately wanted, off at school in the morning and met them at the school gate in the afternoons, still energetic after a short day at whatever office she worked at then. She had remained on top of everything, always prepared. Surely, these three extra hours of work weren't too much to ask.

It had been a tradeoff, she figured. She loved the challenge and the feeling of respect — no, self-respect — at the lab, but she felt tired and cranky at the end of the day. Like today. She exhaled. Like every day, lately.

Traffic was barely moving on the highway. She tried another deep breath; this one came out a growl. Her patience was already drained. Customers, suppliers, the gobs at head office...they all sapped her precious reserves of energy. She knew that. When she dashed to aftercare to collect her kids, she wasn't as present as she used to be, back when they got to be her main focus. She didn't think Maggie and Jack noticed — her systems still worked — and they really did love the after-school programme; besides, the extra two hours of friends, sports and crafts every day meant that she could skip some of the other extracurricular activities that they used to have. Except ballet for Maggie, of course. That still took up an extra two evenings a week. Jack was so patient for those, too;

as long as he had a magnetic building set or, increasingly, a book to read, he was happy to entertain himself.

They were finally getting to that magical point that all parents dream about, where the kids play together, and the parents get to start to be people again.

But which people?

She hadn't been surprised that Grant didn't change and wasn't around more, or more present once the babies arrived. But maybe now...

On the ship, there would be no commute, no conferences to fly off to for two nights or five. There might be video feeds that he'd have to attend, but he'd be no more than ten minutes away, wherever he was. Who would he be when he had nowhere else to go?

She drummed her fingers on the steering wheel. That caused her pause. Would their relationship change on board? There would be fewer pressures, less time constraints and time away from each other. Within the confines of an enormous metal frame, floating through space, would it be like it used to be?

What *was* it like before?

She still felt flattered that Grant Harper had known who she was, that an 'older man' had taken an interest in her, asked her out. She still felt that pull towards him, the same one that had caused her to attach herself and her identity to him and follow him — literally — to the other end of the world, and soon to another world altogether. For him, she left her childhood behind. At the time, that included Ethan too. There had been passion, definitely. But what had they talked about then, other than his ambitions, his dreams?

He found what he needed in a spouse, all right, a partner to follow him from place to place, provide him with a family and a home. He never would have been able to do what he did had he married someone ambitious, interested in pursuing her own career. Someone like Anne would have demanded more of his time and his energy, wouldn't have put her career on hold to move around with him, have babies.

Be fair, Sar. She hadn't demanded, hadn't put anything on hold. She didn't have a career back then; she had simply left her job. For someone with all the systems and plans, she hadn't had one for herself, and she honestly hadn't minded at the time. She was more scared than anything: scared that it would go well, that the babies would be healthy, that... well. The less thought about all that, the better.

This could be an opportunity, though. She thought more about it as she pulled off the highway. The ship would be like a small community. For the first time in fifteen years, she would be in one place with the same people for an indefinite amount of time, not scuttling off after two years or less to the next city, the next university laboratory or CDC lab. Absurd as it sounded, maybe, on a spaceship to Mars, she could actually put down roots.

Maybe she could make real friends. She had a handful of kindred spirits, but they were scattered around the world. They were people that she had connected with for a shortish period of time, then left behind.

In that way, her relationship with Anne and Nancy would hardly change. How often did she see either of them now? Anne was excited for her, had sent her a short email to say congratulations. Nancy hadn't changed her mind or become more enthusiastic but sent her off with blessings and cheer after their weekend. They had spoken twice since then, both heart-to-heart webchats. What difference would it make if they spoke across a country or across a galaxy?

And Linda... Linda was one of her kindred spirits, a friend who believed in her on a daily basis, but Sarah had learned that close friends from work became former coworkers more often than not. True, she would be just a web call away too, but she seemed as supportive as anyone else about the mission. Was it anything more to her than losing her best employee? Was it just Sarah's skills that she'd miss? Couldn't Sarah telework?

And why is there so much traffic today?

She kept fuming. And her parents, why weren't they more upset? *I'm their only child, dammit*. They could web call anytime; maybe it wouldn't feel that different for them. They had seen them once, maybe twice a year until this most recent move. Even now, that third visit felt like too much, like they had taken up a space where Grant's parents could have stepped in for a visit, had they been up for it.

Be thankful for small blessings; *is that how it goes?* At least that guilt would be alleviated.

She flicked her eyes over to the time on the dashboard and grimaced. So late.

On good days, she was cautiously excited for the trip. The futuristic environment of the ship, a sort of ultra-secure, bizarro 1970s-style existence, would actually be freeing for the children. They wouldn't be able to ride their bikes ever again — and here she felt a pang — with the wind in the hair and their feet off the pedals. And true, they wouldn't have the run of the entire ship, but they would certainly have more freedom than their own backyard and wouldn't need her to pick them up from camp. And, she supposed, she'd have freedom too.

She could do... be... *become* anything. She would have the rest of her life to make friends, blend in or stand out. *Freaking potential again.* And she wouldn't need to up and leave everything within two years.

There it was. She was leaving everything she knew for something else, something unknown: not necessarily worse, all things considered, but different. A new world opening up. A one-way, no-return deal. She could reinvent herself again from the following little mouse that she'd somehow become along the way. Or perhaps that's all she had ever been but allowed chance and circumstance to create a narrative that she could blame.

She rolled to a stop in front of the community centre, shook her head, lowered her shoulders. It's my choice. She had chosen to go. She was going to Mars with Maggie and Jack, who didn't really have a vote, but were keen enough, and Grant. The kids would be fine; it was ironic to think that this would finally give them a consistent community, a stable childhood.

Maggie and Jack would be there at the beginning, helping to build something new as they joined the colony, and so would she and Grant. Together.

She reached to open the door.

Chapter 22

Captain Leung's quarters were spacious and sparse. Sarah had met him briefly in a welcome reception during their first week aboard, before the launch, but hadn't seen him since. "Your husband's a brilliant man," he had said then, shaking Grant's hand avuncularly. Tonight, he was sombre.

"Mrs. Harper. Dr. Coyne. I'm sorry to have to tell you this," he began, only looking at Sarah. "There was an accident in the biology lab tonight." A pause, cruelly long. "Your husband is dead. I'm sorry," he said again.

"But I was just there!" Anne responded harshly. "An hour ago! I—"

Sarah grabbed her arm and squeezed it. "What happened?" she said faintly.

"Please, have a seat. Both of you."

The sofa was hard, lacking in decorative pillows. Sarah looked around the room again as she sat and realized how little decoration there was.

A bachelor, she supposed. *What a lonely place to be, alone,* she thought. Then, *Poor Anne*. And then, *Oh*.

He had poured them each a glass of water. Or... he indicated a globe propped open, one of those old-fashioned minibars that would have looked ridiculous in their home but fit right into the spare bachelor pad vibe he had. They shook their heads. The time for a drink had passed, for now.

The centrifuge had malfunctioned, become unbalanced. The rotor failed, and the resulting explosion had shot out metal fragments and shockwaves. They were still piecing it together, too early to tell for sure, he said, but one, if not both of those had killed Grant. He was sorry. The lab was in rough shape, but probably salvageable. The ship was fine, its integrity intact. Grant had been alone. At that, Sarah felt Anne flinch beside her.

Sarah was numb and cold. Her arm was burning only where Anne now held it too tightly. She couldn't tell her that it hurt. It didn't matter. It was all she could feel, and for that she guessed she was grateful.

It didn't matter, either, that the ship was fine, that the hull hadn't been breached, that they'd all go on living and breathing. It didn't matter.

She heard her name from far away. Anne was asking if she was ok. Dazedly, she turned her head to look at her friend and was shocked to see how lost she looked, how old, almost as if her face had slid down her cheekbones. Beautiful Anne looked old and tired, even more than earlier tonight. Sarah just felt cold. *Cold, cold, cold.* Her eyes burned and felt black, like holes sinking into her skull. *The kids*, she realized. *The kids.*

"The kids." It wasn't a question.

The captain nodded. He was clearly ill at ease. These women were being too quiet, too calm. "Mike Davies said that his wife was watching them. They've got the children in their quarters. You can decide if you want to pick them up tonight or..." He trailed off.

Sarah stood up. "I think I'll go." Anne was still clinging to her arm with that terrible face, like a mask. "Thank you," she whispered, for what, she didn't know.

At the door, the captain put out his hand. She took it, like a handshake. *Everything is so surreal*, she thought. *This is probably just a dream.*

"The doctors said it would have been quick. That he wouldn't have suffered." That was kind of him to say. She squeezed his hand a little and her lip twitched into what she hoped was an approximation of a smile. She felt an irrational urge to apologize to him.

The poor man.

He walked them to the elevator and nodded silently as the doors whispered shut. Sarah didn't speak as Anne accompanied her through the corridors to her quarters. This must be a dream. At her door, Anne paused. "Can I come in? Can I... be... here?" Sarah stepped in and opened her arms, and Anne melted in. The two women stood there, holding each other in the empty cabin. There weren't any tears.

Sarah cleared her throat. "Coffee?"

"Better make it tea. We'll need to sleep." They worked side by side; Sarah chose lemon tea bags and Anne filled the mugs with hot water. They brought their cups to the sofa, so much more comfortable and homely than the captain's, and stared out into the universe.

Anne spoke first. "Say something. Please. Say anything."

Sarah took a deep breath. "I followed him. I gave up my whole life for him."

"This is your life, too! This an adventure, and you—"

"Not this part. I mean, since I was twenty-one. I was smart, capable. I had *potential*." She spat that word out, put her cup down on the coffee table. "Since the day I started dating Grant Harper, I've been nothing but a sidekick. A *follower*." She looked down at her hands. They were shaking. "And now what? Anne, what am I supposed to do now?" The tears started, finally. She howled, leaning on Anne, not knowing if she was crying too.

Of course she's crying too. She loved him. She loved him more than I did. They huddled together, and eventually the sobs quietened.

Now what? She was stuck on a ship, on the way to Mars.

Her insides suddenly roiled. She rushed down the hallway to the bathroom, making it just in time.

After, she splashed cold water on her face, avoiding looking at her reflection. She staggered back to the sofa, where Anne waited with a fleecy throw. With it spread it across their knees, the two women snuggled under it, sipping their now-cold tea and looking at the stars.

Chapter 23

Erin pinged her just after seven am. *I'm so sorry. I'll keep the kids as long as you need. -E*

Sarah didn't think she had slept, but she looked over and saw Anne lying on the sofa beside her, looking younger in her sleep. She'd have to pick up the kids this morning; she didn't want them to find out from a school friend or well-meaning parent. She needed to get there first.

Twenty minutes later, she knocked on Erin's door. The shower had felt better than she could have imagined. When she emerged, Anne was gone. Sarah stepped into track pants, as usual, but put on a nice-ish top, then put on a bit of blush and lipstick to make her dead-pale face look somewhat lifelike. And concealer. So much concealer on those purple undereye circles.

Erin answered the door and immediately launched herself at Sarah. "I'm so sorry," she said, her words muffled into Sarah's still-damp hair. "I am here day and night to help." She stepped aside to reveal Maggie and Jack playing cards with Bridget, all still in their pyjamas. "I fed them," Erin said, stepping back. "Just letting them hang out this morning."

Sarah smiled, feeling like her cheeks would crack from the effort. "Lucky kids," she managed.

Mike wandered into the living room, looking out of place and awkward in his own home. "Hey," he said, giving her a hug — a stranger was hugging her — "I'm sorry." He didn't meet her eyes. "If you need anything at all..."

Sarah nodded jerkily. "Ok, kids, this is your two-minute warning. Then you're going to help clean up, ok?"

Erin turned from the oven, where she was removing something that looked suspiciously like a casserole. "Don't worry about all that. We'll do it, won't we, Bridget? Sarah, this is coming with you when you go."

"Thank you, I think? I'll... want to keep things kind of normal, but thanks. Really."

"Hey, I always make casseroles on Saturday mornings. Ask anyone!" Erin's eyes were full of tears. Sarah followed her gaze as she looked at Mike leaning over Bridget.

I know what you're thinking.

How do you tell your children that their dad isn't coming home? How do you sit them down and just... tell them?

The social worker and a psychologist had both reached out this morning, pinged her offers to be there while she talked to the kids, but Sarah had ignored them. Even in this glorified small town, where everybody already knew everything about last night, she didn't want to share this moment. She walked them back to their quarters, letting them chatter on around her, then sat them down on the couch, and knelt before them.

Maggie burst into tears.

"But I want Daddy!"

Jack remained silent, tears running down his face. He kept his head down, repeatedly taking off his glasses, wiping them, then putting them back on. She wouldn't give them a trite speech, tell Jack that he's the man of the house now. That wouldn't be fair. Nothing true would be fair.

"Daddy loved you both so very much." *That was truthful enough,* she guessed.

They sat on the sofa, much the way she had with Anne the night before, wrapped in blankets and huddled together, crying. *What were they thinking, in those little unbrushed heads of theirs?*

✷

Her parents called. They had already heard. Apparently, when a biologist gets himself blown up on a shuttle to Mars, it makes headlines. *Bad news travels fast*, she thought humourlessly. She didn't answer the call.

Sunday passed in a blur. She brought the kids to school on Monday, sad and subdued, but the routine, the playing with their friends would be the best thing for them.

She nodded to the other moms in the hallway at a suddenly silent drop off, smiled wanly at their murmured condolences, let more strangers envelop her in big hugs that she barely felt. Katriahna had pinged her while she was at drop-off. *I will teach tomorrow morning's class for you.* Like she was doing her a favour. That, more than anything else, helped.

She didn't see Anne for the next few days, which surprised her. She heard that she was part of the clean-up crew in the lab, classifying and relabelling whatever was still intact, deciding what could be salvaged, and what would just be recycled. Probably the best thing for her right now, she decided. Anne's passion had always been her work.

She tried not to look at the chest of drawers where Grant kept his clothes, at his side of the closet with his favourite old lab coat; the ones he wore for work were kept in the lab, cleaned and sanitized and decontaminated there, but this was the first one he had ever gotten with *Dr. G. Harper* monogrammed over the pocket. She tried.

She reached into the closet now, held it to her chest. It didn't smell like him, because he never wore it. The whole quarters felt strangely empty of anything that reminded her of Grant, without being strangely empty of Grant himself. He had spent so little time there. The sofa, the paint colours, even the stupid, cheap melamine dishes — all of these had been picked out by the kids, by her. She slammed the closet door.

It wasn't even like he had been erased, but that he had never existed. This wasn't his home, she realized. Not like the lab.

✷

Sarah sat bolt upright in bed.

Somewhere in the ship, a shudder. A scream of metal and a flash of light. A world opening up.

She was shaking again.

It took three days before Sarah was allowed to go into the lab. It had been emptied of the debris, wiped down. Sarah swallowed convulsively. *Don't paint pictures,* she told herself. The captain had been very vague in the details. It had been quick, he said.

Maybe it hadn't been messy.

They had deemed it accidental death, a sudden, unexplainable equipment malfunction.

Do these things just happen?

A sudden shift in gravity, a minute increase or decrease in the speed the ship was travelling, the executive officer had explained, could have... *But did it*, she'd interrupted. *Was there a change in speed on the ship's record*?

She could see the pity in their eyes: the captain, his second-in-command, the doctor.

"We're so very sorry," they all said.

Nobody said, Wow, two weeks into your husband's one-way, nine-month journey to Mars, following his dream, and he's dead. You left everything — everything — behind for him, to never return. So now what, you poor thing?

Nobody said it.

Even before the accident, Sarah knew, the lab had been kept neat. Orderly. Contained and structured, just like

Grant. As much as there was nothing of him in their quarters, he was everywhere here. The carefully-organized cabinets of instruments and freezers full of samples, the label maker he insisted that his staff used, the old one he had brought from Earth — he "didn't have time to read someone's chicken-scratch handwriting" — the lab coats that would have been kept in the cupboard, cleaned and sealed. These last were gone, but he was still here. In this empty, generic lab, he was everywhere.

Anne was there, too, her eyes red. She didn't look Sarah in the eye today. The doctor, the techs and the captain had retreated to a respectful distance. "I've been promoted," she said. "I'm in charge of the program."

Sarah couldn't ask her where she had been or tell her how much she needed a friend right now. There was nothing to say but 'congratulations.'

Chapter 24

"Hello, Astrogirl!" Nancy grinned broadly from the interface in the living room. She seemed to be in a café, judging by the bustle around her. "How's spaaaaaaaace?" She moved the phone away from her mouth for an attempt at a dramatic voice-fade effect.

"It is *so* good to see you, Nance." Sarah felt her eyes prick with tears.

"You too... hang on, gotta pay." The image shifted as Nancy evidently tapped her phone on the scanner, then the world spun wildly for a moment. "Ok... got my coffee... let's go outside."

Nancy looked good. The sun shone on her hair, smoothed back into a ponytail. There were pearls at her ears and on her blazer. Chanel, Sarah assumed. The giant diamond glittered as she took a sip from her travel mug. "I've got..." she squinted at the screen "... ten minutes for you, Sar, but I'm all yours. How *are* you?" Behind her, the trees still clung to some of their autumn foliage, but as she watched, a shower of brightly coloured leaves whisked past.

"It's strange, still, but... fine," Sarah managed, her eyes focusing past Nancy, onto the leaves dancing in the breeze. "The kids have friends — they're settled into school, Grant is loving his work... oh, and I'm teaching dance again." She grimaced.

Nancy cackled. "You're so weird. You're on a spaceship, on the way to Mars, and you're telling me about life as a suburban housewife. Are you on the PTA? No, what's it *actually* like? The stars, the space travel...?

"It's seriously like a small town. It's like growing up in the 70s... but on a spaceship?" Sarah ended lamely, as a question. "It's weird how *not* weird it is. They're all just people, and... that's it, really. There's not much to tell. I miss home desperately."

"Well, it's been rainy lately, and really cold at night—"

"What does it smell like?" Sarah interrupted. "At night. Does it smell like campfires yet?"

Nancy laughed. "You and your 'winter smell.' Um... yes, it did last night." Her smile faded. "Are you handling everything ok?"

Sarah felt her smile dissolve. "I'm... missing outside. I'm missing the wind, rain." She shrugged and ran her hand through her hair. "I'm missing work. The people on the ship are really nice — they really are — but... my world is just so small." She made a face. "I heard it. But the possibility of never seeing anyone else ever again..."

"Novelty's worn off, eh?" Nancy looked sympathetic. "Sar, I think you're so brave. Everything you've done, everywhere you've gone... You've picked up and moved so many times and made a life every time. You *know* you've got this."

Sarah tried to smile. "I know, and thanks. I'm just still in mourning, I think. Hey, how's planning for the Wedding of the Century?"

Nancy rolled her eyes. "I don't want to talk about it; it's going to be incredible." She suddenly straightened up. "But *here's* news: I had a *date*!"

Sarah shrieked and covered her mouth. "Who is he? What's he like? You still have four minutes and I need to know *everything*." They were eighteen again.

✷

But that had been — *last week? Last year?* — Sarah wasn't sure how long ago they had spoken. It felt like years had passed. She felt *old*. When Nancy's image flashed up on the kitchen interface now, she was evidently in her home office. Rain streaked down the window behind her. She had pulled her hair into a ponytail but didn't look sleek or professional this time. Her sweatshirt was definitely not Chanel.

"Sar—" she began, then burst into tears.

Sarah waited for a moment, unfamiliar anger welling up inside. She wanted to scream until her throat was hoarse. *My husband just died. It's not my job to make you feel better.* She closed her eyes and breathed deeply. "Yeah," she managed. "It sucks."

"How are you— never mind, of course you're not ok. How are the kids? Are people helping? Do you have anyone to talk to? What can I do?"

Her words hit Sarah in a barrage.

One at a time. Another slow breath. "I'm... you're right, I'm not ok. The kids are devastated, but... there's some really nice... oh, Nancy." She felt confused, dull, always so cold. "I don't even know what I'm supposed to do."

She had sent Katriahna a ping while walking back to her cabin after her tour of the lab. *I'm sorry, but I can't teach anymore.* There was nothing else to add, to say. She ignored Katriahna's responding pings, three, five, six... they stopped after the third day.

The short funeral was agony, an interminable exercise in maintaining a calm demeanor. She'd had to share Grant's death with BioMars and NASA. She had had to stand with Captain Leung and the children, in front of an official-looking seal, and accept corporations' condolences for her loss in a web call. She was dry-eyed as she had been since the night she and Anne cried together. The coldness had seeped into her bones and decided to stay. She had put a hand on each of the children's shoulders, and Maggie squeaked and jumped as her finger brushed her neck. "Cold hands!"

"Sorry," murmured Sarah.

"Thank you... yes... thank you." She was on autopilot, her face set in a pale mask of a polite smile as she accepted the small silver urn that contained his ashes. This had to be done. It was courtesy, news, PR. She hated every second of it. She would have thrown the urn, tried to see if she could dent it, if she wasn't worried about the ashes and... bits... bursting out. *It would be nice to have Grant around the house again*, she thought, hysteria bubbling up for a moment before subsiding back into numbness. She'd have to tell Nancy that one later.

The calls with her own parents and friends, she let go to recording for a few days. She pinged back a short *Thanks - we're doing ok, but need some time* to most, but forced herself to call Grant's parents. She had Maggie and Jack with her, as a sort of insulation. They stood beside her in the kitchen, already fidgeting as they connected.

An audio call would have been so much easier; she wouldn't have had to look at their faces, pale and drawn into deep, creased frowns. Elizabeth's short grey hair was neat, as always. Lou looked smaller, older than they had on that last visit, the one where Grant barely saw them and Sarah trailed around behind the children, hissing "Don't touch that!" and "Please walk!"

Sarah realized that she didn't know whether Grant had even spoken to them since they boarded the shuttle.

She felt guilty. She could have easily made do with one or two awkward web calls with her in-laws instead of the discomfort of the annual pilgrimage to Halifax. There, she acted as sheepdog to the children, protecting a million little figurines from, at first, their grabby hands, but lately their clumsy legs. Breakables seemed to be on every surface, most of them on tippy little decorative tables that showed fingerprints like they wanted them to get in trouble.

The last visit was five months ago, before she knew they were leaving. It went as she expected. Grant had disappeared to one of the speaking engagements or lab tours that he'd scheduled. Lou had tried to involve Jack and Maggie in helping him build a model of a ship in his office, but they wouldn't sit still. Sarah watched Maggie knock over a small bottle of deep red paint, then saw Jack glue his thumb to a piece of newspaper before dragging them away apologetically.

"Don't worry," he had said.

"Maybe when they're a bit older," she had responded.

She felt her mother-in-law's eyes sweep the room as she entered it, saw how Elizabeth glided over to a table and readjusted a figurine that had been knocked slightly askew. There was never any criticism from his parents — "Children will play" — but Sarah felt strained from the constant watching, the worry. Grant often mentioned how noisy their home was compared to the one he had grown up in, and she could feel it. Their old house was quiet, orderly and peaceful when they arrived, but within minutes, Maggie and Jack found the creaky boards in the hallways and staircase, tripped over a runner or yelled too loudly.

She hadn't, and had never, felt comfortable there. She couldn't tell if the kids felt it too. Though they sat with Grandma and Grandpa for a little while for a story, they spent most of the visit in the basement, playing with Grant's old board games and watching movies on the old chesterfield.

Their goodbyes were brief: quick hugs, dry pecks on the cheek, and admonitions to the children to Be Good, while Grant loaded up the rental car, glancing at his watch. As usual.

*

Sarah tried to smile in an encouraging way, and said, "How are you holding up?"

Jack was quietly poking Maggie in the side, and she giggled. Sarah put her arms around them firmly and said, "Say hello to your grandparents, kids." The children dropped their heads and mumbled hello. "Tell them about school to—"

"Don't bother with that. Let them play." Sarah was surprised to hear her father-in-law's tone, warm and gruff. The kids ran off without looking back, and Sarah shrugged.

"They're doing ok," she said softly.

She was horrified to see her mother-in-law turning red, her lip starting to tremble. "I miss them," she said in a faltering voice. "I didn't see them enough— and I miss my son. And he's gone." She broke down into sobs, while Lou awkwardly patted her on the arm.

"I'm sorry," Sarah said. She had a hard time drumming up much sympathy for her mother-in-law and knew that she should feel terrible for that. *I should but I don't.* No mother should outlive her son, but Grant wouldn't have stayed even if his mom had begged him. Nothing would have made him stay. But she *hadn't* begged. *You've lost something you would have lost anyway, and I've lost literally everything except the kids.*

Anger bubbled up in her throat. Anger at Grant, for dragging them along on this fool's mission, then abandoning them to it. Anger at herself, too. She hadn't put her foot down either, nor pleaded to stay. Not really, anyway. She could have refused to go. *I could have told him the truth and kept the kids on Earth. Then it would be just me and them and I'd have lost him forever... which I have anyway. Along with everything else.*

She stood there, the silence having stretched too long. She wondered if she should show her in-laws the urn she held in her hand, hold it up in front of the camera. Small and cold, it had been engraved with his name and dates and a short quote attributed to Stephen Hawkings. "*To confine our attention to terrestrial matters would be to limit the human spirit.*" She traced her fingers over this statement until it felt warmer. She felt more connected to Grant, suddenly. Another one to tell Nancy: they were both now confined in a metal casing. Except that he was gone, and she was a widow, about to be stranded on another planet without him for the rest of her life.

She rolled her shoulders back. Her neck was aching again as she watched her mother-in-law cry into her father-in-law's arms. She hadn't been listening. *What had they said?* "He loved you very much," she said, the same thing she had said to the kids.

This time, she didn't know for sure that it was true, but she could think of nothing else to say.

Chapter 25

The doors slid open with a hiss as Sarah stepped out of the cold, clinical ship and into a verdant, lush utopia. The lack of transition was unsettling. The air was warm, and she was relieved to find that she was alone. She hugged her elbows and shivered, nevertheless.

She had walked Maggie and Jack to school this morning, as usual. The kids, still pale and unsure, were going to be late for class, but that's what she wanted. Their new morning routine was slower; Sarah wanted to avoid the crowds in the hallway for her own sake. She held their hands tightly in hers and gave them each an extra tight hug as she dropped them off. First one, then the other, each time exchanging a worried look with the teacher. Despite their tardiness, there were still a few adults lingering in the corridor, chatting until they saw her and went silent. She crossed paths with a few of the mothers and fathers — she was starting to recognize the faces, to connect them to the children — each of whom nodded sympathetically or even reached out to touch her arm as she walked by. She guessed that every one of them knew who she was now. Erin had waved to her from the end of the hall, but she slipped into the stairway and kept going. She wanted solitude, away from prying eyes and pity. She hoped that nobody else was in their garden unit.

According to the orientation, the aim of the gardens was threefold. First, NASA and BioMars had tasked the shuttle with maintaining and developing a wide range of species within the challenges of gravity and radiation, to plant and hopefully cultivate on their new planet. The gardens would also grow extra fruits and vegetables to eat and share and generate seeds for sowing in the new soil. And finally, they were a quiet, green space for contemplation, nourishment and meditation to those that wanted or needed it.

I need this.

Last weekend, they had come down with a picnic lunch. They didn't get a proper sleep-in, of course — the kids made sure of that — but they started the day slowly. Their food rations showed up weekly, based on the computer's scans of their fridge and cupboards. There were no real errands waiting for them, aside from keeping their quarters neat and clean, and their only real commitment was Jack's soccer games. It felt almost like still being on Earth. The biggest difference was that Grant was there with them. For the first time in... *years? Ever?...* they had felt like, well, a real family.

She exhaled and tried to lower her shoulders, but they wouldn't release. *How could that have been only last weekend?* The enormity of her loss hit her again, and she staggered, fighting a wave of nausea. After a moment, she took a cautious step forward, then another.

The plot to her right had added a lightweight bench — *great idea* — on a small patch of lawn surrounded by a small cedar hedge. Just past that was a desert-like scape with just succulents. And on her left, the gardeners had evidently taken this opportunity to grow every plant they had ever dreamed of, judging by the multitude of leaves and tangled weeds.

"Everything will grow much faster here," Grant had said, excitedly. His voice rang in her ears. She caught herself turning, expecting that he'd be beside her.

She was alone.

Horticulturalists assigned to each unit supervised the progress of the gardens; even just a few weeks in, Sarah saw drooping leaves in the wild plot next door, with notes pasted on the entrance post: "Plants need water." *Duh.* Her sense of superiority was fleeting, though, when she noticed a note on hers, too. "Please stop your mint!!!"

Three exclamation points. *Ouch.*

Yes, a tendril of mint that had escaped its pot already. She snipped its end, then dug down around where it had dared try to root. The tech had explained that plants on the shuttle would grow at an accelerated pace; the LED light cycles and nutrient compounds would ensure that, whatever the effects of radiation and travel.

She spent some time weeding around her young lettuce plants and checked the moisture of the soil. She didn't need to, she knew. Grant had rigged up moisture sensors for each bed and pot, programmed to that plant's water needs. She smiled. *He's such a nerd.*

Was *such a nerd,* she corrected herself, her smile fading, her stomach flipping again. She kept forgetting. She checked them anyway, plunging her fingers into the cool earth and feeling the damp soil on her hands. *Good, clean, honest dirt*, she thought, finally standing up and stretching out her legs. It felt good to be in here, among the damp, earthy smells, relaxing. It felt natural. Maybe she could do more here, hide here.

Maybe that would pass the time.

She met the kids at school at noon, her hands still dirty from the garden. She felt empty, but more refreshed than she had since Friday night.

*

Jack finished dinner a few minutes before Maggie. She was putting miniscule bites in her mouth, chewing slowly — *was she counting?* — and swallowing slowly, carefully rinsing each tiny mouthful down with water. Her fingernails were nibbled down to the quick. When she finally finished, she popped up and said, "I'll clear the table." She grabbed her brother's plate as well and brought them to the counter, then returned for Sarah's. Sarah watched, wide-eyed, while she picked up the glasses too, then said, "I've got some homework. I'll be in my room."

Jack said, "I'm going to finish my spaceship." This was version number 17, at least. He followed her out, leaving Sarah alone at the table. Dinner had been quiet. She had tried to start a conversation five or six times, but neither of the kids had much to say. School was fine. Recess was fine.

Maybe, she thought, they're really fine.

Or they're really not.

Fifteen minutes later, her kitchen was neat again, the dishes put away. She hung up the wet dish towel and walked down the short corridor. She could hear Jack talking to himself as he built his spaceship. "Another red... another red... another red... a grey..." Even as he coped with the tragedy, he was so *easy*. He had found another Lego fanatic in a boy in his grade and participated the bare minimum at soccer. "Adam doesn't have to play soccer," he had complained twice already. "Adam's mom says that he can choose what he does."

"Too bad I'm not Adam's mom, then," Sarah had replied. "Think of the fun you'll have at soccer tomorrow."

All was quiet in Maggie's room. She knocked. No sound. She pushed open the door a little. "Maggie?" she said. "You ok?" Still nothing.

She pushed her door open a bit further. Maggie's schoolbooks were open on her desk, her bed was still tidied away in the wall, but there was no Maggie. "Maggie!" she called, more sharply, but there was nowhere that the eight-year-old could be hiding.

She's on a spaceship, she reminded herself, trying to staunch the panic that rose sharply to her throat. There's nowhere that she can go. But still... *I can't lose her too.*

Feeling foolish, she ran back out into the living room; maybe she hadn't seen her when she passed by to check on

Jack? But no – she wasn't there. The room was empty. The bathroom was dark, too, its door wide open.

"Maggie!" her voice rasped with terror, knowing that she was overreacting. "Maggie!"

Silence answered her; there wasn't a sound, suddenly, not even the clacking jingle of Lego pieces. Jack's quiet monologue had paused, too. She raced back up the hallway.

"Jack! Where's Maggie?" There was a pause, then—

"I... don't know?" he asked, his voice going higher and higher. *Aha.*

She walked into Jack's room, avoiding the scattered Lego. "Where. Is. Maggie." She tried to stay calm, to keep the hysteria out of her voice. She couldn't have gotten far. Jack's head was down, looking intently at his latest creation. "Jack Michael Harper, tell me where your sister is."

He mumbled; his ears flushed a bright red. Sarah stood over him. "I beg your pardon?"

"She's with Bridget." His voice was hard to hear. Then his head flung up. "Please don't tell her that I told you! Tell her — tell her that you called everyone's mom, and that—"

She hugged him to her, feeling his sturdy little body against hers. *So big, too fast.* "Are they at Bridget's house?" she said gently. "I need to know that she's safe, buddy. You're not in trouble."

He mumbled into her chest, then repeated himself more clearly. "Garden. Mommy, she's going to kill me. I promised that I wouldn't tell."

Sarah got up and put one hand on his cheek. "Ok, stay right here. I'll try not to tell her." She pinged Adam's mom — *Jenny, was it?* — and told her she had to dash out. "Can I send Jack your way for a few minutes?"

She returned to Jack's room. He had put away all of his Lego neatly (Systems!) and was sitting on his floor, holding tightly to his knees. His ears were still pink.

"Ok, kiddo, you're going over to Adam's for a bit." His eyes lit up.

"I'll grab my spaceship!" he cried.

"Nope! You'll grab your soccer ball," she said, trying to keep her voice light. "Let's go."

✷

Sarah paused outside their garden unit for a moment, then slid the door open. If she wasn't inside, she promised herself, she would give in to her panic, notify Security, scream in the halls. She had already been to Bridget's family plot, but nobody was there. If she wasn't inside, she would cause a scene.

For the second time today, she felt the difference in the air as she entered. It didn't quell the tide of anxiety, but it helped ease it enough that she noted, with satisfaction, that the message about her mint had already been removed. There was nothing here but quiet... almost. Had she heard a giggle as she opened the door? A hushed whisper?

Stepping into their plot, she could see just one place that a child could hide. The three apple trees were in raised beds to allow their roots room to stretch down and out. Walking slowly, she started to approach them, then changed her mind. *Life lesson*, she told herself. Her hands shook. *Teachable moment.* She stopped, allowing herself a full breath in and out before trusting her voice.

"Maggie? Are you in here?"

Silence.

Then, a little head poked up over the edge of the bed, with two large, frightened grey eyes. *So much like...* For the first time, Sarah didn't see her own eyes looking back at her. *Later*, she thought. *Add that to the list of things to tell Nancy.*

"Hi Mom." Maggie had dropped 'Mommy' at the end of grade two. It still hurt, even more so now. *Stay calm. Keep it together, Sar.*

"Is Bridget with you? Her mother called me, and she's really worried." A white lie, but worth it. In fact, if she got to Erin first, she could even help Jack save face. Bridget popped up, too, a little more defiantly than Maggie had. *One to watch*, Sarah noted. "I need to bring you home, Bridget, so let's go." The girls followed reluctantly, quietly. Sarah led the way without speaking. Her hands flexed in and out of fists as she walked; as she remembered the last time she had been down this hallway, when she had paused for a long moment before she knocked on this door. Bile rose in her throat.

Like that last time, Erin opened it with a look of concern. She held the door for her daughter to enter.

Sarah forced a smile onto her face. That other time, Erin had hugged her, offered her a casserole. As if that could make her husband's death better.

"You. Inside." The other woman ruffled up her daughter's hair on the way by. "Thanks for finding her," she said, her clear blue eyes sympathetic but twinkling.

"Thanks for calling me," Sarah responded, following her lead. "They were right where we thought they'd be."

"Coffee tomorrow?" Erin whispered.

Sarah nodded and felt her lips form into a real smile for the first time in a week.

"Ok, Miss Maggie," Sarah said. "Let's go home."

Maybe she'd just made another friend.

*

"Honestly, Maggie, you know you can't just leave without telling me!" She could feel her control slipping. Her voice was shrill in her own ears.

"Mom, the ship is safe. You keep saying that. *Everyone* keeps saying that." She hated Maggie's eye roll but had to admit that was true. Every orientation from the very first day mentioned the security measures in place.

"Yes, but—"

"I wasn't running away! We were just hanging out in the garden."

"You left our quarters without telling me! I was worried sick."

"There's nowhere to go, nothing that can hurt me. We can't get lost, and there's no strangers, not really." She pouted. "What happened to Dad isn't going to happen to me."

Sarah flinched. Hard to argue with an eight-year-old that made such good points. Her mind raced; her heart pounded in her ears.

"And there's cameras everywhere. You could have found me without the Snitch." Despite Sarah's trickery with Erin, she hadn't been fast enough with Jack.

"I'm sorry, Maggie," he had cried when they picked him up from Adam's. "She made me tell her where you were!" *So much for teachable moments.* Maggie had glared at him and turned her back. She stalked off ahead, her head high.

Now he was back in his room, already in his PJs, reading to himself, while Sarah dealt with Maggie. She watched herself, as if from a distance.

Stop being irrational. Don't push her away.

She shrugged off her inner voice and spoke louder to drown it out. Her hands were still shaking.

"You're eight. It doesn't matter how safe this ship is; you still need to ask for permission before you go anywhere. We still have rules that have to be followed." This was where she'd usually say, "When Daddy gets home." She paused, as the words hung in the air between them, unsaid. “We’ll talk about your consequence in the morning.”

Maggie turned and stomped off toward her room. “I hate you!” she called back and slammed her door. Sarah crumpled onto the couch and pulled her knees into her chest.

She doesn’t mean it.

She repeated it over and over, but she didn’t believe it for a minute.

Chapter 26

Maggie had dark circles under her eyes. She was quiet at breakfast, sullen. Jack snuck guilty glances at his big sister and gave her the yellow vitamin. Her favourite.

"You can have it," she said icily.

The chill lingered in the air throughout breakfast and while brushing teeth, right until they stepped into the corridor for her school. Maggie stalked ahead, her head up, her jaw set. *A teenager already?* Suddenly, a group of Grade Five boys ran past, jostling and playing tag. Maggie jumped back against the wall of the hallway, but Jack wasn't quick enough. He stumbled and fell, his glasses skittering ahead of him.

Maggie stood in the middle of the corridor now, her feet planted wide, and shouted after the boys. "Miles and Harry, you bullies!" She then turned to pick up Jack's glasses, folding them carefully before bringing them back to where he sat examining his skinned knees. She knelt down to hand them to him. "Hey, are you ok?" She shot a dirty look over her shoulder. "Those boys are jerks. I'll tell their teacher they knocked you down, ok?"

Sarah forced herself to stand back and watch as Maggie brushed off Jack's knees and helped him to his feet. She suppressed a grin. This was ok, then. When they got to Maggie's classroom, Jack waved to her and said, "Bye, Maggie! Bye!" until she turned and waved back.

Sarah hesitated – for too long? – then softly placed her arm around Maggie's skinny shoulders. "Good job, Miss Maggie," she whispered.

Her daughter's smile faltered, and she looked at her toes.

"I'm sorry, Mom… about yesterday. Mom— Mommy, I… don't hate you." A tear dripped off her small, pointy nose.

"Oh, Maggie, I know you don't." She engulfed her into a close hug. "I know you didn't mean it. I'm just— none of us are feeling like ourselves without Daddy." She gave her a little squeeze and kissed her cheek. "Try to have a good day today, ok, sweet girl?"

Sarah was still smiling a little to herself when they passed Erin and Bridget on the way back to the stairway. Erin touched her arm on the way past and said, "Coffee on Deck 12?"

Sarah watched Jack push ahead into the river of other kids on the stairway, his large backpack jutting out on either side of him. She didn't want to let him get too far ahead. "Give me ten minutes," she said. "I'll meet you at the coffee shop."

Erin's hair and makeup were perfect again, and her clothes were neatly pressed. As a rule, Sarah didn't wear clothes that had to be ironed unless she must, and then only for work. Definitely not on board, for school dropoff five decks down.

The café was bright and cheery, with the few tables surrounded by comfortable red armchairs. Elaborate gold-coloured frames surrounded views of the stars.

"I was a lawyer," Erin said, blowing on her cappuccino.

You gave up a career to come along, Sarah thought to herself. *Why do I find it so hard to realize that everyone's done the same?* She had to stop thinking of the other wives on board as pampered housewives, not partners, people who had given up as much or more.

"You *are* a lawyer," Sarah corrected her.

Erin shook her head. "No. California income tax laws won't be applicable to anything we come across on the ship, or on the colony, at least not for decades. I get to be 'Bridget's mom' now. And—" she hesitated. "'Mike's wife.'" Mike was an aerospace engineer and helped with the maintenance of the shuttle's energy system. The few times she'd seen him, he appeared to be a quiet, smart guy. Sarah had seen the two of them together at the second school orientation session, where Bridget and Maggie had first smiled at each other shyly. And then when she picked up the kids that morning.

Sarah laughed without mirth. "I... don't know *who* I am. Grant's widow?" Erin reached over and squeezed her hand. She felt the warmth seep in and blinked a few times. "Thanks. I've got... a lot of thinking to do. Not that it will change anything." She took a sip of her tea.

More melamine, she noted sourly.

"Take your time. Nobody expects you to jump back in. You'll find a way to contribute to the mission when you're ready. What did you do on Earth?"

"First, this is— *was* Grant's mission, not mine. I was literally just tagging along. On Earth, *God,* that sounds weird,

I managed a lab. But I'm definitely not ready to be in a lab right now, not after... and the kids need me, and Maggie..." *Stop it. Maggie's ok.* She took a shaky breath. "And besides, I don't think there's a place for me here. Maybe I'll stick with teaching ballet." Another sip. "But not right now." She tried to smile, to take the bitterness away, to not mess up this chance at friendship. It came out as a grimace, and she shrugged apologetically. "Sorry, I'm feeling a bit bleak."

I thought my daughter was gone. I thought she was dead. She pushed these unbidden thoughts away, then changed the subject back to Erin abruptly. "But surely we'll need your expertise in interpreting rules and laws around here. I mean, it's only a matter of time until human nature takes over."

"Hasn't it already? What were those girls thinking last night? She's eight and is giving me teenager attitude and problems already. I didn't sign up for this!"

Erin was treating her like a normal person. Not a victim, not someone to be pitied and cajoled and danced around. It felt surprisingly good. After all, she had literally two options: wallow in self-pity or don't. She considered the woman across the table, who had had a career of her own since university and had taken the bare minimum of time off after Bridget's birth. She and Mike had been fortunate in having been able to work and progress in the same state, no uprooting needed. That must have made leaving her work, her home, her identity behind even harder. She had never *had* to be 'Mike's wife' until they boarded this ship.

Dust yourself off, Sar.

Erin was a kindred spirit. The two women sat there for three hours, eventually ordering more tea and some banana bread to share. Sarah felt herself relax; she laughed for the first time since Grant's death, first covering her mouth and smothering it, feeling guilty, but then again, louder. *How long, she wondered, before I stop measuring in firsts again?* But Erin was funny, found the same things about motherhood absurd. Sarah debated whether she had really been lonely for her whole adult life, or if she had intentionally kept others at arm's length. She'd been ashamed of her missed potential and judged others for what she perceived was their judgement of her. *I'm a snob*, she realized.

They had to walk quickly to get back to the classrooms in time to pick up the kids for lunch.

Sarah walked ahead, like she was pulling her along.

"It's a steep learning curve," complained Erin. "I'm having to learn how to be a mom, a cook and a supportive wife all at once." She paused. "It either means that I've had a really good run so far, or that I've missed out on a lot of things."

"The first one," declared Sarah. She paused, just before they reached the stairwell. "Can we do this again?"

"Definitely, but next time, we'll do this over wine." When Erin hugged her goodbye, Sarah squeezed back.

✷

Maggie was in a better mood at lunch and seemed to have forgiven Jack completely. When they put their shoes back on for their afternoon at school, Sarah leaned against the doorway and took a deep breath.

"Maggie, do you think you can walk Jack down to his classroom?"

Maggie looked at her, shocked. "Me?" she squeaked. "Really?"

"You're going to be nine soon," Sarah said with a nod. "And you're right. It's a safe ship. *But*. Straight there, then to class, and straight to his class after school and straight home. No fooling around, no sneaking out. You can have freedom as long as you tell us where you're going and who you're with. Deal?"

Before her eyes, Maggie grew taller, older, more responsible. "Deal." She called out to Jack, "Come on! I can't bring you back to school late!" Jack's bewildered eyes turned to gape at Sarah, who made a production of sitting down on the couch and opening a book. "Let's go!"

After the door closed behind them, Sarah counted to ten, then dropped her book on the table. She raked her hands through her hair with a long, shuddering inhale, then blew it out loudly. Right. What was she going to do now?

What would Grant do?

Even more than his voice echoing in her mind, the conversation with Erin had invigorated her. What *was* she going to do? She had been looking at this, the rest of her life, like a punishment, but maybe it could be an opportunity. She could create herself again, but better. She had the time and tools to apply to her art, her dance, her fitness. *At my age?* She had access to millions of books, journals and courses of study. The ship was pretty much a commune, so whatever she created or harnessed for herself, she could really, actually make happen. She could be... she could be...

She had no idea what she could be, or what she even wanted. No, that wasn't true. Despite the opportunity to remake herself, she knew what she wanted.

She wanted her old job back. She wanted to see her parents again. She wanted Grant. Sarah slumped back against the sofa cushions and pulled the blanket around her shoulders.

She wanted to go home.

Chapter 27

Sarah was still on the sofa. She lay on her back, clutching a cushion to her chest. She'd watched the stars for about five minutes before she laid down, wallowing in self-pity for what felt like hours. She could have celebrated the tiny bit of freedom she'd just given her children and gained for herself, but instead, her mind whirled. There had to be a way to get home. *Get a grip, Sar.* When she finally stood up and stretched, she was surprised to see that less than an hour had passed. She had at least another hour and a half till the kids got home from school.

Right then.

She got up stiffly, poured herself a glass of water and sat down at the interface in their kitchen.

She had done the basic training on it during that first week before takeoff. The interface was fairly similar to smartphone technology, but with enough small differences to make sending messages back to Earth or signing up for an online Master's degree in Biology, for example, seem unwieldy and overcomplicated. She had quickly got the hang of pinging people on the ship. She now added Erin to her favourites list, which so far had only Anne, Katriahna and Grant – she wasn't ready to delete him yet — but needed to put in some time to make sure she knew how to use the interface fully. It would be idiotic not to. And it would keep her busy till the children got home.

By the time the kids piled in the door after school, she had a headache. She had worked her way through two tutorials and created a schedule for dinner for the next week. Small victories, but she felt like she had started something. She had also downloaded a new book, subscribed to a moderately-academic science publication, and checked over the ship's inventory of art supplies. She grudgingly tore herself away from the screen to prepare their snack. Apples, graham crackers and peanut butter. Easy.

"We came straight home," Maggie announced proudly. "Jack was dilly-dallying, but I told him that we had to walk quickly and not stop because Mommy was waiting for us and because I was in charge, he had to do it." Sarah suppressed a smile at both Jack's somewhat sullen look at his superior big sister and the inadvertent 'Mommy' that had slipped back into Maggie's lexicon.

"We'll go out again after snack, Jackattack," said Sarah. "I'm proud of both of you. Thank you for helping Maggie, Jack." She knew what usually worked with these kids, and she was glad to see his little shoulders start to descend away from his ears as she smiled at Maggie over his head. She'd have to make him responsible for something, too. "Hey, do you think you could lead us all the way to the playground?"

He flushed a little and stood up straight. "I can do it. I know the way." She knew he could. His sense of direction was the best in the family, far better than hers and slightly better than Maggie's.

She brought along their water bottles and her smartbook. The kids dashed ahead and around her as they headed to the playground, passing other people — neighbours, she supposed she should think of them — in the corridors. So many of them were familiar faces now, when only two weeks earlier they had all been strangers. Quite a few smiled and nodded or greeted her on the way by. There was still pity in their eyes, but caring, too.

It's a small town, she thought. It's safe and friendly.

The playground was overflowing with children. The unit was divided up into a large, grassy space for younger kids to play without being run over by the older ones, and a functional playground space for school-aged kids. On the other side of a glass wall spread a great big patch of turf, where three or four games of soccer were already underway.

The benches were all full, so she sat down where she was, her back against a potted tree. "I'll be here," she said, opening up the file for her new book. "Go play, but don't leave the complex."

Off they ran. She watched them only for a minute to see that they found friends to play with — they did — before starting to read. She found it easy to become absorbed in her book. The sound of so many children shouting, laughing and crying washed around her to make a thick, heavy white noise that didn't exactly help her headache. Suddenly, though, a new sound rang out. She lifted her head from her book. Was that... a dog barking?

The rest of the playground paused for a beat as well. The volume dropped suddenly from a solid 9.5 to a 3, very quiet for a hundred children. Then — squeeee! — the sound of those hundred children making squeaky cooing sounds over a — no, two... no, *three* puppies. On a good day, without a headache, this would be a lot to take. Sarah's forehead creased in pain, and she covered her eyes with one hand. That helped a little.

Where did the puppies even come from? she wondered. They had been given enough attitude about wanting to bring Rupert along. *Nobody said there would be puppies!* Keeping her eyes closed, Sarah leaned back against the tree. She didn't nod off, not exactly, but she was startled to find Maggie right beside her, tugging at her sleeve.

"Mom! Mommy! Look how sweet he is! Can we have one?" Sarah squinted one eye open to see her daughter and Bridget kneeling down beside an objectively cute golden retriever puppy. She couldn't tell which one of them looked happier or more in love. A few feet away, Jack stood tentatively watching. She sat up straighter.

"Jack, come here, buddy. Come sit with me and pet this dog." He kept his eyes on the puppy. She didn't know how it started but right about when he started walking, the sight of a dog or a horse would make him even quieter, and he'd nonchalantly move to stand behind whoever was with him. He did it so coolly that most people wouldn't notice. If they did, they'd think that he just didn't like animals.

It had even been there to a slight degree with Rupert. *Rupert*, whom Jack had loved so much. He wasn't a hugely friendly cat to begin with, but on the days that he got a little can of wet food as a treat, he would wind in and around the bearer's legs, purring. If it was Jack, he wouldn't reach down to pet him, necessarily. He'd stand there, instead, with bright eyes, pink cheeks and an odd little smile on his face, kind of an 'I know I'm supposed to be enjoying this, so I'm trying to enjoy it' look. On the extremely rare times that Rupert had jumped up onto his lap while he was sitting watching tv, Jack would sit very stiffly and still, and very awkwardly move to pet him. You could tell that Rupert hadn't really been into it either. Afterwards, Jack would simply glow. "Rupert was on my lap," he'd say proudly.

Now, Jack slowly walked around the tree, keeping Sarah between him and the puppy, whose mouth was wide open in a doggy smile. He sat down beside her, tucking his feet underneath him with his hands under his knees.

"Come on, Jack," coaxed Maggie, burying her face in the silky golden fur. "I love you," she said to the dog. "I love you; I love you; I love you."

"What do you think, Jack?" Sarah said softly. She put her hand on his back. "Do you want to pet him?" He stared with a rapt look on his face, then dropped his head quickly. "It's ok."

Bridget tried to make the puppy look at her. "Sit!" she ordered. "Sit! Puppy! Can you sit? Puppy! Puppy! Sit, Puppy!"

Sarah had had enough. Her head was throbbing. She stood up stiffly, took Jack's hand and pulled him up to her. "Let's go home."

Maggie looked up from the dog. "Can I stay with Bridget? Her mom's here." She pointed over to one of the benches where Erin sat, squished between two other moms that Sarah recognized.

Erin looked over and waved, and Sarah indicated the girls, then pantomimed walking away and leaving Maggie with her. Erin grinned and gave her the thumbs up.

Get me out of this noise.

The hallway was blissfully quiet, though muffled sounds of children playing and shrieking could still be heard. Sarah leaned against the cool wall, then pulled Jack in for a hug.

"Hey buddy," she said. "Sorry, Mommy's got a headache. I don't know if it's... well, what did you think about that dog? Pretty cute, eh?"

Jack's head was down, and his ears were red. His voice was small. "I like dogs," he said. "But I don't want them to bite me."

She chucked him lightly below the chin. "Hey. No dog has bitten you yet, right? Maybe it's time that you started thinking like a scientist."

He looked up at her, thinking. "You mean like Daddy?" He looked tired, too. *I wonder how he's sleeping.*

She smiled as her heart panged. "Yeah. Like Daddy."

"Let's go!" Jack pulled on her hand and took her to the nearest stairway. He led her down, down, down then halfway down the length of the ship until they were in the corridor that Sarah recognized as the biology lab. She had only come here once, after it had been cleaned up. She had never — literally never, in all their years together — showed up at his lab unannounced. *Or announced,* she corrected herself. Not since he was her TA had they been in a lab at the same time. When they got to the lab door, she hesitated. When had Jack been here?

Jack reached up and tried to open it.

"It's locked," he said.

"Of course it's locked, Jacko. They can't leave the lab open for anyone to just wander into! They keep dangerous stuff in there!"

His eyes were huge behind his glasses. "What kind of dangerous stuff? Like santifoos?"

"Centrifuges aren't dangerous — not usually," she reassured him hastily. "They keep precious stuff in the lab too, seeds and germs and compounds to grow things and help people. And if they got mixed up or dropped or dirty, it would make everything much harder to do, here on the ship or on Mars when we get there..." He wasn't listening anymore. He was tapping on the access screen at a speed and with a skill that Sarah envied. In the haze of her headache, she was mesmerized. In a moment, Anne's terse voice rang out through it.

"Yes?"

"Hi! Can I see Daddy? It's Jack. Can you open the door?"

Silence.

"Anne," Sarah broke in, in a strangled voice. "I'm sorry. Jack just led me here and—" Her heart beat fast. "I'll talk to him. I'm sorry. Sorry." She grabbed Jack's hand and tried to pull him away.

"No! I want Daddy!" His face was red. He planted his feet.

"Daddy's not in there, sweetheart. Remember?" She wrapped her arms around him. *I don't want to have this conversation again.*

"Um, listen, Jack, it's not a good time. I still have at least half an hour in here, then I have to clean up before I go home. Can I see you another time, buddy?" Anne's voice was leaden.

"Maggie wants a puppy. I want to ask Daddy if he'll let her have a puppy." Jack had lifted up on his tiptoes to try to speak into the interface.

"What? They let the puppies—" Anne swore, and Jack's eyes widened. "I've got to go. Sar, I'll come over tonight if I can, ok?"

The connection ended abruptly. Sarah looked down at Jack, fearing that he'd be upset. But no, he was all smiles. "What are we making for dinner tonight? I saw you made a schedule."

She pasted a smile on her face and ruffled his hair. "Let's take a walk, first, kiddo. Then we'll go back to the playground to pick up Maggie, and then you can help me with dinner."

✷

Jack nodded his head as he led her up and down corridors that he seemed to know by heart, that all looked the same to her. She wasn't sure that he was listening as she explained again that Daddy was gone, from the lab, from the ship, but that he was still in their hearts, would always be in their hearts. "All the things he taught you, they're still there, and the way you felt when he smiled," she recited. *I've already done this. It's not fair that I had to do it once.* They braved the deafening playground and dragged a reluctant Maggie home, then she set them in front of a slideshow of family photos while she prepared dinner.

Sarah had fallen into bed as soon as the kids had been tucked in, leaving the dinner dishes soaking in the sink.

She lay on top of the covers, a cold cloth across her eyes. It had been a hard day, but... a good day? She wasn't certain of that, but there was a lot to work through. A new friend, new freedom for the kids and for her. Sudden realization that, at thirty-eight, she still had potential (ugh), and tangible steps toward a new goal, and this raging head.

It must have been the extra hours in front of that screen, she thought to herself.

When she woke briefly to change into pyjamas at ten o'clock, she stumbled out into the living room, disoriented in the dim light. Grant wasn't home yet. She reached for her smartbook, to ping him, to ask him where the hell he was, then remembered that he was gone. It hit her again, a physical blow that bent her over double for a minute. When she caught her breath, she slowly straightened up, then stalked over to where his urn still sat on its shelf. She picked it up listlessly. It warmed against her cheek as she looked at the stars.

"Look where we are," she whispered, the words heavy in her mouth. "Look where you left us." She slammed it back down, then, pausing only for a minute in front of the interface to stab at his name — *Delete* — she went back to bed.

Chapter 28

Anne pinged her the next morning.

Can I pop by in 10?

Sarah considered.

I have, literally, nothing else to do.

She deleted that, and replied, *Ok*, instead.

She was still surprised at how quiet everyone had become around her. She stopped conversations by walking down corridors. She was pretty sure that most of them had never even met Grant, but perhaps they all felt bad for her — perhaps they all put themselves into her shoes every time they saw her. It was a relief to get back into her quarters, to imagine that, as soon as the door closed behind her, the ship sprang back into life instead of trying to mourn with her.

She pulled two bright mugs from the cupboard and set them out, then a plate with a few cookies. She pondered, then added two small bowls of yogurt and spoons, the same snack she'd sent in with the kids this morning, sweet and nourishing. Easy.

She stood, her hands by her sides, still. Waiting. Anne's knock woke her out of her stasis.

"I'm sorry about yesterday," she blurted. Then, "Come in." They hugged for a long time. Anne was dressed casually, and she made a face as she glanced down at her sweater.

"Mental health day," she explained. Her voice caught. "I haven't taken a day off since..." She stopped. For an instant,

Sarah was glad she didn't finish the sentence but then watched in horror as her friend's face crumpled.

"Coffee?" She felt guilty about how relieved she was to turn away, to go through the motions of tea and coffee, to sit down at the table with steaming mugs that were too hot to drink from. Sarah dipped a cookie into the smooth, cold yogurt, then let it crumble on her tongue. She watched Anne, unsure about what was expected from her, irritated that she was crying, that someone else wanted her to comfort them. *It's not fair. What about* me*?* Surely, she had earned the right to be selfish while the kids were at school, at least.

Then, *Of course she's crying. She loved him. She loved him more than I did.* Again.

And there it was. Under the grief, the despair, the bleak what-am-I-going-to-do and how-can-I-tell-the-children, she felt the depth of her friend's hurt.

Sarah wrapped her hands around the smooth plastic sides of her mug. It burned, hot against her palms. Melamine didn't insulate as well as her old stoneware had. She didn't relax her grip but instead squeezed tighter, relishing in the pain. She wanted to feel it. Maybe she could focus on something other than the pain she felt about her life. Her identity and her husband, both were gone forever. Even her favourite freaking mug was lost to her.

She sighed, gave in, and rested her hand over Anne's.

"I know," she said. "I know."

*

Damn puppies.

"Sorry, buddy." Sarah reached down to ruffle Jack's hair. "Why don't we invite Adam over to our place instead?"

The playground was closed for two days for treatment, the research team announced.

Ever since that day at the playground, the puppies seemed to be popping up all over the ship. One of the crew members' dogs had had a litter while in quarantine, a bulletin explained. The puppies had been too young to be separated from their mother at the time, so, with a complete lapse in judgement, they'd brought them along. There weren't enough to go around but families could be matched with a dog if they wished.

It was a terrible idea.

A spaceship, and the colony too for that matter, is a fully *inside* experience with small, controlled pockets of nature cultivated here and there. Neither were ready for even three puppies running loose. From a biological point of view, it made sense to keep the dogs healthy and active, to make sure that when they joined the colony there were viable specimens to add to the biodiversity they were trying to encourage. But there was pee everywhere.

They walked and scampered through the hallways to the grass-covered playgrounds and garden plots. This was fine; due to the close community vibe of the ship (or perhaps the state-of-the-art surveillance cameras), the dog people — as they were quickly branded — *were* trying to be responsible. But there is a difference between picking up dog poop up from a sidewalk outside or from a hallway inside. There was no rain, for starters. *What about the residue?* somebody asked. So, dog owners were expected to carry around cleaning cloths and a vinegar solution, to wipe the hallway down after they'd absorbed the puddles of urine or scooped.

It caused far more conflict than the animal team anticipated. What they had expected to be a treat, a novelty, a pleasant diversion and a recall to life on Earth, became a dividing point between the families with dogs, and without. Those that had to clean the hallways complained the most — and the turf was immediately made off-limits — but the people frequenting the playgrounds and gardens were a close second. For their part, the dog owners quickly realized how much training and exercise a growing puppy needs, and, despite the huge size of the ship, complained about the lack of adequate facilities on board for growing dogs to play.

They reached a compromise. The playground became 'dog-friendly' for one hour each morning and one hour each evening, where the dogs could run free and tumble together at will, and nervous kids like Jack knew to stay clear. The rest of the time, the dog owners' garden plots served the purpose, as long as the solid waste was removed and disposed of in the ship's sanitary systems.

The other animals on the shuttle were contained in labs; their care, feeding and waste collection processes were carefully defined and managed. Sarah would have loved to sit Grant down, to ask him what the bioscience team had been thinking. *Of course* he *would have analyzed the effects before releasing them.* But then again, he hadn't released them, and it would be an insult to even ask the question of Anne. *And besides, they're managing it now.* By closing the playground for two days.

There is a difference between a lawn on Earth and a hydroponic patch of grass in space.

On Earth, the natural cycles of nitrogen and hydrogen generally regulate how it is absorbed and assimilated into plants and nature. In theory, as in the lab, it would work the same way on the shuttle, breaking down, enriching the soil. But it didn't, apparently. As much as they tried to replicate it, the microbiome on board had not yet progressed to that point. It was a fine balance between healthy plants that produce edible products and barren land. Everything here was necessarily artificial, from the light source to the fertilizers. One little change in pH, moisture or temperature could destroy everything, and they were rightfully concerned that the urine might throw off the balance. The treatment was a harmless 'but smelly' compound of additives, fungal matter and bacteria that they applied to the playground soil the night before. Dog owners' garden plots were scheduled to be sprayed once the playground reopened.

This was just a precaution, they said, to maintain that balance. Everything was fine. The puppies were nuisances, but adorable ones. And Jack was happier building rockets with Adam in his room, anyway.

Sarah's self-betterment plans continued. By the end of the week, she was comfortable with the console and had populated schedules for herself, Maggie and Jack. Hers was nearly empty, but she set aside blocks of time to review the lab manifests and protocols. She wanted to learn more about why the growth cycles were accelerating and maybe what additives were in the garden treatments. She created a reading list of classics and scientific texts to review and had bookmarked three different courses that would help her towards her Master's.

She added her gym time to her agenda, cross-referenced with the spinning class schedule and her favourite instructor. She still avoided the dance studio, making sure to stay out of the way of Kahtriana. Her messages had started again, and Sarah had felt guilty enough to promise to start teaching again next week.

After the kids went to bed on Friday night, Sarah hopped in the shower. She hadn't had a chance after her workout this afternoon, but took the time now, letting the hot water sluice over her sore muscles. It felt good to be tired after doing something, she realized, not just feeling tired of having nothing challenging to do. She stretched her neck side to side and noticed that it was a little sore, but nowhere near as sore as it had been in the last months on Earth.

Chapter 29

This was wrong. All wrong. She checked her notes again, looked up the references she had bookmarked. *How different could it be in space?* she wondered. *Completely different in absolutely every imaginable way*, she answered herself. She didn't know enough about Grant's work to figure in the radiation and gravity issues, but she knew the Earth protocols and substrates, their compositions and interactions, cold. She must be wrong. *I'm not wrong.* She was certain, but not 100% certain. Not enough to ask anyone. She worked her way through the lists on Saturday and Sunday nights, staying up late, way past when she knew she needed to head to bed.

On Tuesday, she waited till the kids had left for school, then poured herself a glass of water and sat down in front of the console. *Please don't be busy.* In a few seconds, Linda's face beamed clearly from the screen. Behind her, the familiar painting hung against the grey walls of her office. Her own little popsicle sculpture sat on a shelf just to her right, beside the cactus. It looked good there, like it belonged.

She hadn't spoken to her friend since the night before everything fell apart, before Grant died. They had exchanged messages — Linda's warm condolences were appreciated; Sarah had responded primly.

"Sarah," Linda said, a sympathetic smile on her face. "It's good to see you. I won't ask you how you are" — *This is why we're friends,* Sarah thought — "but I'm here if you want to talk. To what do I owe the pleasure?" She looked fantastic, as usual.

"Strictly business this time, I'm afraid. Do you have a few minutes?"

Linda checked her calendar. "For you, I have an hour if you need it. What's up?" Sarah wished she had taken a minute to put on some mascara. Linda knew her too well. She hesitated. No need to tell her about the ridiculous dog situation. That way lay madness, hysteria, and she didn't want to fall apart in front of her old boss.

She explained what she had found in the biology documents, how the protocols were different from what she had expected. "I have some numbers to run by you. They seem off to me, but I might be wrong."

Linda leaned forward and rubbed her hands together. "If they seem wrong to you, they're wrong, but I'll take a look. Send them over?"

They spent the next twenty minutes bantering back and forth, comparing their numbers. Suddenly, Linda looked past her screen. "Ethan! Come take a look at this!"

Sarah shook her head, her eyes wide. *Her unmascara-ed* eyes. She shot daggers at Linda, then brushed her hair back and put on a smile as Ethan's familiar face filled the screen beside her.

"Hey, Sar!" He frowned. "I'm so sorry for your loss—"

She closed her eyes and shook her head. "Just... don't, ok?"

Ethan seemed to understand. "How's Mars?"

"She's not there yet, Ethan. She's still got... how long now?"

"A little more than eight months," said Sarah weakly. "I've only really been gone three weeks."

"It feels like longer." *So sweet*. He cleared his throat. "What's up?"

She repeated herself again, ending with, "But I still don't know what the exigencies are for orbit, space travel, artificial gravity, artificial environments... I could be way off base here."

His grey eyes crinkled as he looked at her, then moved to take a closer look at Linda's screen. "I've been at Corporate for too long and I don't know enough about the 'space factor'-" he used air quotes, his eyes twinkling. They both hated air quotes. "But yeah, I would never have mixed this enzyme substrate complex at this concentration. I'd have to go back to Bio 101 to remember why, though." His eyes skimmed over some of the other substances she had highlighted. "Let me take this to the lab. There's some really smart guys there that still know how to 'do science.'"

"The space thing, though, Ethan. I could be totally wrong."

"I'll ask that. Interesting stuff. Are you sure this isn't classified?"

"Nope, it's all in our common-access folder. All good. And thanks, I appreciate it." It was almost like being there, even almost like being back in school, working together in the lab and in the library. From here, at least, there was no chance of misbehaviour.

Linda had almost been pushed right out of the screen. "Ok, great then. Ethan, out you go. I need to have some girl talk now." Was she imagining it, or did he blush?

"Ok, ok! I'll get back to you as soon as I can. Sar, it's good to see you. Aside from..." he drifted off. "Is it absolutely amazing?"

She smiled into his grey eyes. "It's pretty cool, yeah. And thanks."

He left the frame. She watched Linda's eyes follow his path to the door. "Ok, he's gone. Phew!" She fanned herself with her hand. "That was warm."

"Stop it!" Sarah burst out laughing. "And thank you again. What's Ethan doing there?"

"He's here a lot. He sits in your office when the new hire isn't there, takes care of your plant. He's impressed by everything you've done; you know. Now." Linda leaned forward and put her elbows on her desk. "What's really going on up there?"

Sarah tried to keep the conversation light, away from her tragedy and her anger. The kids, their activities, an impersonation of Katriahna, the puppies.

Linda laughed out loud. "They gave puppies out? On a spaceship? The world – no, the universe – has gone mad. How did they ever get that past Grant?"

That sobered her up a little, but then she giggled. "Yeah, they didn't think it through. The breeding program falls — *fell* — under Grant's authority, but I don't think he would have signed off on that part. He wasn't short-sighted." She explained the physical challenges and disruption on board, then switched over to mention the issues they were having with breaking down and reassimilating the urine and fecal matter. "Girl talk," she grinned again. "—Oh my God, the time." She realized with a guilty start that she had five minutes to get to Studio 2 for her class. "I have to run, but thank you! I'll call you soon!"

She was only on the third day of her Better Sarah plan, and already she had slipped. She threw on track pants and a light top. There was no time for mascara. At least her dance bag was already waiting by the door, packed with her shoes and water bottle (Systems!), but she was still going to be late.

✷

She ran through the corridors — *how undignified* — and down the stairs. Thank goodness for Katriahna. She had let the little ones in and had them sitting in a semicircle while she checked attendance. Her eyes flashed as Sarah burst in the door. *Those eyebrows.*

"I'm terribly sorry," gasped Sarah, dropping her bag by the interface and taking her slippers out of her bag. That darn piece of hair flopped over her nose. "I absolutely detest being late." It worked. Katriahna's lips twitched into what, on anyone else, might have been a smile.

She pinned back her hair as the children shuffled over to find their places at the barre, calling their names and moving apart those that needed to be separated. She quickly stepped into her slippers as she started the music, then began to lead the warmup.

Down-two-three-four. Up-two-three-four. She was finding it hard to concentrate but she could count to four on autopilot. *Something else I'm good at,* she thought, feeling Katriahna's eyes burning into the back of her neck.

"We cannot be late, Sarah."

The last child had gone off with her mother, and Sarah watched the dear little thing walking away proudly, tutu bouncing with each step. She hoped that it wouldn't be a long lecture but knew that she wouldn't get away scot-free. Her brain was still racing from her conversation with Linda, and she wanted to get back home and take a look at the documents again before the kids got home. She wanted to be sure.

Katriahna was vibrating a little more than usual today. Or maybe she was picking up on her energy. Either way, she was tense. "I'm sorry. It won't happen again." Better to apologize and act humble than make excuses.

Even though any excuse I make should be good enough right now.

"I'll mark it down. Should this happen again, there are other instructors who would love to fill your shoes." Sarah couldn't believe her ears. *My husband just died*! Her first thought was that, if there really were other people on board who were desperate to teach two preschool ballet classes a week, then let them. She barely stopped herself from asking which sport allowed only two strikes before you were out. She almost told her to Eff off. She took a steadying breath.

"I'm sincerely sorry, Katriahna. I'll see you Thursday."

"On time, please, Sarah." Katriahna's voice rang out behind her as she grabbed her bag and walked quickly out, not bothering to change out of her slippers first.

Chapter 30

Sarah's cheeks were still burning as she let herself back into her quarters. *It's not life and death,* she fumed. *It's preschool ballet.* She downed a large glass of water, then grabbed a handful of dried fruit and nuts. She kicked off her slippers harder than she meant to, then retrieved them and put on flats. Still seething, she grabbed her smartbook and headed back out. She could do some more reading in the garden plot, maybe clear her mind.

Cool, moist air welcomed her as she slid open the unit door and stepped onto the brush mats. She breathed deeply as she walked, feeling instantly lighter-hearted, over to her garden. She had brought a little folding stool down on Sunday afternoon to keep in here, and it fit in, the perfect addition, she thought again smugly as her heart rate began to slow. She would work for a bit, weed and water. Then, when she was calmer, she'd take a look at that first page again, the one with the anomalies. She placed her smartbook on the stool and just stood for a moment, breathing deeply.

It wasn't home, she knew she wasn't outside, but the abundance of life in here, the greenness was... *healing? Was that the right word?* She rolled her neck back and forth, then walked among the rows of little green shoots.

Exhale the bad, she told herself. *Exhale Katriahna.*

Their plot was doing well, she gloated silently. The plants were absolutely thriving, growing steadily. They hadn't borne fruit yet — any of them — but the root vegetables, incredibly, should already be ready to harvest in about a week. Science sometimes felt like magic.

She started at a muffled cough. Turning quickly, she saw a neighbour that shared their unit, kneeling down two plots over. He lifted up a large, dirty hand in greeting, and she returned the wave. *Not today*. She wasn't in the mood for small talk. Maybe he'd stay where he was. The man, dressed in jeans and a light t-shirt, raised himself to his feet smoothly and approached her. *Maybe not*.

"Dave! How are you?" She had already practiced insincerity with Katriahna this morning. *Why not perfect it today?* Dave was a few years older than Grant and worked as a massage therapist. He was a muscular, slow-moving, kind man, and Sarah felt guilty for feeling intruded upon.

His forehead was creased today. He looked puzzled and worried, but not pitying. She wasn't sure that he recognized her, mostly because he didn't immediately offer his condolences. He shook his head slowly. "I'm not sure. My plants just don't seem right." He gestured at her plot. "How are yours doing?"

Sarah looked around at her plot. It looked lush. The rows of seedlings stood up in varying shades of green, some with bushes of red-veined leaves, some with delicate fronds. She hadn't received any notes from the garden staff today, so figured she had solved most of the problems of groupings and overwatering (*one time!*). She had been feeling competent.

“They’re good, I think.” She took another deep breath through her nose and smiled up at him. “It’s amazing how fast everything has grown. God, I love it down here. What’s going on with yours?”

“No flowers,” he said abruptly.

Sarah gestured to her plot. “We didn’t choose any flowering plants,” she said. “I’m not very good at them anyway but thought we should focus on growing food and herbs and such.” *Oh dear*, she thought. *Now I sound preachy.*

“Not just the flowering plants,” he interrupted her earnestly. He didn’t seem offended. “There’s no flowers on my tomatoes... or zucchinis... and no flowers mean no fruit. And,” he continued, “the roots aren’t... well, they’re not right. I wasn’t a big gardener back home but look at this.” He held out a handful of three sausage-sized shoots of what could have been beets or carrots, but they were uniformly a dingy brown. He poked at one with his other hand, and it quivered like jello.

“Do yours do this too?”

Sarah frowned. “I don’t think so. We pulled up one from each row about a week ago, and they were looking pretty good. I think they’ll be ready next week.” Definitely more beety and carroty than the grub-like roots in Dave’s hand.

She walked over to the last row of her plot and looked closely at the little plants. Their greens looked crisp, slightly veined with red, and were visibly bigger than they had been even three days ago. No new weeds had popped up. All good. She reached down and wiggled one of the beets, then gave it a little tug. It came out of the soil easily, and Sarah felt a queasy sensation in her stomach. Last week's test had shown a small, but definitely purplish-red root. This... *thing*... was a round ball the size of her fist, but like Dave's, it had a muddy colour, and was oddly squishy to the touch.

"That's not right." Without thinking, she had echoed Dave's statement. She crossed over three rows, to the carrots. They had crowed over the one they had tested: thin, but already five inches long and bright orange. They were going to be beautiful. She went to the middle of the row, grasped a healthy-looking frond, and pulled. It was... well, it looked like a long thin bag of brown gelatin. She dropped it, then stepped back, brushing her hands off on her pants. "Was it like this yesterday? Have you told anyone else about this?"

Dave shook his head more vigorously. "Just noticed it today. I was about to ping Central when you came in."

"Do it. I'll send a message too and will ask around in the meantime. And I'll call Anne."

Chapter 31

Sarah and Dave stayed in the garden unit until one of the gardening gurus arrived, and then another and another. Several biologists dashed in carrying augers and trowels sealed in clear plastic, then, what felt like a long time later, Anne. One of the technologists slipped in behind her and pulled a large metal trolley in behind him, loaded up with empty containers. She nodded at Sarah, then looked away quickly. Her large eyes looked frightened. They hadn't seen each other since that brief visit after their short exchange through the lab door.

Anne uttered terse instructions to the group as the technician handed out gloves and little plastic containers to the bio team. They fanned out among the rows of plants, each white-coated person taking a small sample of earth in their bottle, then pulling one vegetable up and placing it in a second container. Each looked the same: squishy and brown. Anne stood by the door, armed with a clipboard, a pile of stickers and a sharpie. She asked her team quietly which plot, which row, and handed out labels. A neat stack of containers grew on the trolley.

The captain's executive assistant appeared for a few minutes, then walked brusquely out of the unit. As the door slid open, Sarah saw two other trolleys in the corridor, also piled with boxes. More white coats awaited Anne's instructions.

Sarah stood back as long as she could. Her offer of help had been politely refused, so she stood by the door beside Anne. Only once did she speak up; one of the younger technicians said, “Harper plot, row E, turnip.”

“It’s a beet,” Sarah interjected. “If you got it from row E, it’s a beet.”

Anne’s marker paused, hovering over her sheet of stickers. The technician glanced at Sarah, then back at Anne.

“It was row E,” repeated Sarah. “You picked that from my plot, in the row decorated with elephant stickers.” Jack had made that one after Sarah helped him shower off all the dirt from planting. They had made a craft out of decorating each row marker, something that would have been impractical to do at home, where there was rain and, well, actual weather. Even Grant had joined in, striping his marker in yellow and black paint.

“It’s for the beans in row B,” he had said, his eyes twinkling.

“But it looks like a bee.” Jack looked confused.

“A bee!” shouted Maggie. “A bee for B! *Daddy*!” The kids had collapsed into giggles, and Grant winked at Sarah, the corners of his mouth tucked in not quite enough to hide his dimples.

Sarah looked at Anne pleadingly, and watched as she wrote down, *Harper plot, Row E, Beet*, and handed the two stickers to the tech. As the young woman turned away, she whispered out of the corner of her mouth, “Thanks, Sar.”

Sarah nodded. "I'm going to go. Do we know yet if it's in other units?" she asked softly.

Anne's smile was weary. "I only know what you know. I think it'll be a long night, though." She refocused her attention on another technician approaching, holding two boxes of samples from Dave's garden. "I'll call you later, ok?"

Sarah backed out the door. Maybe a quick session at the gym would clear her head.

"Williams plot, row B, sweet potato."

✷

Sarah, freshly showered and only a few minutes late, rushed to meet Jack at his classroom. She hadn't been down here since she had let Maggie take responsibility for the back-and-forth to school. He looked up with his close-lipped smile when she called him, pushed his glasses up and swept his crayons into his tub of school supplies, then waved goodbye to the friends whose moms were still chatting in the hallway. Jack held her hand as they walked up the stairs to Maggie's class. Maggie and Bridget were the last two in the room, whispering and giggling together at a table, and Erin was leaning against the doorway, scanning her smartbook.

"Well, hello! I guess Maggie was... just about to leave to meet Jack?"

"I was just about to remind her," Erin said. "What's up? Got time for coffee?"

"I don't think—" Sarah started, but then changed her mind. "Yeah. Coffee would be great. At mine?"

They took the long way around, pausing at Erin's while Bridget dropped her backpack and grabbed a bag full of doll clothes. *Maybe they're not growing up so fast after all*, thought Sarah, and thought she saw the same thing mirrored in Erin's eyes. Jack stumped along after the girls and within a few moments, they were inside their home.

"Welcome to HQ," quipped Sarah.

Maggie rolled her eyes. "Harper Quarters," she groaned to Bridget. "So embarrassing." *Maybe not.*

"Go play, kids. We'll call you when your snack is ready."

The two women worked together, taking down mugs, cups and plates. Erin helped herself to the coffee maker, and Sarah made tea for herself, then paused. "Will Bridget drink tea?" she asked. "The kids enjoy it if I make a big deal out of it."

A few minutes later, Jack, Maggie and Bridget sat around the coffee table on pillows. In front of them sat a plate with scones, a jar of jam and a little pot of clotted cream. Sarah winked at Bridget as she poured them each a half cup into a melamine mug. "Go easy on the sugar," she said, then brought the tea pot to the kitchen table where Erin sat waiting.

"You are something, Sarah Harper." Sarah grinned and spread some clotted cream onto a scone.

"The freezer's well-stocked. And just look at them!" The kids, obviously feeling that they were getting something special, were putting on airs, speaking primly and behaving beautifully. She looked back at Erin, who was still sizing her up. "We spent two years in London before we moved to Ottawa," she admitted. "I developed a taste for afternoon tea. They'd be rolling over in their graves if they saw this melamine tea set, though."

How uncanny to serve tea in her own home, something else that she hadn't done in years. Despite Grant's death and the hollow feeling that came with it, every day on the ship she came closer to a feeling of normalcy, such that she hadn't experienced since she was a kid. Her children were going to grow up without a father, and they, like everyone on board, had left everything behind on Earth. But today, they were three kids at a tea party. Sarah smiled, and tears came to her eyes.

"Hey, are you ok?"

She shook her head and wiped her eyes. "I'm a mush," she laughed. She cleared her throat. "Kids, just leave your plates there. But go wash your hands before you play!" The three disappeared quickly, whooping down the hallway. Erin looked at her expectantly.

"I'm fine. It's still a lot —it's always going to be a lot, but I don't want to talk about... *him* right now." Erin nodded sympathetically. "But thank you." Sarah waited a minute, till she was sure the kids were out of earshot, then said casually, "How's your garden doing? Been down there this week?"

Erin grimaced. "I haven't. I've been neglecting it a bit. Turns out that people that don't garden on Earth don't just become super gardeners when you put them into space." She made a little tick mark on an imaginary clipboard. "There's another experiment done. Besides, that message this afternoon, that they're all being checked by the horticulture staff for the next little while, that we wouldn't have access for a bit..." She stretched. "So now that I really, really want to garden" — she winked — "I can't. How's yours going? You're down there all the time."

Sarah smiled. "I miss my yard," she admitted. "Am I a terrible person? Of all the people, all the world that we left behind, I miss a patch of grass?" She rubbed her eyes. "And my mugs." She indicated the dishes. "I hate these things so much." She paused. Nobody had told her not to say anything. "There's a problem with the gardens, with the vegetable patches, at least. Well, with the root vegetables. I was down there this morning, and they've all gone... weird. Weird and brownish and gloopy." She paused, shook her head. "That's my professional opinion, and those are scientific terms."

"Are you kidding? What's weird and gloopy?"

"Ah! A fellow scientist! Well, Doctor, all the beets and carrots and turnips and such in our unit — they were fine last week, almost ready to pick, but this morning, Dave — you know Dave Williams? The massage therapist?"

"I'd *like* to know Dave the massage therapist."

"Dave has a plot in our unit. This morning, he found that his turnips were... well..."

"Gloopy. Brown. Weird."

"Exactly. And so were mine. And my beets and carrots. We called it in, and the place was suddenly swarming with lab coats. They were checking the other units when I left. I don't know how far it's affected..."

"What does Anne say?"

Sarah paused. Anne had barely acknowledged her this afternoon. Apart from anything else that was going on, she couldn't blame her for that today; this a big deal, whatever this was, something new and exciting. Grant would have been in his element. Biology. Yeah. But could she tell Erin that—

"She... um... probably won't tell me, not until there's an official answer."

"What? Your best friend won't gossip with you over something as weird as this? Really? Who are you going to tell about it?" She waggled her eyebrows and smiled ingratiatingly. "Besides, it's probably nothing. At most, it's a bunch of turnips rising up to save us from having to eat turnips."

✷

Sarah had dimmed the lights once the kids were in bed. She put her PJs on and curled up on the sofa in front of the universe, reviewing the notes she had made in her smartbook and wondering how to approach this. The numbers were wrong. The quantities and measures just didn't add up. She wanted to be 100% sure before she mentioned it to Anne, and she was almost there, 95% at least. But what were the chances? These documents had been checked by Grant and probably several other people much smarter than she. And perhaps, no, *probably*, there was something she was missing, some sort of element of *space* that they accounted for, something that wouldn't have been proper for Earth but was absolutely right up here, that took in microgravity or radiation. Like the way the plants grew extra fast. *Or did before they turned into brown jello*. She would talk to Anne.

The door to their quarters buzzed, and she got to her feet. When she opened it, she gasped. Anne was *filthy*. She was dirty, disheveled and looked bone tired.

"Anne!" She reached for her arm, but she pulled back. Even her face was covered in dirt.

"I can't come in," she said. "I'm leaving a trail."

"Come. Use my shower. I'll lend you a robe." She sat back down, book set aside, and listened for the water to start. After five minutes, she got up and made her a cup of lemon chamomile tea. She put it on the coffee table beside a bright-coloured plate holding two digestive cookies.

Nice and calming.

She sat again and could hear that the water was still running. A few minutes later, she heard the water stop. She made a second cup of tea, claimed the first for herself — it still wasn't quite cool enough to drink — and waited for her friend to come join her.

Anne walked to the sofa like an old woman. In Sarah's old robe, she looked taller and thinner than she had last week. Her cheeks were sunken in a bit. Sighing, she took a seat and leaned her head back against the cushions, then placed her hands over her eyes.

Sarah waited.

Anne didn't move for what seemed like forever, then said, "It's bad. It's... it's every unit."

Sarah didn't say anything. She twisted her fingers together.

"All the vegetables. Not just the tubers and taproots. Anything that roots. That's... every plant."

Sarah squeezed her hands tighter. "I made you some tea."

Anne kept her hands on her eyes. "The trees. The grass. If it hasn't already, it's just going to rot. But it has already, so..." Her head still lay back against the cushion, her neck extended.

"Can we plant again? We have seeds, we have—"

"It's the soil. The soil is rotten, infected. We have to—I have to find a way to clean it. I have to clean all the goddamn soil on this entire ship. I don't even know what happened to it—" There was a catch in her voice, an odd note that Sarah had never heard before Grant died. Anne was always so calm, so in control.

"But everything was fine last week, wasn't it? The carrot we checked looked fine. How could anything move so fast?"

Anne finally shifted her head to look at her. Her eyes weren't a gleaming green tonight. They were dull, tired. Old.

"I mean, the one we checked. Maybe the others were already bad by then," she babbled. "What about the food stores on board—?"

"They're fine. They wouldn't be affected by the soil. It's just the plants, Sar." There was an edge to her voice. She dropped her hands to her lap, twisted her fingers together. Her lips were set in a firm line and she looked away, then down at her hands.

"What about the compound you sprayed? Could that have—"

"BioMars hasn't— the compound wasn't approved yet." *Oh.*

Sarah sat up and picked up her tea. She took a tiny sip, then wrapped her other hand around it too. She closed her eyes and took a deep breath, inhaling the steam. This is how she had handled Grant when he was upset.

Stay quiet, don't ask stupid questions, Sar.

Anne picked up her mug too and sat there with her tea, watching the stars outside. The steam made little puffs around her face as she breathed deeply, her eyes looking dark, hooded. "Everything is going to be fine. I just need to figure out how to fix it. Grant would have figured it out by dinner. It's just... a lot for my first week as boss. My first decision was..." She left the thought unfinished.

"Hey, at least you won't be bored." Sarah tried to put a teasing note in her voice.

Anne's eyes stayed fixed on her hands. She nodded. "Grant would love this, wouldn't he? I... I miss him, Sar. He was supposed to be here."

I know.

They sat together, like they had the night Grant died, not talking, just looking out at the stars. They were moving at 26 kilometres per second. The stars travelled even faster, but everything looked motionless, unchanging.

A while later, Anne sat up abruptly. "It's late. I'm sorry for barging in. Thank you... for the tea, the shower..." she glanced down at the robe. "I'll wash this and bring it back." She stood up, still moving stiffly and slowly and picked up their mugs, each containing a spent teabag. Sarah lifted the plate that still held two digestive cookies and followed her to the kitchen. A low light illuminated the space, the time displayed on the console. Twelve-fifteen.

"It's going to be fine. I'm going to figure this out, and there's nothing to worry about." She didn't sound convincing. No hug tonight, but Anne rested her hand on Sarah's shoulder for a moment before trudging away down the corridor.

Sarah composted the waste, then slowly washed the dishes, leaning them into the drying rack carefully, trying not to make any noise. She wiped down the counter and took care as she dried each dish and put it away. She folded the dish towel into thirds, then hung it back on its rail, smoothing it nicely.

She walked slowly back over to the sofa and rolled her stiff shoulders back as she gazed out into the stars again, so bright and numerous in the infinite blackness. She tilted her head towards one shoulder, then the other, wincing at the flash of pain. Maybe she should make an appointment with Dave.

She was unsettled, that was all. Nothing more. She wasn't scared. Everything would be just fine. Anne was qualified, a professional. She wasn't hiding anything or lying to her. That was all there was to it.

She turned away from the window and headed to her ensuite to brush her teeth. Anne's dirty clothes were crumpled in a heap beside the shower. She dropped them in the laundry hamper, then washed her hands and climbed into bed, willing sleep to fog her mind.

Chapter 32

Sarah rolled over, enjoying the last few minutes of sleep. She stretched, then slowly opened her eyes, blinking in the sunbeam. A warm breeze floated in through the window and she could hear a lawnmower running outside.

What day is it? she wondered lazily.

"Mommy! We're going to be late for school!" Sarah sat bolt upright in bed. Right. Overhead light. Fan. Lawnmower... *huh.* No lawnmower. She swung her legs over the side of the bed and stood up, then sat down again abruptly as the room whirled around her head. *Woo.* She slowly rotated so that she faced the bed, her hands supporting her upper body, her head down. *Slowly does it.* And... she was up.

The wall interface said 7:40. *Dammit.* She had ten minutes to be up, feed the kids and leave to get them down to their classrooms. *This seems to be my new thing. I wonder what happens if you're late*? she wondered, then shook her head. *No. On it.*

"Let's go let's go let's go!" She clapped her hands, then swiftly stepped into a pair of track pants and a baggy sweatshirt. Hair up in a messy bun, glasses on.

Glamourous as always.

Jack and Maggie were somehow already dressed. Maggie was in head-to-toe violet today, Jack in contrasting stripes. *Doesn't matter*. Their beds were unmade but it would have to do today. Oatmeal, banana sliced overtop, milk. No time to chew. Teeth brushed, ish. Flipflops. Fine.

They jogged to the classroom decks, their feet slapping on the tiles. That humming sound seemed to follow her. Had she not noticed it before? Was it just because she was so tired that it sounded too loud in her ears?

Maggie, dropped off. Jack, dropped off. *Ten seconds to spare.* As soon as Jack's teacher closed the door behind him, Sarah sagged against the wall and yawned.

"Late night?" asked another mom, ferrying her smallest child to the kindergarten class next door. Sarah smiled wanly and nodded. She waited another minute against the wall, her mind flopping between slipping back into bed and going to the gym.

"Sarah! Coffee?" A third option. Even better. She pushed herself up to standing and saw Erin poking her head out of the staircase. "I thought I saw you flip-flopping by this morning." She grinned as she looked her up and down. "Rough night?"

*

They sat at Erin's table today. Sarah was interested to see how different her quarters looked: different furniture, colours, laid out for three instead of four... *the kind of apartment that we should have now, I guess.* But it made her feel better, too, like they were living in a home rather than just a cookie-cutter apartment. She hugged her tea, feeling the vibration through her seat, through the table. She remembered noticing it when she first stepped aboard, like the ship was alive. She must have gotten used to it, that's all.

"Ok, so I'm a lawyer, not a scientist. Scientists are... well, you're a different breed." Erin was put-together again, blonde curls pinned away from her face, spilling down her back.

"Everybody hates lawyers," Sarah snapped back, laughing

"This is why we're friends. So, Anne's not worried, though."

"That's what she said, but..." Sarah hesitated, then went on. "She was lying. She doesn't lie. I think... I think it's pretty bad. Her face... she looks terrible. I know she hasn't been sleeping very much over the past few weeks, but yesterday— she looked fifteen years older."

Erin shrugged. "Mike hasn't mentioned anything. The ship is running fine. They'd tell him if there was an issue." Her coffee sat on the table in front of her. The cups were melamine, too, but a different shape, a cream colour speckled to look like stone, a blurry teal edge. They were pretty. They suited this space, and Erin. Sarah watched concentric rings appear in her tea, in sync with the vibrations.

"Do you— do you feel that?" Maybe she was just exhausted.

Erin shrugged again. "There's always a slight vibration. I barely notice it anymore."

"But can you *hear* it too? The humming?"

Erin put her head on its side, considering. "Yeah, there's a hum, but I don't think it's new. I think I've gotten used to it. Are you sure you're ok? I mean, considering everything...?"

"I... don't know." She pushed that lock of hair off her forehead. "I mean, the kids are doing great, I'm doing *stuff*, this isn't the first time I've been floating—"

"— in space—"

"— at loose ends, not sure about what to do with myself. I've been... reading some of Grant's scientific texts."

Erin snorted, then pretended to nod off. "Sorry, what were you saying?"

"I was saying that lawyers are the worst. But *before* that, I was saying... I think I've found some errors in Grant's work. Not his experiments, but in the concentrations of the substrates and..." Erin was looking at her with a pained expression. "Never mind. I'll call Linda and bore her with this instead. Hey, what's black and white and looks good on a lawyer?"

"A pit bull." Erin raised her coffee cup to her lips. "I've heard that one before."

"I should reach out to Anne. I mean, she's crazy busy, but she's in there, hands on, and has been working so closely with Grant— had been," she corrected herself. "And if *anyone* can understand Grant... what?" Erin was looking at her oddly. "What?" she asked again.

"Nothing."

"Erin, *what*?"

Erin put her cup down and stared into it for a beat too long. "I'm your friend. I care about you. And it doesn't matter now." She stopped. Sarah waited her out, stared her down. "Anne... well, she joined this mission to work with Grant, right? She left everything behind to follow *him*. And look at her." Sarah glanced down at her own hastily-put-on clothes. "She's been a total mess since he died. I'm not saying that I believe anyone but she's not a parent, she doesn't mix with the other moms, but *everyone* knows who she is. There's been ... some comments made at drop off, some mornings."

Sarah could feel her cheeks burning. "Anne is my friend," she said. "I've known her for ten years." *I haven't seen her for ten years.* "Longer. And Grant was oblivious to the world. The only reason he married me was because... I was there. No," she continued. "You didn't know him, and you don't know her. They're both brilliant, they're both professionals. No. Tell your—" she waved her hand around "—*sources* that they don't know what they're talking about." She drained her cup and stood up. "I should probably just go."

Erin stood up too. "Don't go," she coaxed. "I'm an idiot. *They* are idiots, and I shouldn't have repeated what they said."

Sarah forced her mouth into the shape of a smile. "It's fine. I know. And I'm not mad, and I'm not worried. I promise.

But I'm going to check my numbers with Linda. We'll do this again soon, ok?" She put her cup into Erin's sink, and turned back to her friend. "I'm ok. Really."

*

She returned to her quarters, shook her hair out of her bun and pulled it back again. She splashed cool water on her face, then patted it dry. First, mascara, then Linda.

She pulled a chair up in front of the interface and pinged Linda, who answered within seconds. Sarah grinned.

"I feel that maybe you don't have enough to do."

"I'm making time for my favourite ex-employee and you're giving me grief? What's up?"

Sarah stopped short. *What can I tell her?*

"I'm calling more as a friend."

Linda's face softened. "It must be so hard," she said. "I'm sorry — I keep getting caught up in the so-cool-that-you're-going-to-Mars that I forget to be sensitive. I'm sorry," she repeated.

"No, don't be," Sarah said. "It's just that, well, Anne is acting weird, the ship's in chaos, and—"

Linda cut her off. "Which one do you want to start with? Weird or chaos?"

Sarah chuckled. "Both, I guess. And I need a friend who can *also* give technical advice, then. Here goes."

She took a deep breath. She started with the garden issue, what Anne had said. How Anne had avoided her after the accident, her mood. The rumours.

Linda's face darkened. "Ok, whoever is spreading that around, especially *now*, has a special place waiting for them in hell. Why would you even listen to that garbage?"

"Because I'm tired. And it's stupid, but... it makes sense. She gave up her life to follow him. They were spending more and more time at the lab—"

"That's not unusual, with anything you've ever told me about him. But hell, I only saw him, what, four times in real life?"

"I know that you don't know her, but Anne was avoiding me until... that night, and she was distracted and snappy then. I saw her last night and she's stressed and worried, and... defeated, almost. I couldn't tell if it's grief, or because of the gardens. Or if it's compounded because she's responsible, or because she's *responsible*... like it was her mistake, her oversight." *Or maybe having a suspicious, jealous friend isn't what she needs right now.*

"Have you talked to her about it?"

She hadn't. They hadn't talked at all, really. She hadn't asked her about the substrates and odd concentrations. And she hadn't asked how the puppies could have been handed out without Grant's sign off, or what part, if any, she had played with the sprays they were applying to the soil and gardens. Had she not fully assessed the impact of these choices? Had someone acted without her permission? She had simply assumed that these things weren't in her responsibilities, but they were. Of course they were. Even as Grant's second-in-command she would have had full awareness of all of this, and now, as the lead biologist, even grieving, she was responsible.

"Don't mind me. I think I just needed to hear all my thoughts out loud. I could have said all this to the fridge."

"Hey." Linda put on a mock-hurt face.

Sarah smiled and pushed her hair back behind her ear. "You know what I meant. I didn't need to unload all this on you. Everything already felt weird before Grant died, but now with the gardens... And we're all tired, and I'm struggling. It's like sometimes I'm completely fine and I feel like I can find my place here, then it comes rushing back, and I feel so guilty that I've forgotten him, even just for a minute. How can I forget him?" She shook her head. "And I'm still working through my original stages of grief. What's the one after 'gets on a spaceship, never to see friends and family again,' but before acceptance, and then your husband dies?"

Her smile had fled. She exhaled. Linda looked stricken.

"Sar—"

"That was supposed to be a joke, but I guess I'm not—I'm sorry. Changing the subject, how's Alex enjoying the car?"

"Not changing the subject. It's a lot, far too much for anyone to deal with alone. Do you have friends to talk to there?" Sarah heard a knock, and saw Linda look past the screen towards her office door. She shook her head and waved her hands to dissuade any interruptions. Linda waved away whoever had been at the door, then her gaze returned to Sarah. "I'm always here, and Ethan. He's worried about you too, you know. I think he'd be good to talk to."

It had been a good chat, overall. She managed to avoid any further mention of Anne or Ethan, and Linda just threw out, one more time, "You should really talk to him."

*

When she shut down the interface, it was lunchtime. She had barely five minutes to throw together quick sandwiches before the kids flip-flopped back into their quarters. With the brightly coloured plates and cups set up by the window that framed the out-of-this-world view, they laughed and chattered. Everything was fine. No, *good.*

*

When they went back to school, this time in proper shoes, Sarah hopped into the shower. She'd do the dishes later. *Systems,* her own voice mocked.

Dressed, lightly made up, and far more presentable than she had been for the first half of the day, she pinged Anne. *I know you're swamped, but we need to talk.* She frowned. *What was* that *about?* She deleted it. *I know you're swamped, but come over again tonight? Or I can come to the lab*. That wasn't scary at all.

Chapter 33

10 years ago
Wellington, New Zealand

It's a different world down here, Sarah thought. The wine was stronger, for one.

They'd been living in Wellington for a little over a month. Their little townhouse had been unpacked and set up, and Rupert was litter trained and adorable.

She had come to meet Grant at the hotel for the reception. She hadn't felt like going out, like being 'Mrs. Harper' at a hotel ballroom with a bunch of nerds wearing name tags. But what else was she going to do? She had already been to spinning today. Her office had been shut down at three thirty due to a power outage, so that was done. *Let's face it*, she told herself. *You have no friends.*

She had just finished her first full week at her new job but hadn't yet met a kindred spirit. The other admin assistants seemed a bit cliquish at lunchtime and on breaks, warily eyeing up the new girl with the degree.

I didn't tell them about my degree, she grumbled to herself. *It must have been that damned HR lady.*

She looked in her closet for a good ten minutes before choosing a navy-blue sleeveless dress. An attempt at a smoky eye, twelve minutes with a straightener, and she felt presentable. No, *stylish*.

"New Sarah in New Zealand," she said out loud to her reflection. She slipped into navy pumps, slicked on some lipstick and walked to the bus stop at the end of the block. March meant autumn, and by the time the bus came, she was a bit chilled. She could feel that her hair was no longer smooth.

The bus was efficient, though. She arrived at the conference hotel twenty minutes earlier than expected and helped herself to a glass of red from one of the uniformed servers. The ballroom was only sparsely populated with the attendees. The last sessions wouldn't let out for another ten minutes or so.

Sipping her wine, she tried to look interested in the scientific posters hung about the outer walls of the room, pretending that she was still part of this world. She recognized various bacteria and viruses by their Latin names — *I've still got it*, she thought — and read the writeups intently, if only to avoid interacting with any of these apparently brilliant, tweedy strangers.

She heard a discreet cough at her elbow and glanced up to see another besuited waiter with a tray.

"May I offer you another?"

She stared at the glass in her hand that was somehow already empty, and slowly placed it onto the empty table beside her. He wasn't the same server who had given her the first glass, so she grinned. *Why not?*

"Yes, thank you." She took another glass and swallowed another mouthful. "It's lovely wine."

Still smiling, she looked past the server to see a couple walk into the ballroom, their heads close to each other. The man was tall and lean, wearing a well-fitting dark suit. The woman, in a light grey suit whose jacket nipped in tightly around her waist, tossed her shining dark hair over her shoulder as she touched her companion's arm and laughed up at his bright blue eyes. His face dimpled into a smile.

Anne!

Sarah's smile stretched wider across her face as she recognized her friend. It had been hard to move away from her. After years of loneliness, of being a rock and an island, she'd had almost two months of coffee dates and wine nights in Cambridge before they moved. That time had made her realize how tired she was of being lonely. Rupert, cute as he was, hadn't been able to replace her. Though, it was sweet of Grant to think of that.

Grant.

She hadn't even recognized her husband, she was so excited to see her beautiful friend, who now reached up to brush his cheek with her other hand. He was gorgeous, even more than usual beside that stunning woman. He stood there, smiling down at Anne, while she touched his face. Sarah's smile faltered.

Don't be silly, Sar.

She took another large swig from her glass, lifted her chest, and walked steadily over to where they stood, still gazing at each other. As she approached, Anne turned, and her perfect eyebrows rose just a bit. She dropped her hands from Grant, squealed, "Sar!" and grabbed her in a fierce hug.

Sarah held her wine glass out to one side and hugged her back, one-armed. Grant took the cue and relieved her of the glass; he stood a step away from the women, a small smile on his lips.

"I didn't know you'd be here!" said Anne, just as Sarah said, "Grant didn't tell me you'd be here!" They laughed, still hugging.

"God, I've missed you. Now, let's get us some wine."

"More wine," Sarah corrected her.

Anne linked her arm through Sarah's, then raised a finger. A young server rushed over.

✷

Anne had responded to her ping after dinner. *Tomorrow? 8?*

She sat quietly on the couch, staring out at the starry expanse as Sarah tucked in the kids and kissed them goodnight. She looked up only when Sarah lowered herself beside her.

"The lab's been busy."

"Yeah."

They had never been like this. They had never had nothing to talk about, or too much to talk about but not sure how to say it. Sarah sipped nervously at her drink. She had made them each a Moscow mule with the ginger kombucha that Anne had brought over as a gift. She had poured them too strong. Anne tapped her fingers on the base of hers. She drew lines in the condensation that fogged the glass where the cold liquid touched it. Her nail polish was chipped, and her hand shook a little.

"Is the ship going to be ok?" Sarah started to say, just as Anne spoke.

"I was in love with Grant."

Oh. And there it was. It made... so much sense. They would have seen each other over and over, through the years. Conferences and symposiums, lecture circuits. All that travelling. The rumours, then, whatever she had denied and not even allowed herself to consider, were true.

Sarah felt nothing but cold, detached. "Does he— did he feel the same?" Her voice sounded alien to her, distant.

Anne waved her hand as she finally took a sip. She winced. "I have no idea. It's not like we were having an affair." She looked straight at Sarah, saw her eyes. "Oh my God. Sarah, no! I would never— he would never— oh, shit, Sar. I'm sorry. I shouldn't have said anything."

In the light of Sarah's living room, she looked tired, yes, but more than that. Old. The lines around her eyes and lips had deepened since Grant's death and had etched themselves even more since she had last sat on this couch two days ago. She looked down at her hands again. "He doesn't— I *know* he didn't love me. He couldn't. He needed a wife, someone to take care of him. I'm not that. He's too proper, too focused. I just came along because I couldn't lose him. On Earth, he was always there, somewhere, but this was just too permanent. I... I shouldn't have said anything. Nothing has *ever* happened between us, I swear."

She reached across the sofa. Sarah moved her hand away, placed it into her lap. *What am I supposed to think?* Poor, beautiful, brilliant Anne, working with him so closely, knowing that she'd never have him. Excelling in her career, travelling the world. Not an object of pity, exactly.

"I believe you," she said, keeping her hands in her lap. "I... don't know what else to say right now."

She *did* believe her. And she felt the injustice of it all. If only Anne had come out to her sooner. If only she, Sarah, had been brave enough to stand up to say 'no' to Grant before they had moved for the fifth time. Before she had fallen into Ethan's arms the first time. Before they had boarded a spaceship. She had kept what Anne would have killed for. She had cheated them both out of happiness.

She would never be able to tell her about the kids, about Ethan. *I'll never be able to tell her the truth.*

They sat in silence for a moment.

"How's work?"

Anne put her elbow on the arm of the couch and rested her forehead against it. "I'm so tired." She spoke, then, about the soil, how whatever happened to it was spreading — had already spread — faster than any spore, any pathogen she had ever heard of. Between researching possible origins and past outbreaks and their management — some solved and some just slowed — and reviewing theories molecular and organic, testing samples to see if any of the soil on board could be saved, she hadn't slept more than four hours in a row for the last two days.

The pathogen *was* a spore, she said, or at least, acted like one. It seemed to be *like* bacterial soft rot, a crop disease that was worrying enough on Earth. But it shouldn't be able to affect so many plants, so quickly. It wasn't anything she had seen before and shouldn't have been able to be produced from the fungal compound they had applied to mitigate the dog problem.

"... But you said the treatment wasn't ready yet, wasn't approved."

"It *was* ready. Maybe BioMars hadn't approved it yet, but they would have. And whatever this is, it's not that. It's something new."

"Listen..." Sarah began carefully. "I've been reviewing the lab supply manifests."

Anne gave a small grin, lifted a perfectly shaped eyebrow. "For fun?"

Sarah returned her smile, awkwardly. She shrugged. "It's what I know. They were in the open folders, and... well, the concentrations all seem... off. Obviously, I don't know what the soil levels are now, but the starting values just weren't right, for Earth, at least. Maybe that could have contributed? I could talk to Linda and Ethan..." She trailed off as Anne gave her a hard stare. She felt her cheeks grow hot.

"Linda's my— she was my boss at LabX, and Ethan's... an old friend."

Anne took a swig from her glass and grimaced. "Old friend, eh?" Pinker. She was blushing pinker.

"Yes, a friend. But they can help! I have a network that we can access. LabX is huge, and—"

"NO!" The forceful response made Sarah jump. She knocked her still full glass and caught it just in time. A small drop splashed onto her lap.

Anne pulled her shoulders back, took a breath. "No. This soil issue, the plants dying; it's all— all classified. We're not pulling Earth into this. We can't. If this gets out..." She shook her head, her hair whipping around her face. "Whatever's happened... I have been trying to figure out how, but—" She placed her glass on the coffee table and stood up suddenly.

"I need to get back to work," she mumbled. "The soil is still a problem, and everything is dying."

Chapter 34

No entry. The sign was pasted in the centre of the door, which was locked against her anyway. She paused, then walked on.

Sarah missed her little garden plot even more, she felt, than she missed Grant. Maybe it was too much to process, and she needed to touch the earth, to lean against the still too slender trunk of her apple trees, to use the green and the freshness to start to heal.

But the apple trees were dying too, Anne had said. The unnamed pathogen had now affected the houseplants in the cabins. Their roots, just like those of the vegetables – *had it really only been a week ago?* – had swollen with fluid. The outer layer had stretched and cracked, leaving the brown substance within to ooze out into the soil. Some plants looked healthy for longer than others but once the roots were affected, it would only be a matter of time before the stems became spindly and pale, droopy. The plant in Maggie's room had shed its leaves.

Sarah had enough background in biology and had listened to Grant mutter to himself enough to connect the dots. The spread of destruction could be plotted fairly easily. There *could* have been transference of organic matter between the garden units. The horticulturalists could very plausibly have tracked fragments from one to the next on their rounds. And some of the gardeners would have tracked more into their own quarters. Microscopic bits of the bacteria could certainly have found its way into a houseplant here or there. But Erin's plants had died too, their roots bloated and watery, and she had neglected them even more than she had her plot. Whatever it was, it had infiltrated the whole ship. It had survived the air-cleaners and filters.

They had sealed off the gardens, quarantined them completely, shut down the air transfer from the units. Technicians collected samples from each plant and its soil, whether showing signs of infection or not, and the soil and plants themselves — each and every bit of growing vegetable matter on the ship — had been gathered up and incinerated. They were left with a mountain of bacteria-ridden samples and soil that needed to be cleansed of the infection.

They were fine, the captain's announcement assured them. The ship's supplies were plenty, the food stores were unaffected, and the unmanned supply shuttle was due next week. They were just fine.

Fine is relative, mused Sarah.

✷

She had sent Anne another message. *I want to go over some numbers with you.* Anne had protested. She was far too busy to deal with supply lists, but Sarah insisted. *No. I need to show you this. Ten minutes.* Grant wouldn't have let it go.

The next morning, she waited for Anne in the conference room closest to the lab. She was prepared for Anne's brisk, don't-waste-my-time demeanour; she flashed her notes up onto the screen without preamble. "This isn't right. It *wasn't* right. None of it." She had compiled her own observations with research she had found, further annotated by Ethan and Linda's efforts. "First things first. These manifests were signed off like this before boarding, and I can't understand why. The concentrations, the nutrient breakdown in the soil... they're all... *not right*. And the added nitrogen from the puppy urine, and that compound..." Anne scanned table after table, her brow furrowed, biting her lip. She was silent for a long time.

"I told you this was classified, Sar— " she began.

"These are the original manifests, open-access documents," Sarah shot back. "I haven't shared anything further. I promise, but this is important. You have to listen to me. *This* is where it started."

She looked up at Sarah swiftly, appraising her. "I'm sorry. But yeah. You're right. You start after lunch. You're going to sort this out while we keep working on this."

Sarah shook her head. "What do you mean, 'sort this out?' I'm not the scientist. I'm not capable of—"

"You *are* a scientist, and you *are* capable. You're right. You've told yourself for years that you're not, that you missed your chance. But this is your chance. Tap into that potential, baby." She grinned at her briefly. "Call up your boyfriend and put his big brain to work, too. We need all the help we can get."

Sarah blushed hotly. "Ethan isn't my boyfriend. And I haven't—"

Anne stopped smiling. "What he is, or was, I don't care about. We can talk about that later, but right now, I need you. Your kids need you, but so does everyone on this ship. I'm not Grant. I'm asking for help. Do it for his memory or not. Mourn him or hate him for dragging you along, but everything will *die* if we don't figure out a way to clean this pathogen out of the ship. Finding out where it came from is a huge part of that. You can work with me when the kids are in school." She dropped her chin a little. "Know your enemy and know yourself..." she trailed off.

"What's that?" Sarah asked.

"Sun Tzu. *The Art of War*."

"How will assigning blame to Grant—"

Anne's eyes flashed, and her cheeks grew red. "I'm not blaming him. We're not discussing whose fault it was — at least not right now — but identifying what it is, is important to beating it. And we need to know what caused it so we can prove to Earth and the colony that it won't happen again. I'll get permission to share this with your lab. The bacteria is still alive on the samples, and the soil is still rife with it. It's... everywhere. We need to cure the ship." She stood up. "I've got to get back to work." And that was it. Once they could find it, they could name it. Things that had names could be overcome.

*

Sarah would be working in the lab, among, but separate from those that did 'real science'—

"Stop it," said Erin, whom she reached out to as soon as she got back to her cabin. It would be good for her, she insisted, and good for the ship. Sarah drank a rare cup of coffee as she cleaned up the lunch dishes, wincing at the bitter taste. She sent the kids back to school, then took a deep breath as she buzzed the lab door. Inside was kept cool and sterile. On entering, she felt the now-familiar chill, the hospital-like smell creep into her veins and settle into the pit of her stomach. *This is where it happened. And Anne has been in here every day*. She patiently participated in the safety briefing, donned protective gear and manned her console. Anne spared her a quick look and a nod, then turned back to her microscope.

The spores had travelled throughout the entire ship, found not just in vegetable matter, but in dust, on equipment. On people.

Everyone seemed healthy, so far.

The pathogen hadn't shown up *in* people yet, just *on* people. Medical staff had been tasked to collect samples of cheek cells, just little swabs, little scrapes, then snips of hair and nails. There were checkpoints on each deck, rotating between fore and aft decks to collect as much data as possible.

They took small blood samples during routine physicals and checkups. The number of data points was huge and growing. On top of the soil from each garden unit and houseplant, and the passenger tissue, there were now air samples being taken from each deck, each section, each room.

This was her specialty. She sorted and catalogued. She used Grant's antiquated label maker, smiling at herself at first, then appreciating the ease of updating and autofilling the information. *Systems,* she thought wryly.

✷

The afternoon passed quickly. The ship propelled along its trajectory, unable to return to Earth anyway. This was set up to be a one-way trip, like the first two shuttles that had gone before, the original settlers. *The first two* successful *shuttles,* Sarah reminded herself. There had been others before, sent off with great pomp and circumstance, only to not make it. The first went dark after some fifty days of travel. The second didn't survive the landing.

The last two ships had been successful. The passengers — no, *pioneers* — had assembled the preliminary shelter, then added on and reinforced it, ensured that the life-support systems and multiple backups were functional. When the second shuttle landed safely, the colony more than doubled in size, becoming more of a community than a family.

They started to grow crops and create real, sustainable processes, so that one day — eventually, far in the future — Mars could be as inhabitable as Earth. And one day — even farther in the future — they might be able to even send ships, and shuttle people, maybe even Maggie and Jack, back to Earth. But not yet.

This ship couldn't go back to Earth. It wasn't meant to go back to Earth. It couldn't land on Earth's surface with Earth's gravity, and its fuel wouldn't like re-entry. The supply shuttles were the same. Once they transferred their contents, they were deactivated. There was no return, no going back.

She had known all this. But now Sarah's mind raced as she watched Anne try to concentrate on the slide in front of her. She looked sad and exhausted, but she also looked scared. Her hands shook.

"Hey." A new thought occurred to her. "What are the puppies going to do now? I mean, they can't go in the playground or gardens anymore. Are there going to be puppy pads all over the place, or..." She trailed off, seeing the creases around Anne's mouth deepen.

"Sar—"

The bottom dropped out of her stomach. "The puppies. You didn't—"

"They were euthanized. Sar, we had to. They shouldn't have been allowed on board in the first place, and they may not have caused this problem, but they exacerbated it. I had to make the call." Anne's eyes, suddenly shining with tears, pleaded with her to understand. “This is... serious. Really, really serious. It’s life and death.”

Oh. It felt like all of the air had been suddenly sucked out of the room.

“They’re... not going to let us land, are they?” she said slowly. “Unless this is sorted, we’re a danger to the colony, to everyone. We’ll contaminate their crops. We’ll kill everything.”

Anne finally looked at her, her still-beautiful green eyes bloodshot, dull with grief and fatigue. She nodded once, then turned back to the screen.

So, that was it. They were stuck on this ship to Mars, and there was no way back and no guarantee that the colony would even let them get close. Would it be better to attempt to land and get shot at? Blown up while in orbit? Attempt to return to Earth and die on the way?

Anne nodded again, a jerky motion of her head. “No pressure,” she said. “At least we have six months to figure it out.”

Chapter 35

What would Grant do?

She couldn't count the number of times that thought had passed through her mind since his death. Well, he wouldn't receive such a bombshell then leave at three pm to meet the kids at home, that was certain. She went through the bio lab's decon process like a robot, removing her mask, gown, shoe covers and gloves, sorting them into the proper receptacles — *just like riding a bike* — making sure that she was clean and safe. Not that there could be any guarantees.

She half-jogged to her quarters, barely inside before the kids tumbled in the door, clamouring for a snack. Overall, they had rallied well from Grant's death. They were still sad, of course, quieter than they had been, then louder, prone to bursts of anger and tears, but they were going to be ok. They didn't mind that they were still going to Mars, didn't seem to see that the entire universe had shifted around their family. Maybe it was because Grant hadn't really been around much, so his absence was more manageable, Sarah supposed. *Or maybe just because they're kids.* She didn't know.

She was rallying too, sort of. The gut-punch realizations that he was gone came less and less frequently. She was angry, no, *furious*, with him, but his loss was less of a physical pain with each passing day.

A knock at the door revealed Adam and Bridget. *Did I set up a playdate?* she wondered, searching her memory, then shrugged and let them in. The noise at HQ increased sharply, then dropped off as they disappeared to their rooms. Adam and Jack were building an intricate new spaceship, and Maggie and Bridget were... well, she didn't know what they were doing, but there was giggling. That was good.

She pinged their mothers to let them know they'd arrived safely, then hesitated for only a minute before pinging Katriahna, too. *I'm needed in the lab. I can't teach anymore for a while.* It took everything she had not to add, *Bitch.* There. Let her think what she wanted.

She splashed cold water on her face from the kitchen sink, but knew she looked pale and terrible. Her eyes felt swollen, but her head was clear, if unfocused. She felt twitchy. She had known that it wasn't a good idea to have too much caffeine in the afternoon, and that coffee really had been awful. She was so tired.

She sat down in front of the kitchen interface and called Linda.

"Hi," she said, smiling wanly. "I've only got a little while, until the kids emerge from their caves."

Linda took off her glasses and patted her hair back from her face. Her eyes were anxious. "Before I call Ethan, how are you?"

"I'm... managing. Or I'm not, but I don't have much choice, do I? But let's get to this. We can do a social call another time." She clapped her hand to her mouth. "I'm rude. I'm sorry."

"No, *I'm* sorry, Sar. And don't worry about it. You have carte blanche for behaviour, for as long as you want. Hang on." She put her glasses back on and typed something into her keyboard. "Ethan should be here in..." she squinted "...one minute."

"Linda? Thanks. For everything. For believing in me, for—"

"Hey, Sar." Ethan pulled a chair up beside Linda and put an open laptop off to the side.

"Hey." In her coldness, a warm feeling spread in the pit of her stomach. "Thanks for meeting. But enough of this. I need help."

"We can help. They've authorized any and all of LabX's resources to help you fix this." Ethan stared earnestly from the interface. *How did they both know already?*

First, *that was fast*. And then, *Crap*. If Head Office approved it, that meant that Head Office knew. That Earth knew. That BioMars and the colony knew. Sarah didn't want to search it up. She could imagine the media storm, the panic on Earth and on Mars, coming so closely on the heels of the tragedy – of *her* tragedy – it would make it seem even worse, if that were possible. Of course they would have had to inform the colony, *of course they would*, but she wished that they had waited another week, another month, long enough that they could have solved the problem and made sure that everything was safe, then tell them in passing, like a 'guess what just happened?'

Linda was typing again. Sarah saw a message flash up in her inbox, and there was the official communication from NASA, with BioMars authorizing the sharing of information with LabX. Just below it, she saw that Anne had forwarded it to her, as well.

What a coup, if LabX could help them. Professionally, it was already a huge pat on the back that her lab was recruited to help — "Because of *your* work," Linda had said — and if they helped solve it, it would be the gold seal on an already steep trajectory. International acclaim. Funding. More capability. And here she was involved with it again, able to contribute meaningfully, albeit this time in from afar. *Very afar*. It would have been flattering, if it hadn't meant that her life depended on it.

"Take some time, Sar." Linda's face was concerned. Ethan's eyes were soft.

"I'm fine," she responded, running her fingers through her hair. "And we don't really have time. I need to work. I need to. Because otherwise we're all going to... I need to work."

"We're here." She could almost feel Ethan's hand over hers. "Ok, then. What do you need? Tell us where to start."

It felt almost normal and infinitely comforting, to see Linda and Ethan sitting side by side in the familiarity of Linda's office, against that peaceful canvas of blues and greens. The interface worked well. She could stare at Ethan without feeling self-conscious. *What if I had told him, or told Grant? Or never left him in the first place?*

She transferred the files: the ship's log of plants and vegetation on board, as well as the manifest of lab supplies, with the anomalies she had identified highlighted, her notes. She attached the lab analysis of the soil, its makeup upon loading, then recent concentrations.

She took a steadying breath, pulled her shoulders away from her ears, and began.

"It's some kind of bacterial soft rot." In front of her, Ethan started typing. She watched their two sets of eyes scan what was probably the same entry she had read. She cleared her throat and continued.

"The pathogen was noticed in taproots first. The effects of soft rot on Earth are similar to what we're experiencing, but they're much more severe than they should be and spreading faster. From what I've researched, it's not uncommon, but it's hard to treat without starving or dehydrating the soil: essentially, killing the rest of the vegetation. Also, this is far more pervasive than it should be, and has spread to most of the vegetation on board. The known forms shouldn't be able to affect anything but taproots and the like. My theory is that it was triggered by the increased nitrogen from—" Here, her breath caught. She smirked, a pained look on her face, "—dog pee, and exacerbated by improperly-balanced soil substrates and fertilizer compounds— I've sent you the list of suspect substrates — not to mention the unknown effects of space radiation and microgravity." She smiled feebly. "That's... that *was* Grant's specialty.

"True rot would travel via water supply only, or insects, but this one seems to be producing spores, which makes this tricky, because one, soft rot doesn't produce spores, and two, it's probably being transferred through the ventilation system and not being filtered out. We're dealing with something either very small or unknown or both. It's new. It's got to be some kind of mutation."

Ethan looked at her with a mixture of pity and admiration. "There's my girl," he said.

Sarah blushed as she felt her eyes fill with tears.

Linda nodded and nudged him. "What did I tell you? You've got this, Sar, and you've got us. Whatever you need."

18 years ago
Kingston Ontario

"Shhh!" Nancy hissed. "He's looking!"

Ethan and Sarah pinched their mouths shut and put their heads down, his over the microscope, hers over the slide she was preparing. Their shoulders shook.

Nancy was at the next station over with a quiet girl named Michelle, who looked pained to be involved with such immature behaviour. The TA, tall and serious in his rumpled lab coat, stopped at their station first. "Alright, let's see what you've got here." He carefully picked up the three prepared slides for inspection.

Nancy and Michelle stood silently while he slid the first under their microscope. Michelle looked nervously at Nancy, who stood confidently behind him and winked at Sarah. "These are excellent," the TA said. *Did he sound disappointed?* "Well done."

Ethan still had his eyes to the microscope as Grant moved towards them, but Sarah could tell he was watching the TA's approach. She pushed her hair behind her ear as she stepped back from the bench and waited for him to review her slides.

She didn't know why she was nervous. She was sure her — that *their* work was good. She had studied the protocols last night and reviewed them again before starting today. Ethan, for all his joking around, was a great lab partner. They worked well together. She had set up their workstation, while he collected the samples from the lab's freezer. He sterilized the equipment while she calibrated the microscope. They were a team.

Grant cleared his throat behind Ethan, who slowly straightened and moved away from the microscope, one arm behind his back. He used his other hand to flip the hair out of his eyes. Sarah and Ethan were careful not to look at each other as Grant peered at their slides, one after another. When he stood up, his face was impassive. "Well done," he repeated, his back rigidly straight.

Ethan reached a cartoon-like right hand forward. He was wearing a latex glove inflated and held in place around his wrist with an elastic band. "Thank you, sir," he said with a straight face, looking Grant in the eye. "I really appreciate it." Grant extended his hand automatically, then jerked it back. Nancy snorted and Sarah turned her head away, biting her lip.

Grant flicked a bright blue glance down to her, then back to Ethan, while Michelle tried to telegraph empathy to him. He turned away and walked over to the next group. "It's a good thing we're so good at this, Sar," muttered Ethan, poking her with his ballooned forefinger. "Stick with me, kid."

"Mmm-hmm. You take a look, and I'll record."

"We make a good team."

"Stop poking me and get observing." She pulled off her own gloves, grinning, and recorded his observations carefully on the workstation keyboard.

They switched places. "Do you know what I think?" she said, gazing at the slide in front of her. The one-cell-thin section of mouse kidney on it looked colourful and orderly, the cells all arranged in beautiful symmetry, the purple walls of the closely packed cells contrasting with the red-stained nuclei. There were always patterns.

This morning, the slide preparation process had taken two and a half hours to complete; the third years applied three different stains and let them develop for prescribed times, up to an hour each. While they were waiting, the students preserved other samples in formalin and prepped and labelled slides for the first-year labs.

Sarah's notes were printed out and covered in her neat handwriting. She had read up on stains while she ate dinner alone — Nancy had been out with John — her head propped up on her elbow. There were new substances that could be applied instead, combinations that would highlight the same structures, with less time needed to develop. She mulled these over and added to her notes as she prepared the slides.

"We could cut at least an hour if we used some of these new fluorescents. It would save time, save the school money..."

"... Save the world!"

She lifted her head to smile into Ethan's grey eyes, so much like her own. "Exactly."

They submitted their work and cleaned the workstation. They returned the slides to the autoclave, cloaked the microscope with its cover, and dropped their lab coats in the bin by the door, where Nancy stood waiting.

"What took you so long?" she greeted them, shrugging into her jacket. "I'm starving."

"Sarah's finding efficiencies again," Ethan said. "She's going to fix the world."

"There's always a better way," insisted Sarah as Nancy rolled her eyes. "Why not find something, *do* something new?" She wrapped her jacket around her and followed Nancy and Ethan out, glancing back over her shoulder just before the door closed behind her.

Grant was staring at her, his long, thin hands still on his desk. His eyes were so blue they almost glowed.

Chapter 36

During the days, she fell back into her role of administrator, organizer. She mapped out the shuttle, revised the testing rotation based on bacterial hot spots that LabX's analysis revealed. When she gave direction, the lab staff no longer glanced over to Anne for confirmation. This time, she didn't feel like she was just putting in time, filling the hours to try to contribute, but actually supporting something big, making a difference. This was important. This was life and death, for three and a half hours every morning and three hours every afternoon, then however many hours she could handle after she tucked Maggie and Jack into bed at night.

She dashed to meet them in their classrooms straight from the lab, and spent her afternoons with them, right up until the comforting familiarity of their bedtime routines. She watched over them closely, looking for their reactions, their fears and their sadness.

Somehow, it had been easier to tell Maggie about her father's death than that of the puppies. Her reaction, then, had been quieter, not angry, not screaming so loudly that she gagged. She was eight; how much more tragedy could she handle?

"I'm so sorry, Maggie," she whispered into her hair. "I'm so sorry."

She had gone back to walking them to school and back, twice a day, on the way to and from the lab.

“Mom, I can take us.” Maggie rolled her eyes.

“I know you can, Miss Maggie. But let me tag along, ok?” She didn’t want them to know how hard she was trying to memorize everything, to learn them by heart. It wouldn’t be fair to tell them what she was working so hard for, what she didn’t want to think about, how they might not make it to Mars. She pushed down the knowledge that she was being irrational: if they didn’t, these memories wouldn’t do her any good anyway.

She fed them their meals and snacks and watched them as they ate. She tucked them in at night, with "Good night, Jackattack" and "Sweet dreams, sweet girl," everything she had done before, but now with an intensity that she couldn’t let go of.

She brought Maggie and Bridget to the dance studio and dropped Jack off to Adam’s quarters on the way. His mom, Jenny, gave her a sympathetic smile. “Anything you need, you call me,” she said.

“Thanks,” she responded. *Everyone is still being so kind. Let them.* “I’ll be back in about an hour to pick him up.” They headed to the studios, passing a team of technicians in the hallway. She gave Maggie a quick peck, and tried to slip away quickly, unseen — she wanted to fit in a workout — but wasn’t fast enough. Katriahna pounced on her, her claw-like hand closed over Sarah’s forearm.

“Sarah, I am sorry.” Under the heavy, dark eyebrows, her brown eyes were intense, but kind. “I lost my husband and my daughter a few months apart, and I know it is hard. That’s why I came. I had nothing left, so I came." She pulled Sarah into a tight hug, her bony arms clamping around her waist. "I understand what it is like, the pain. And you are strong. You are not alone." She looked up at her. "You are a good teacher and when you are ready, you will come back." She patted Sarah on the cheek once, then turned away, her attention already on the class. She clapped her hands sharply. "To the barre, girls! You are here to dance, yes?"

After that, she let Maggie walk to her ballet classes with Bridget. She stopped going to the gym.

Nights, she did pushups and situps in her living room, mountain climbers and burpees and jumping jacks, getting up off the sofa for a set every twenty minutes or so, to stay awake, to keep alert. She pored over her notes, the lists she had made during the day, reviewing documents and studies forwarded by LabX or BioMars. There had to be something she wasn't seeing, something critical that everyone had missed.

The days that she called Linda or Ethan, she made sure to do so as soon as the kids were in bed, talking for a short time only, trading information and formulas. The rest of the time, she was alone with her notebooks, her interface, her research. Sometimes, she'd wake up on the sofa in the early hours and drag herself to bed. More often, she'd spend the whole night there, getting up to fall into bed only minutes before her alarm went off.

"Sarah." Erin had pinged her so many times, with no response. She was waiting for her at school dropoff on

Wednesday morning. Bridget was already inside. Maggie gave a quick wave before slipping into the classroom.

"I have to drop Jack off..." she started to back away towards the stairwell, but Erin stepped forward.

"I'll walk with you."

"No, I— I have to rush off to the lab, and—"

"I'll walk with you," she repeated.

Sarah dropped her head, then nodded. She was so tired. There was so much to do, and she was wary about inadvertently telling Erin too much. Those that knew the extent of the problem agreed that they mustn't cause panic: the medics, the technicians, the captain and his most trusted staff. *I'm one of them.* She felt a pang of pride. Mustn't tell the passengers that their lives depended on what they did and didn't find out, how close all of them were to dying. *No pressure.*

She gave Jack a hug goodbye, quickly, so his friends wouldn't see, and watched him saunter into his classroom. Out of the corner of her eye, she could see Erin leaning against the wall, waiting for her. They walked slowly towards the lab, Sarah's hands in her pockets. Erin stayed silent for a few minutes, but then said, "Listen. Mike's going to watch the kids tonight. He's going to take them all to a movie, and we're going to share a bottle of wine."

Sarah stopped walking. She looked at Erin, and said, "No. I— I can't. The kids..." She went quiet, leaned against the wall. "They need me right now."

"They need a break, and so do you. You've been together almost every second since Grant died." Sarah flinched. "It's true, and you know it's true. They'll have a good time. Mike won't let them out of his sight. If it goes well, they can spend the night." She put her hand on Sarah's shoulder. "You need a night off. You need a friend, and I miss mine. Please."

Sarah's shoulders slumped. "I know. Thank you." She looked down the corridor. "I have to get to the lab, but yes. Tonight."

Anne looked up as Sarah walked in. She was in the biosecure section of the lab. She had a smile on her face, the first genuine one Sarah had seen in almost a month. She lifted one thumb up.

"There he is. We've got the sucker." Her voice carried through the speaker between labs, triumphant. "So now we've just got to get rid of him."

The trays of new samples, stacked as high as her waist, awaited her. She sat down, opened up her interface, and set to cataloguing the specimens. They could do this. It was science, plain and simple. All she had to do was spot the right pattern.

*

The wine was good. It felt wonderful to sit with a friend, to be normal for a change, with no secrets or heavy knowledge between them. Anne was an old friend, a dear friend, but there was too much history, too much pain for them to spend time like this together right now. *Too much shop talk. Too much guilt.* With Erin it was simple, easy. She was the only person Sarah had laughed with since Grant's death.

The kids were in good hands, she knew. She tried not to think of the last time they had stayed over. With everything else, it must be hard on them to have her hovering over them every waking moment. She didn't want to talk about Grant. She had told Erin about the work, but not why she was working so hard. *Let her think that I'm hiding from dealing with Grant's death.*

Well, aren't you? another voice demanded.

She talked about how it made her feel like she was a part of something again, which she hadn't felt since—

"Since your job on Earth."

Sarah paused. Well, yes, but... "Yes, since then." Was it just the work? The meaning, the desperation? Or was it the calls to LabX, the connection with Linda and, yes, Ethan. It felt like it had in university: easy, familiar.

I'm a terrible person.

When she let herself into her quarters — *HQ*, she thought wearily — she was more than a little tipsy. Without the kids sleeping down the hall, it felt empty of everything. She wrapped herself in the throw on her sofa and lay down, staring at the stars with burning eyes until she fell asleep.

Chapter 37

That was how she slept now, when she slept at all.

Now that she had to, she didn't like to sleep alone anymore. When they were first married, she used to feel lonely when Grant travelled without her, and she'd curl up on her side of the bed with his pillow behind her back. Then, as she got used to it, especially once they had the kids, she embraced it. A whole bed to herself and a whole routine of long-sleeved pyjamas, foot cream inside of fuzzy socks, and sometimes a sheet mask that she'd find wadded up on her pillow in the morning. And Rupert behind her knees. Sometimes she dabbed lavender oil on her temples and rubbed cuticle cream into her nails. Even with two busy kids and her own job, then career, the nights alone had been an opportunity to pamper herself, to sit up reading as late as she wanted.

That was all done. She didn't even bother changing into her pjs anymore. Her dreams were haunted by dirt. She dreamed of plunging, wrist-deep, into black earth, feeling the soothing silkiness of the soil flow between her fingers. Of washing her hands over and over, never coming clean. She dug under the tree in her backyard, and pulled out the box that had held Rupert, instead finding inside one of the puppies, its fur filthy, its stomach bloated and slimy.

After weeks of frenzy, of worry, of laser-sharp focus, of not sleeping, Sarah was exhausted. *It's not grief*, she told herself. *It's failure.* For every small step they took forward, identifying a new component of the Space Rot — which they had started calling it, flippantly at first, but the name stuck — they spent days forced up against brick walls. Each time they sequenced its genome, it had changed.

Anne and the captain had daily briefings with NASA and BioMars, usually no more than five minutes long. Anne always returned from these in a foul mood.

The samples weren't cooperating. There was no evidence of spores, but how else could it be spreading? Why couldn't they kill it? How could it be surviving without the vegetables and soil to feast on? There didn't seem to be any sort of order to its distribution, not the kind you'd see on Earth. The bacteria itself was affected by lots of things: temperature change, radiation, oxygen deprivation and dehydration, which was positive, but they couldn't *kill* it. It all just didn't make any sense.

"If you could only send us some samples to work on-" Ethan began.

"You'd get them in two months, and they'd probably mutate on the way." She pulled her face down with her hands and sighed. "And there's no way to get them to you anyway."

Everyone was exhausted. They were frustrated and worried, and made too many mistakes, which Anne pointed out sharply, overtired and stressed herself. The other researchers and technicians cut her a wide swath, trying to avoid her wrath, and Sarah could tell that they were tiptoeing around her as well. She and Anne didn't fight, not exactly, but layers of grief and fatigue were stopping them from communicating well. They were civil, but that was it.

Sarah took her lunch break with her kids as usual, then quickly washed the plates before rushing back to work. Anne had stayed at the lab again, quickly swallowing a cup of soup and another coffee, before getting back to work. She was jittery and bad-tempered, and snapped back when one of the senior researchers suggested that she take the rest of the afternoon off. It was only one-thirty. Anne's eyes blazed for an instant, then dropped. She quickly decontaminated, and stepped into the outer lab, where Sarah sat in front of the interface with bleary eyes.

"You too. Out."

Sarah rolled her neck on her shoulders and yawned. "I just want to get through this last—"

"Nope. Out."

Sarah mock-glared at her friend, then sighed. "What are you going to do, fire me?"

"I'm going to buy you a cup of tea. Let's go."

The corridors were almost empty. All the children were still at school and only the turf-carpeted playing fields were open for the preschool children today. Had the corridors ever been bustling? What had it been like, only two weeks ago, before the soil was poisoned? Or three weeks ago, before Grant died? *I can't even remember.*

The coffee shop at the aft of the ship was designed to be homey, industrial-chic with finishes that looked like wood, wrought-iron and cement. *Yet here am I floating in a tin can,* she found herself humming. Anne shot her a look and she stopped. The young man behind the counter slid their orders to them, his eyes never leaving Anne's face. *Tyler*, his nametag said. *They really haven't missed a trick with this place*. They brought their drinks and a pastry each over to a high table with stools.

"You'd think they'd have kept only the comfortable parts of a coffee shop," Anne grimaced as she climbed up onto the stool. "I hated these things."

"The other one has comfier chairs. This feels like home, though." Sarah wrapped her hands around her mug, more melamine disguised as mock stoneware, of course. She could feel how much warmer the air was in the coffee shop, anywhere outside of the lab, but she still shivered. She was always cold these days. "Aren't you... are you homesick at all?"

Anne had done the same with her mug of coffee. Her nails were short as always, speckled with remnants of the nail polish she must have last applied before the Captain told them that Grant was dead. Her hands were largish, dry from decades of constant handwashing. She had pulled her sweater down over her wrists and shivered too. "I'm not." She caught Sarah's glance. "Really. I mean, science has been my life forever. I would have been a fool not to take this opportunity-" she shrugged "— or make this opportunity. You know I begged Grant to hire me?"

Sarah hadn't, but she wasn't surprised. "Do you miss him?" she asked abruptly.

Anne's gaze didn't waver. "Every moment. Every time I'm in the lab, I'm looking for him, wishing he was there to tell me a better way of doing it. Whatever *it* is." She laughed huskily. "He was such a know-it-all. What about you?"

Sarah fidgeted with her cup, rubbed a mark off the rim with her thumb. *Do I?*

"I don't… it depends on the day," she finally managed. "He wasn't really… there… a lot, for me and the kids. I know how it sounds—" she could see Anne open her mouth "— and I'm sorry he's gone." She kept her head down and spoke quickly. "It's a totally inadequate way to talk about my husband, and *inadequate* is the wrong word too. But there's so much to do, and there's not time to grieve right now. Later." She looked up at Anne, who still looked horrified. "I *know*. But we are all— all of us— going to die if we don't figure this out. Whatever happened, whatever mistake was made that caused this, it doesn't matter. What matters is that we clean this up, or they'll kill us all."

There was a clatter behind them. The young man had dropped a full tray of mugs on the floor. They jumped and whirled around on their stools, Sarah gripping the table dizzily. He scrambled to pick them up, and Anne squatted down to help him.

"It— it's fine," he stammered. He had overheard what she said, or at least part of it, Sarah realized. He would know who Grant was — of course he would — and *every* man on board would know how Anne was, she was sure of that. She telegraphed her panic to Anne, who was smiling calmly and picking up melamine mugs from the cafe floor.

"There we go, no harm done," she said. The boy's face was white, confused and sick-looking. He was still staring at her as if mesmerized. "Do you have a cloth that I can mop this up with?"

"Dr. Coyne? What's wrong with the ship?"

Anne shot Sarah a look, then looked back at him with a relaxed smile. "The ship's fine, Tyler." She had read his nametag.

"No, sh— she said we were going to die, that someone was going to kill us. And... and the puppies. They're gone."

Anne shook her head, her dark shiny hair settling nicely on her shoulders as she smiled into his frightened eyes. "Oh dear, I think you misheard us. We're working on the problem with the gardens right now, on whatever's infecting the plants!" She gazed at him intensely, then licked her lips. Sarah watched, amazed at this performance. She had never seen Anne turn on the charm, but... if she had wanted something with Grant, Sarah couldn't imagine anyone being able to withstand this. "The puppies were sick, and we couldn't make them better. It's just the plants that are dying, that we have to kill. There's nothing to worry about, I promise." She looked back at Sarah. "I'm going to go wash my hands. Be right back."

Sarah sat there awkwardly, still holding her cup tightly between her hands. The small warmth seeping into her hands wasn't enough to erase the chill inside. *What had she just done?* Would he believe Anne? She wasn't mentally equipped to be the cause of a ship-wide panic right now. *And the kids.* She held in a whimper. Tyler had returned to his post behind the counter, a dazed look on his face. Anne certainly was a force of nature, she admitted to herself. No wonder she'd been able to talk herself onto this shuttle.

Anne was back from the bathroom. She *was* brilliant. Sarah had to give her credit for that, however uneasy she felt about her lies. Her friend smiled once at Tyler over her shoulder, then turned back to Sarah. "Now, never talk again."

Sarah cringed again. "I'm sorry."

"Don't be sorry, be silent. Ok, so the two of us are going to take the weekend off. I mean it. You do what you do, hang out with the rugrats and your Mommy friends, and I'll do what I do—"

"What *do* you do in your time off? I only get to see you in the lab, and before that, just at parties or bars."

"I drink. Now, quiet. We're going to come back Monday morning, *having researched nothing* and we will be refreshed and able to look at the problem with clear heads. Yes? And *we will talk to no-one*. Drink your tea. Now, tell me about the spinning classes on this ship. I think I'll take up exercise."

Sarah made a gagging sound. "Oh God, you look like that and you don't even *exercise*?"

Chapter 38

"Hey."

"Hey. Don't look like that." Sarah tried to laugh but failed. "I already know."

Anne had sat her down before she left work, pulled her aside so that the other scientists and technicians wouldn't hear. NASA wouldn't send more people, more plants or animals, to Mars, not until they knew what they were dealing with on this shuttle. Until they could eradicate the space rot for good and know how to prevent it for next time, the shuttle programme — the *Mars* programme — was stalled.

It made sense.

The next shuttle had been scheduled to leave six months after their successful arrival, long enough to ensure that lessons learned from the landing and transfers were incorporated into the planning. They could identify what else was needed to expand, to shore up the shelters and infrastructure. The personnel selection was ongoing, with more space for families — not pets yet, as per their disaster — and a bigger cross-section of, well, humans to be represented. They had been trialling materials for transport to start mining. But now everything was on hold, indefinitely.

"So what? Say we can't solve this thing and they don't let us into the atmosphere. Then that's it? We're gone, yes, but the colony is just left there? They'd just abandon it?"

Anne had shrugged. “Indefinitely. The unmanned shuttles will continue, but that’s all I know. The captain’s going to make an announcement... not that it matters to us.”

“Of *course* it matters to us!” Sarah had protested. Then the immense weight of it hit her. It wouldn’t matter.

Over Anne’s shoulder, she saw two technicians frozen over their stations, pretending that they didn’t hear.

How long have they known? she wondered.

Sarah hadn’t been hungry for dinner. She’d been unable to sit still, thoughts whirling around in her mind. *What are we missing?* She busied herself with organizing; sorting Jack’s Lego by colour, then cleaning up the craft cabinet. She made dinner for Maggie and Jack but didn’t join them. Instead, she hovered around as they ate, cleaning the kitchen thoroughly, sweeping, then mopping under their feet.

“Mom, you’re driving me crazy,” Maggie complained.

“Lift your feet,” responded Sarah.

The colony wasn’t pleased. *That’s putting it lightly.* There had been urgent communications, professional but with a tinge of panic, flowing in for the past hour. It was only a matter of time before everyone on the shuttle realized the situation they were in. While the unmanned shuttles would still make the voyage, their contents would now be reduced to inorganic matter, sterilized and irradiated to make sure that nothing could infect the men and women that were already living there. But it couldn’t grow as a colony. And, if anything went wrong with their own systems... They were putting all of their hopes on hold until this problem was solved. This problem, whose solution was so close Sarah dreamed about it most nights, had for months. She could almost taste it. *But what if we can't solve it?* They weren't just trying to save their own lives anymore, but now of everyone in the colony. *Four months left. No pressure. Now, let's clean the oven.*

She put the kids to bed and continued cleaning. HQ was practically gleaming by the time she realized how hungry she was. She popped some noodles into a bowl, poured over boiling water and sprinkled in just enough MSG to make it tasty, then leaned against the counter to eat. When her interface had lit up with an incoming call, she had assumed that it would be Nancy, Linda, her parents. Not Ethan.

"It's ok," Sarah insisted. "*I'm* ok. This actually makes absolutely no difference to us. Either we'll solve this and beat it and they'll start up again, or we won't, and we won't get there anyway." She saw a flash of pain cross Ethan's face. "Sorry, dark humour," she mumbled. She twirled ramen around her fork, chasing a little rehydrated green onion around her bowl.

"Yeah, about that, Sar. One, it's *not* funny. And two... I was— I mean I *am* on the list. For the next one, whenever it goes."

Sarah choked on her onion.

He wore a faded T-shirt and his hair looked damp, like he had just stepped out of the shower. She hadn't spoken to him alone like this before. It had always been with Linda, in her office. But he must have been at his own kitchen table. It felt intimate, different somehow. She felt shy. *Around Ethan.* He pulled an open beer into the frame.

"I think I'm going to need to join you in that." She reached past him onto the counter, and tipped some red wine into a glass, then a bit more. It might be a school night, but the world was ending. Again.

"That's a respectable pour." Ethan's eyes crinkled as he lifted his beer. "Cheers."

"Cheers." She smiled and took a sip.

Linda and Ethan had come through with every resource they had. LabX — and Earth — had been helpful, but they were starting to understand that Earth wasn't going to be where the answer came from. On Earth, geneticists were sequencing and resequencing the genome. A network of phytobacteriologists worked virtually around the globe, but all on terrestrial bacteria. With each new proposed solution and premature celebration, the *this is it* and rising of hope, they realized anew that whether it was due to radiation or microgravity, substances responded differently on the shuttle than they had on Earth. There was no way to send bacterial samples back, so that they could have a true sample of Space Rot with which to play, to experiment.

The last unmanned shuttle had arrived a week ago with a shipment of vials containing hopeful cures — *Earth* cures — that were already two months old by the time they reached the ship. Two months behind the research they had done since then, on two-months' different strains. There should be more materials arriving any day now, but they were working in the past.

We can't go back.

"It's like trying to use an interface with a dial-up modem," Anne had exclaimed in frustration.

Their best hope was the team on board. Not only were they brilliant researchers, but they had daily experience with the bacteria, and their expertise was growing. They were hands-on. And they were more motivated than anyone else by the literal do-or-die challenge before them.

"Bad news: still no cure on Earth. Good news? Everything seems to be completely different in space, so... maybe you'll need to pack your suitcase after all." They started to snicker.

She topped up her glass. And looked at him steadily.

"Distract me. Tell me what you do for fun," she said.

"I play hockey on Tuesday nights," he said. "And Barney and I go for romantic hikes every weekend."

Sarah sat up straight. "Who's Barney?"

Ethan grinned at her. "Barney is the love of my life." He shifted his screen to show a scruffy brown hound resting its head on his jeans-clad knee. He scratched the back of its head, leaving a few pieces sticking up. "I... uh... still play guitar a little bit... to Barney, mostly. What about you? You can't be in the lab *all* the time."

Sarah catalogued and ordered during the day, reviewed the team's notes and research in the evenings. She checked each outcome, checked the composition of each sample, the concentration of each substrate, double checked everything for accuracy, up to rigour. She found at least one error a day, but she kept checking. She had to be sure. Everything had to be perfect. That's the only way they'd beat this. *Life and death. Life and death.* Her mantra beat behind her eyes whenever she wasn't focused enough to drown it out. She loved the work because it had given her structure, something to keep her mind off... well, everything else.

Grant had been gone — *dead* — for almost two months. His urn still sat on the shelf. He'd become part of the decor. The kids had settled back into school and life. And she was putting in time.

"I've been dancing again, sort of." She grimaced as she said it. Katriahna had invited her to participate in an adult ballet class on Monday evenings, after the kids were in bed. She declined three times before Erin, obviously recruited to the dark side, bullied her into it. She had gritted her teeth and showed up for the first session, worried about Katriahna and what she would say to her and was surprised by how much she had enjoyed herself. There were three other women in the class, each who had evidently had dance training, and one, Nicole, who had danced professionally. The lessons were challenging but not too discouraging. The stretching and strengthening were another welcome distraction from... well, everything else. She was sure she was getting better. Last week, she had even gotten a nod from Katriahna after her warmup at the barre. High praise, indeed. Maybe the woman had a soul after all.

"Hey, do you remember first year, when you stained your fingers purple for a week?"

"I still think Nancy poked a hole in my glove."

Ethan was someone that let her laugh, remember, *be* somebody that wasn't Grant's widow all the time.

It felt too soon; wrong, but easy. Nice.

She shook herself, then drained her glass. "Well, this has been fun, but I've got to get some sleep. I've got another big day tomorrow of saving all of our lives. After everything else, I owe the kids their future, whatever it turns out to be."

"I know you can do it. And then I'm coming to join you." Their eyes, matching greys, met tentatively. They smiled, then the interface went black.

She walked slowly around her living room, trailing her fingers along the smooth plastic of the walls, the taste of wine still sweet on her tongue.

Was that a date?

She stopped in front of the small box that lay just inside the door. She stooped to pick it up, then, a little dizzy, braced one hand on the frame to help her stand again. She had brought it in when Maggie and Jack came in from school, distracted and hungry, and dropped it there when she was cleaning. It must have come on the unmanned shuttle. A cardboard box addressed to Dr. Grant Harper, it had already been opened, then re-taped shut.

She set the box on the coffee table then sat down across from it, staring at it apprehensively: a piece of home that had travelled all this way for a man that wasn't here anymore. Her eyes travelled to where Grant's urn sat on a shelf, beside the photo of them on the bench that fall day.

It's so small, she thought again.

She shook herself, then grabbed the box and ripped off the tape. The packing material had been disturbed. It had obviously been checked and repacked. She gasped as she pulled out a blue stoneware mug, the twin to the Danish mugs that had broken.

Just the one.

She slouched back against the couch, hugged the mug to her chest and burst into sobs. Hours later, she pulled a throw over herself and fell back into a fitful sleep.

Chapter 39

"From our point of view, we recommend that you jettison—"

"Jettison?" Anne interrupted. She was exhausted, belligerent.

"Expunge. Forcefully expel... all remaining infected plant matter, the soil." Linda wore another power suit — *How many of those does she own?* — and spoke calmly and confidently. "Any seeds could be infected."

Sarah and Anne sat in the Captain's conference room. A scientific team from NASA, and Linda and Ethan shared half of the large interface on his wall. Two directors from BioMars were on the other half; Sarah had met them at one of Grant's Christmas parties, but their names washed over her without being familiar. Captain Leung and the ship's Chief Medical Officer sat across from them.

"We want the seeds for the colony." One of the BioMars men spoke up. *Greg. That was his name.* He coughed, looked to the side, then said, "Best case scenario, you all get to the colony, of course. And if — *when* — you do, we want to cultivate more crops. Can we just irradiate instead of... uh... jettisoning?"

His associate said, "We can always send more seeds on the unmanned shuttle." The NASA team visibly winced.

Greg continued. "Have you fully explored freezing? Dehydration?"

Anne responded. "We've proven that both freezing, and dehydration stop the bacteria from reproducing, but it's only dormant, not dead. It will come back, reconstitute as strong as ever once it thaws or water is introduced."

Like my green onion, thought Sarah.

"As long as there was never a chance of being exposed to any heat or water again..." she made a wry face. "Impractical, so no. Besides, we think dehydration may have played a part in it spreading outside the plots. We know the bacteria causes the plant to produce a saplike biofilm, which is absolutely teeming with more bacteria. This acts as a protectant for the plant, for the bacteria, allowing it to thrive longer. We're cautiously certain that they're not producing spores, per se, but it's possible that the bacterial ooze, once dried out, has particulated and spreads through the ventilation system. It's not being filtered out."

"It's actually good news," added Ethan. "The particulate versus spores, I mean. Spores are extremely resistant to bacterial warfare, and would make this problem... um, much worse," he finished lamely.

"The bottom line, please, Dr. Coyne. Can you kill it?" Greg squinted into the screen.

Sarah glanced nervously at Anne, then at the captain. Captain Leung leaned back in the chair beside her, his face impassive. She saw a muscle twitch in his jaw.

"We *can*," Anne started slowly, "via sanitation and sterilization. We could clean everything with a light bleach or formaldehyde solution. In the lab, that actually kills 100% of the active bacteria, and we're confident that it will also kill the spores... or aerial particulate, as we're going to call this."

"That's all good news. So, what's the problem? What do you need to be certain?" *Why haven't you fixed this yet?* Greg seemed to be saying. Sarah held her breath.

"That's... our main issue. We can do it easily — *so easily* — in a vacuum, and we have. Repeatedly. We can scrub the soil, clean the air, clean the water. The bacteria on inorganic surfaces." She paused. "However, the spores— er, particulates are still being found in passenger samples."

"We know that already. There has been no evidence whatsoever that it can harm people. I thought we confirmed that." Greg looked to his fellow director who nodded.

Anne looked directly at the interface.

"The people that have moisture in their skin and air in their lungs?"

"Those are the ones."

A heavy sigh. She waited for it to sink in. One of the men at NASA spoke first.

"So, in order to get rid of this thing once and for all..."

"We have to get rid of the people. Or dry them out, freeze them, or flush them with bleach. Yeah."

"Huh."

"Yeah."

Chapter 40

Volunteers had created new schedules for the common areas, rearranged the activities for kids and grownups on the turf fields and gymnasiums, and introduced new art classes, cooking classes, yoga and movement classes.

Despite this, the atmosphere on the ship was charged with new tension. Everywhere Sarah went, technicians were swabbing passengers and surfaces. After dropping Maggie off at her classroom, she witnessed one of Anne's senior staff being cornered by some of the moms. She ducked her head and walked past quickly; her eyes averted.

"What aren't you telling us?" She heard their voices raised as the stairwell door swung shut behind her.

The sealed gardens were frozen. The soil was removed to a secure area for irradiation, and the units, implements and ventilation systems scrubbed out with a simple bleach solution. Cleaning crews circulated, wiping down every surface.

Sarah still felt keenly the void left from the gardens, but there was something liberating about not pretending to be outside anymore. They weren't on Earth and never would be again. If this was going to be their home, why not get used to living their new lives as they would be on Mars, inside. If they made it to Mars, that is.

"They're flattening," said Linda. LabX had pulled in all of its resources. The shuttle lab sequenced the Space Rot genome in the living samples every 48 hours. Sarah tracked, recorded and shared sheet after sheet of new data daily with Earth for their analysis. Trouble was, it kept changing. Slight variations, sometimes none, but LabX's data analysts were charting the changes in the living samples, looking for patterns. "The mutations are slowing down. It's not stable yet, but it's slower. That's something. We'll win this yet."

Sarah and Anne had started eating their lunch together in front of the interface with Ethan and Linda. Erin and Jenny insisted on taking Maggie and Jack on these days. Sarah took a bite of her sandwich and held it up, as if to say, Cheers. Ethan did the same, as they ended the connection.

Anne's smartbook pinged and she cast an eye on it. Sarah didn't notice. She was smiling to herself at Linda and Ethan's positivity. And Ethan's smile.

Silence. She looked up, saw that Anne had stopped chewing.

"What is it?" Sarah asked.

"It's in the food supply," choked Anne, her mouth still full. She chewed for another moment, then swallowed before she continued. "They've found it in the potatoes. They're sequencing it now." She pushed her bowl away and dropped her head into her hands. She was still.

Sarah took the smartbook and read the message. *Oh God.*

She put it down slowly, her hands shaking. "Ok. *Ok.* But it's only in the potatoes so far, Anne. Don't give up hope.

You *can't* give up. Come on." She put a hand on Anne's forearm.

"But if it's in the potatoes, that means it could be—" Anne's voice was muffled.

"Could be isn't *is*. We don't know yet. We'll test and we'll isolate. We can beat this." She opened the interface and tapped through a few screens.

"I'm not Grant." Anne lifted her head and stared miserably, with red eyes, at Sarah. "He's the one who could figure this out. He's the one who—"

"Who isn't here. He's gone, Anne. He's left us here and we have to fix this." Sarah's voice sounded harsh to her own ears. She took a deep breath and rolled her shoulders back. "I'm sending this to LabX."

The screen lit up within seconds. Ethan and Linda looked grim.

"So, it's still... here. And spreading."

"Do you have to tell NASA?"

Anne dropped her head onto her hands again.

✷

They were back in the conference room. The NASA team was larger this time, headed by Marc, the lead flight controller. Greg and a man in a lab coat represented BioMars.

"How? You told us that the food stores were unaffected." The lead from NASA looked panicked.

"We're not sure. They were, but... Our best guess is that dormant particulate found its way to the food stores and rehydrated. Probably on a human carrier."

"We sequenced it immediately. It's quite different, wildly so from the first samples." Anne was composed. She spoke slowly and clearly.

Ethan chimed in. "It's a new strain, we think. We compared the new sequence to the others. You should have heard James, one of our lead analysts; he squealed like a schoolgirl." Ethan chuckled, then sobered. "Sorry."

"Right. So if we follow protocol, it means getting rid of – sorry, *jettisoning* – what, all vegetable matter on board? What are we left with? What do we eat?" A flush rose in Anne's pale cheeks.

"Not all yet, just the infected matter. We're still dealing in unknowns. I understand it's only the potatoes so far." Ethan looked conciliatory.

"They're currently testing the rest of the organic matter. We've scaled up the rotation, but we don't know yet what else if affected, if anything." Anne's back was straight, her voice level. "I want to be honest. We don't know yet."

"Ok, spitballing here." Greg said. "Bleach is the only proven kill right now, right? Let's revisit the bleach idea. How much bleach would we need to... uh... 'wash the air' with?" He used finger quotes. Sarah saw Ethan's mouth tighten.

"The concentration is actually pretty low: 10-15 ppm," Ethan reported stiffly, scanning a page. "It's well within the safe range for humans and has shown consistent results in destroying the Rot."

"That's good. Ok, so we only need a light mist of bleachy air. Effects of breathing in bleach fumes in humans?" Greg leaned forward.

"Short-term exposure at those levels would lead to... uh... burning and discomfort and can aggravate asthma or perhaps reveal or exacerbate underlying respiratory tract problems."

"Ninety-nine percent of those would have been detected in pre-boarding testing, right? There shouldn't be any surprises on board." Greg smirked. "There it is."

"... But it needs to be a constant wash for ten minutes to be sure that we got it all."

"Dammit." Greg sat back in his chair. He did genuinely seem to be sorry.

Sarah smacked the conference table and saw Anne jump. "We can kill it! That's why this is so frustrating. We have the answer in front of us, but it's going to beat us." Sarah let her hands fall heavily into her lap.

"It's not. But we're going to starve to death." Anne's voice was quieter now.

The Captain cleared his throat. "We have more than just potatoes on board. We will salvage what we can and ration what's left until the next shuttle arrives." His jaw twitched again, almost imperceptibly, then glanced at the doctor. He sat up taller. "I think we need to address the elephant in the room. If the food supply is affected, if we're not going to be able to land... sooner or later, someone's going to have to make the call. How long are we going to wait? What is the plan?"

Greg and Marc shifted uncomfortably in their seats on two different screens. *They've already had this conversation*, Sarah realized.

Marc spoke first. "We don't have a 'plan' as such. It's not something that we want to happen, or to have to do. But if we do have to... take action... dammit, Captain, this isn't easy for us either!"

"I know." The Captain squared his shoulders. "But I need to know. When the time comes, is it better to tell the passengers, give them the chance to say goodbye? Or to just... do it? It will be very quick." He glanced guiltily at Sarah, who had paled and stared at him, her eyes wide. "I've had time to think about it. It's my *job* to think about it. What would you want? Would you want to know?"

✷

Jack was already asleep, tired out after his soccer game on the turf fields. Without the playgrounds and gardens, more passengers came out to cheer them on, adding to the excitement and the distraction of the little players. Maggie, showered after her ballet class, was lying in bed, reading.

"Hey, Miss Maggie." Sarah sat down on the edge of her bed and brushed her hair away from her daughter's forehead. "Did you have a good day today?"

Maggie lifted one finger as she finished the page she was on, then closed the book and lay it on her stomach. She studied her mother seriously. "It *was* a good day." She paused and ran her slender fingers over the cover of her book, studying them intently. "Do you think Daddy can still see us? I mean... wouldn't... his *spirit* be way behind us? We've gone millions of miles since he died."

"Oh, sweetie." She lay down beside her and put a hand over Maggie's. "I think he can because he's in our hearts, not out there in space. I think he's watching over us and feeling proud. He wanted this adventure more than anything, and... well, he would travel one *million* million miles to see you get to Mars, to grow up and explore all the places that he dreamed of going with you."

Maggie nodded. "I think that too. Did you know that Ms. Katriahna said I'm on track to be *en pointe* in two years? She said my feet are strong enough now, but I have to wait until I'm eleven. Maybe ten."

Sarah shook her head and kissed her temple. "Don't rush it. You're my baby." She took Maggie's book from her and put it on the shelf.

"Jack's your baby. I'm your princess."

"Ok, goodnight, Princess. I love you. And... Daddy loves you too."

"I know."

"Sweet dreams, sweet girl." She closed the door softly. The smile left her face and her shoulders sagged. *Just keep going. Don't let them see.* She had changed into leggings and a T-shirt before Jack's game, and now pulled a soft flannel shirt overtop, inhaling the collar deeply in hopes of smelling the man who used to wear it.

Sarah wandered out into the living room and looked around her aimlessly. *HQ*, she thought bitterly. Grant's sleeves hung down well below her fingertips, so she rolled them up, then interlaced her fingers and stretched her arms overhead. She exhaled with a sigh, then released her stretch and collapsed down onto the sofa facing the window, where the view changed so imperceptibly that it was constant. *The only constant here.* That and Grant's urn and feeling bone tired. *Just make the call, Captain.* She wasn't scared. She was sad and lonely. Defeated.

She picked up her smartbook and pulled up the day's data, then went back to the beginning. She scrolled through the various iterations of the bacteria. *I see you.* There were slight changes to its structure, almost imperceptible as she flipped from one to the next, not 'wildly different' at all. Ethan's analyst was obviously grasping at straws. She rubbed her eyes. *Pattern. There's always a pattern.* She flipped through them again, a little faster this time. *When would it be too late? When can I just give up?* She created a new folder, copied the images over. She clicked on every second, then every third image. Sarah gave a sharp intake of breath. *Wait.* She went back a few samples, then compared it to the most recent image.

She was sitting up straight now, flipping back and forth between the two, her eyes open wide. She typed quickly.

Tell me I'm not imagining things. Tell me I'm not too tired and exhausted and making this up because it's what I want to see.

It felt like an eternity before the interface lit up behind her, its reflection a bright rectangle superimposed over the stars.

She exhaled loudly, then used her hands to push off her thighs as she stood up. She stumbled over to the kitchen. *Linda.* She answered, and Ethan and Linda flashed up, still at the office with Linda's watery painting behind them. Ethan was holding up her popsicle sculpture, making it gallop across the screen.

"Hey, wh—"

"We see it." They were bursting with suppressed grins. "Grab Anne and get to the lab. We'll send over the documents on the way."

"Tonight? I was just heading to bed. Can't it wait till-" she shook her head. "No. I'm on my way."

Tell Maggie? No, she wouldn't sleep. She scribbled a note in large letters and centred it on the floor in the hallway. *I'm at the lab. Ping me if you wake up. xo Mom*

How times change.

*

"We can't go back," Sarah said. "Everyone kept saying 'one way' and 'no return.' The shuttles are two months behind. The samples keep changing. *We can't go back*. But we have to!"

The lab report was up on the interface in front of them. The coloured rows were all puzzle pieces that she had catalogued. Sarah unfocused her eyes. *There were so many rows*, she thought. Anne leaned in to look at it.

"Vinegar? We missed vinegar? No... we didn't. We tested it—" Anne looked to Sarah for confirmation. She, too, had been on her way to bed early. She wore a sweatsuit and had her hair pulled back with a thick band. *Still gorgeous, though.* Sarah wished she had changed out of Grant's old flannel shirt. *Focus, Sar. Pay attention.*

"That was weeks ago," Ethan interrupted eagerly, taking off his glasses. "This is what James found, but we just didn't make the connection. Sar, you're right. The last four mutations over the last eight days have a weakness here—" he indicated a bond in the molecular structure "— and acetic acid, even in a tolerated concentration, kills it. Denatures it here so it can't reproduce, can't survive. We had already crossed it off the list. But there's a new vulnerability. It'll do it."

"What concentration? How tolerable?" Anne looked wary.

"10-15 ppm, nothing more. Like that light mist of Greg's 'bleachy air'" — finger quotes — "but with acetic acid. It's going to be uncomfortable, but better than bleach. Coughing, chest pain, maybe some vomiting, but it's not going to kill anyone. And Sar... it's going to *work*." He smiled into the camera, his light grey eyes sparkling for the first time in weeks.

Linda jumped in. "But you have to act quickly. There still isn't a linear pattern that we can see, and if we lose this window, if it closes..."

We're back where we started. "I'll call the Captain now," said Anne.

Chapter 41

It was past midnight when they gathered in the conference room with the Captain, two of Anne's lab team, and two engineers. Linda, Ethan and the groups of now-familiar faces were already up on the interface. Aware of her own sloppy attire, Sarah had buttoned up Grant's old shirt to her chin. It didn't help much, but it was the middle of the night; everyone was dishevelled. She was happy to see that Greg looked like hell.

Captain Leung outlined the announcement he'd make first thing in the morning. He had to handle it carefully, not divulge too much information. Though, most of the ship's staff would be briefed or have heard whispers by the morning, would already know the consequences should this fail.

The information for the civilians must be minimal and matter of fact. They had to sanitize the ventilation system, neutralize the spread of the bacteria to preserve the food supply. They would be using a low concentration of acetic acid for a period of exactly fifteen minutes, and there may be uncomfortable side effects. He was counting on the passengers to not panic, to not overload the medical staff that were positioned in each corridor, ready to assist. All families and non-essential passengers were to stay in their units for the duration. Those with known respiratory issues would be confined to sickbay, cared for as best as possible, though the medical staff would be suffering the effects of the vapour themselves.

"No, they can't wear PPE," Anne snapped at the head of medical services. "No filters, no masks. It won't be fun, but everyone needs to breathe this in for the full fifteen minutes."

"But how are they going to help anyone if they're inhaling it too?" The men from NASA and BioMars nodded. He made an excellent point. Ethan had explained that the 'discomfort' would be very close to debilitating.

Anne's lips thinned. "We're going to have to count on the fact that most people will be too 'uncomfortable' to be able to stagger out of their quarters looking for help. We can't take the chance that *anyone* avoids treatment, or it will all be for nothing."

"If my staff are incapacitated, what's the predicted mortality rate?" The Chief Medical Officer wasn't backing down. "For that matter, what's the rate even *if* they could provide care? We don't have enough information for me to approve this. It's too risky."

Anne glanced at the Captain, who responded quietly but firmly. "The mortality rate on this ship will be one hundred percent if we don't try this. I'm sorry, Doctor, but I've made the call. We're going to proceed. Vet your team for anyone with respiratory difficulties. They can suffer through it in sickbay with the rest of the compromised passengers. I'm ordering you to brief your team. We start at 0900."

The interfaces went blank.

"The rest of you, get some sleep," Captain Leung said. "Dr. Coyne, Ed, please walk me through this one more time." Anne smiled tightly at Sarah as the door closed behind her.

She let herself back into her quarters quietly, observing that her note was still on the floor. *Good.* She bent to pick it up, then straightened quickly as her interface lit up again.

"Ethan."

He was sitting in Linda's office, fiddling with the little popsicle again. He looked worried, exhausted, but his eyes shone.

"Linda's gone home already but I just wanted to tell you from both of us, this will work." He cleared his throat. "I know it will, Sar."

Her lips curved softly. She hugged her arms across her chest. "It'd better. Good night." She yawned, covering her mouth with her sleeve.

"Good night, Sar. I'll see you soon."

She suddenly felt wide awake. "No," she blurted out. "No, you won't." His forehead creased in confusion. "Ethan, it's been wonderful— it *is* wonderful to work with you, but you can't just give up the rest of your life for me, to follow me. It's too soon, and we're not... we're not *us* anymore. I'm not... who you think I am." She sank down onto the stool and looked at him pleadingly. Her arms with their comical, too-long sleeves flapped once, then rested on her knees.

He stared back, through the interface, bewildered.

"Sar, I want to be a part of this. Whatever happens with us, we don't know how that will go, or what the future will bring. But this whole Mars thing... it's something I want to do, someplace I want to go. I can't not try to save you, and I won't not want to be part of it." He scrunched up his face. "That was barely even a sentence. But I'm coming to Mars, as soon as I can."

It was now or never. She had to tell him about Maggie and Jack *now*. She closed her eyes and took a deep breath.

✷

Sarah had made a simple breakfast of toast with a smear of jam. Watered-down apple juice for the kids, weak tea for herself. It just needed to be something easy to digest. She had barely slept, and her stomach was in knots. *Life or death. Life or death.* The ghost of a smile played around her mouth as she noticed the slight change in her mantra. *Deep breaths, Sar.* She explained in few words what was going to happen, and why they had to try. Maggie and Jack looked at her blankly, then followed her to the couch where she sat between them and went through a slideshow of family photos. So many with Grant, so few with her. Always the photographer, for once she saw it as a blessing. When the Captain's calm voice gave the five-minute warning, she bundled them each up in a light blanket and herded them into their bathroom. She gave them each some Lego and they sat on the floor, quiet for once, quiet for whatever was coming.

A faint scent of vinegar built quickly to an overwhelming assault, scorching a path into her nose, the back of her throat, even her lungs. The kids screamed and struggled. She held them, tears streaming down her own cheeks, not just because her eyes burned like hell. She found it impossible to suppress her own whimpering for their sake, distraught that she couldn't make it go away. Praying that it would work, that it would really and truly cleanse the air for all of their sakes. She coughed and retched, grasping Maggie's hand here, trying to squint through bleary eyes enough to pat Jack's back.

It had taken only fifteen minutes, total, from when the first vinegary mist emanated from the ventilation system until the filters and fans turned on full blast to clear the air of the stinging fumes. Not quickly enough. It had felt like an eternity. It had been... *vile*. The smell, the taste, the choking and burning. The fear that it would never stop.

When it was all over, Sarah sat with her arms wrapped around the kids as they sniffed in great, shuddering breaths. Jack had been sick but didn't have the strength to get up at first. She put both children in the shower as she mopped up the floor, letting them sit in the tub as the water streamed over them like rain, rinsing out their eyes and ears, then showering herself off. She put a load of sheets and pjs into the washing machine. Her sofa, the cushions, everything they owned reeked of vinegar.

She tried not to think how much worse it must have been for Anne, who had been down in Engineering with members of senior staff, monitoring the flow of solution into the fans, somehow overseeing the process while struggling to breathe in the acid air herself.

Or for Katriahna, all alone in her little cabin. She'd never know. Katriahna had been found in her bed after the air treatment, the lone casualty of the process, "a success," Greg would crow at the next debrief. Losing an elderly ballet teacher to heart failure wasn't a tragedy at all, if the treatment had worked. Sarah wanted to reach through the interface and punch him in the face.

*

When they emerged into the damp corridor, many of her neighbours were already out there, standing and sitting in groups, red-eyed and weak. The medical personnel looked just as miserable as everyone else. She walked among them, touching an arm here, a shoulder there. This was her community.

At the end of the hallway, barely visible between the little clumps of shaken people, a tall, dark-haired figure in a white lab coat emerged from a stairwell. Sarah's eyes flooded with tears and she sagged against the wall, suddenly dizzy.

A hand on her waist, a kiss on her cheek.

"I'm sorry, I thought I saw... I'm fine." She smiled weakly at Anne; her red-rimmed, bloodshot eyes looked calmer than they had for weeks.

"It's done." She pulled her close for a hug. "Now, we test."

She smelled strongly like vinegar, like everything would for days, and even now, almost two weeks later, Sarah still caught a slight whiff of it now and then and flinched from it.

Chapter 42

Sarah stretched; her eyes still closed. The Saturday lawnmower, the warm wind across her face... all faded away as she opened her eyes to see that Grant's side of the bed was empty. He must have... *oh*.

Was it already four months? For the last week, she had slept on her side of the bed again. Her bed was so much more comfortable than the couch.

Six o'clock was definitely too early to be awake. She pinged Linda once, to say that she was taking the weekend off.

Good. The response came quickly.

She rolled back over and dozed.

Nicole, the dancer from Sarah's adult class, had brought the class of ballerinas into the auditorium for a rehearsal on Friday afternoon. There, on the stage, with the glittering expanse of the universe as a backdrop, the small group of girls stretched and flowed as music surrounded them. There was only a faint tang of vinegar still sharp in the air.

Erin had begged her to come watch.

"She won't want me to see until the recital," Sarah had protested. Despite the morning in the bathroom, clinging to her and begging Mommy to make the vinegary mist stop, Maggie was back to acting distant. Sarah wanted to be careful of her daughter's boundaries. She felt uneasy as they snuck in, but they weren't noticed in the darkness of the back seats.

Nicole led the warmup with a very different energy than her predecessor. She had taken over teaching the classes, her posture as elegant as Katriahna's had been.

Amid the four other girls in matching leotards, each with hair pulled tightly back into buns and similar lean leggy grace, Maggie stood out. There was something in the way she moved, the rapt expression on her face as she pliéd and turned, the carefully exact arm positioning that she made seem so natural. A long, turned-out leg stretched out in front of her and she paused for a second, silhouetted against the stars. Sarah felt Erin's arm around her shoulder.

"Look at them," she whispered. "Look at our girls."

When she touched her cheek, she felt it was wet with tears she hadn't known she was crying.

She had gone to bed shortly after the kids on Friday night. They had all gotten into their pyjamas right after dinner and snuggled up on the sofa under a blanket to watch *Pete's Dragon* with popcorn and candy. When they'd finished, she helped them floss the popcorn kernels out of their teeth and tucked them in. She walked through the cabin, picking up the night's dishes of cups and the popcorn bowl, and stacked them on the counter. She'd deal with them in the morning. Time for some new systems.

She woke again, this time to find the two kids reading books on Grant's side of the bed. They used to do this when he was travelling, sneak into her room in the early morning, sometimes falling back asleep, but more often just lying there, turning their pages quietly until she noticed them.

“Read me the paragraph you’re on,” she said sleepily, rolling over and putting her arm across Jack’s belly. He slowly read her a few sentences about dragons and warriors. “And Maggie? Your turn.” Maggie read clearly, enunciating extra clearly, showing off a little. Her book was about mythical creatures. Her drawings, lately, had been a little less ballerina-focused, with a few more unicorns.

Sarah yawned, then wandered into her bathroom. She splashed warm water onto her face, then patted it dry and looked in the mirror critically. *Who are you?* The woman who looked back at her: who was she? A widow. *Is this what a widow looks like*? Her hair was still dark and tangled, with only a strand of grey here and there. Her skin was pale from the seven months on board with no sun. She had stopped taking in her timed UV sessions. These were required for all the passengers onboard, but she hadn’t gone to her appointments since... well, for four months now. She was somehow still healthy.

It was Saturday morning, and she was a widow. She was a single parent. She was... *A scientist?* In this reality, on the ship, in the colony, she didn’t have to have a job. She would be well taken care of just because of who Grant was, who he had been, but she was contributing. She was part of this community. She had found her place.

She was going to be ok. She and these kids would make it to Mars, and they’d start their new lives on an alien planet with a small colony to welcome them. They’d help build new and better structures, branch out and explore the new world around them. And, if the sampling stayed clear, another ship would arrive, and another, then another, maybe one day with friends — *with Ethan* — on board. He was still insisting on joining the colony. She was glad, after all, that she had faltered and chickened out again. That she hadn't told him the truth about herself and his children. Maybe one day, she would tell him. But maybe not.

One day, they would have the capability to return to Earth. *What then?*

First things first. First, she had to keep sampling, keep working, be *sure* that the rot was gone. That the treatment had worked, that it would never return.

But today was Saturday, and she had promised Anne that she wouldn't even think about it again until Monday morning.

She poked her head out of the bathroom, and the kids were right where she had left them, stretched out on the bed, books held above their heads. How was it possible that so little had changed for them after Grant's death?

So little, except being on a spaceship headed for Mars, she reminded herself. *For Grant.*

They'd have that as his legacy.

"Pancakes?" she called out.

"Yay!" they answered in unison, without closing their books. *Smart kids.* It would take her at least half an hour to get breakfast on the table. They weren't going to move until they had to.

In the kitchen, she pushed the popcorn bowls off to one side and opened up the cupboard. She had put her new pottery mug at the very back. She reached for it, poured herself a cup of tea, and touched the interface. A folk song filled the cabin as she gathered the ingredients for pancakes. Flour. Sugar. Baking powder. Salt.

She dug behind the salt, past the vinegar. She shuddered.

Powdered milk. Powdered eggs. Oil. She was a widow. She'd left everything she knew behind except for these kids, and her g-d husband died in his own g-d lab. Mixing bowl. Pan. Her kids were lying in bed with books like any Saturday morning, as space streamed by outside their window. She started to giggle, whisking the dry ingredients together, then mixing the eggs and milk with water in a liquid measure. They were on a one-way trip to Mars. She was laughing out loud by now, sloshing a bit as she added the oil. And the whole shuttle was still technically condemned. Tears streamed from her eyes, and she gripped the counter as she shook with laughter. *What has* happened *to me?* she thought. *I used to be sensible.*

The interface pinged and she looked up. Her parents were calling. *Woo.* She wiped her eyes on her sleeve, then accepted the call. She held up one finger, still snorting with laughter, and stepped out of the frame to blow her nose.

"Hello!" she gasped, a broad smile on her face. "It's so good to see you!"

Her parents looked the same, no different from eight months ago when they watched her leave so stoically. They both grinned, unsure of the joke. She had talked to them only a few times since Grant's accident. She had finally thought to about a week afterwards, when she didn't have many details to share with them about his death, about the pathogen. She must have been in shock, she realized.

I probably still am.

"It's good to see you too," her mother said. "Are you alright? What time is it there?"

Sarah sniffed. "It's the same time as it is there, I've told you. We're set to stretch out the clocks in about a week, though, for the last two months of approach. How are you?"

They were chipper and chatty, completely unconcerned with pathogens and peril. *The media doesn't have the full story, and I will never tell them.* She had learned her lesson about revealing too much to Linda, to Nancy. *I'm good with secrets.* The weather, the yard, the neighbours. They were 'only parents' of an only child, she had always teased them, but they certainly had let her go pretty easily, she thought now. Following your husband is one thing, but letting go of your daughter, that would be another, she thought. Through the open door, she could see Maggie's feet. She had rolled over onto her stomach and was kicking her feet back, alternating, her toes perfectly pointed. *How could you just let me go*? she wondered. Then, *I've let Grant go.*

It's just part of life. Moving on is moving on. Maybe one full night's sleep hadn't made up for three weeks without.

"Come talk to Grandma and Grandpa!" she called out, interrupting her father. The kids squealed and came running.

She didn't know what he had been saying, anyway. She turned back to the pancakes, watching them start to bubble, the edges to brown. Today was just like any other Saturday, she thought again. All that was missing was a lawnmower outside, crisscrossing the lawn, leaving stripes and checks and that sweet smell of newly mown grass wafting on the breeze.

She popped in and out of the frame as she cooked. Maggie posed and pirouetted to the music that was still playing, and Jack ran back and forth to his bedroom to show them this Lego figurine or that set he had built, passing Grant's urn without seeing it. Grant had become part of the apartment. Her mom started to tell a story about a rude woman at the library and her dad pulled out the newspaper. Behind him, new curtains hung in the kitchen window.

The pancakes were ready. Maggie and Jack dragged the table over in front of the interface. When they all sat down around it, it felt almost like having Grandma and Grandpa at the table with them. Her dad pretty much ignored them, except to ask for a word on the crossword now and then. Her mom disappeared for a few minutes and came back with a cup of tea and a piece of toast.

It felt like a pretty good start to the day, considering. Maybe later, she'd make a mosaic out of the pieces of the broken mug.

The End

Acknowledgements

The premise of following a spouse to a new colony isn't new. I wanted to explore the human side of those that tag along on others' grand adventures to somewhere without any chance of returning. Where could a family go, today, that they couldn't ever come back from? The only place that fit the bill was Mars, and *Ground Control* was born. With the resurgence in space exploration, from Space Force to SpaceX, this story really isn't that implausible, or won't be for long.

In the course of writing this book, I spent weeks reviewing NASA, Canadian Space Agency, SpaceX and MARSOne information, from generalities about space travel to shuttles to Mars and experimental biology in space. I took as few liberties as possible with what is actually possible now, or what is *about* to be possible.

There are scraps of songs and stories throughout this book that have inspired me for years, and I borrowed them with the deepest humility.

I.S.S. (Is Someone Singing) - Barenaked Ladies and Chris Hadfield
Space Oddity - David Bowie
An Astronaut's Guide to Life on Earth - Chris Hadfield
The Restaurant at the End of the Universe - Douglas Adams
A Little Princess - Frances Hodgson Burnett

I'd like to thank Dr. Ron Howard, P.Ag., for his time, humour and patience during our discussions about plant pathology and bacterial rot in potatoes. Your input and advice were invaluable to my creating a (somewhat) plausible way to save the shuttle. Any errors are mine.

I'd also like to thank the wonderful women in my running group who had to listen to me talk about soil diseases and bacterial soft rot for eight miles or more, for weeks at a time. You are all heroes.

To author S.M. McEachern, whose advice and wisdom really made me believe that I could do this, thank you for your friendship and for believing in me, too!

To my beta readers, Andrea, Laurel and Lisa, who saw this book at its very worst, you gave me hope that I could make it better. I hope I did.

To Vaughn, Ailsa and Tamsin, thank you for letting me work on this while trying to be your mom at the same time. You'll get to read it one day.

To the exceptionally creative Kaleigh West, whose design skills brought my book cover, trailer and graphics to life, you are, truly, a ninja.

And finally, to my editor, LaNae, it was an absolute pleasure to work with you. (You know what I did there.)

K.A. Hough is a Canadian writer who balances her passion for exercise and science with her love of cookies and nonsense. She currently lives in London with her husband, their three energetic kids and a codependent dog. In her spare time, she writes personal essays, teaches boot camps in the parks and drinks tea.

Visit her at www.karenhoughwrites.com

CPSIA information can be obtained
at www.ICGtesting.com
Printed in the USA
BVHW050953240921
617236BV00002B/6